Calliope O'Callahan and the Psy Syndicate

Psy Syndicate, Volume 1

Tantlian

Published by Tantlian, 2023.

Calliope O'Callahan and the Psy Syndicate
By
Tantlian

Copyright Page

CALLIOPE O'CALLAHAN AND THE PSY SYNDICATE

First edition. July 15, 2023.

Copyright © 2023 Tantlian.

ISBN: 979-8988717812

Written by Tantlian.

Chapter One

Amber

"**D**on't Poop on Me," read the white sign with the figure of a dog in a defecation position. The sign was positioned prominently on a lawn that would make a golf course envious. Kentucky ryegrass grew perfectly green with no signs of weeds or yellowing. Only six- or eight-footed insects on a prescribed list were allowed to make their abode in or even consider crossing that lawn. The yard that Amber Biggs was passing by at that very moment belonged to the Hartfords, otherwise known as perpetual contenders for Yard of the Month. The white-posted mailbox had a document-sized flag of fall leaves fluttering below. Marshmallow-shaped boxwoods surrounded the post like sentinels, and the driveway was free of oil spots. The house itself was a two-story of at least 2,500 square feet and had a brick exterior mixed with gray siding. A white rocking chair sat at a perfect angle on the small front porch. The rosebushes, having lost their blooms, ran along the edge of a curved walkway from the driveway to the front steps. This was a typical house in Amber's planned community, where all the colors were muted except for the occasional flower or flag.

Having lived the entirety of her twelve years in the neighborhood, Amber was immune to its charms, rather she thought of it as the most obnoxiously boring place on earth. Her parents had chosen this neighborhood carefully, examining its proximity to a good school system and its inhabitants' mean income. Her father was all about the way things looked, not about how things really were. Amber's life up to that point had been planned just as meticulously as the neighborhood. She was on track for an Ivy League education, doing all the extracurriculars necessary for an impressive college application whether she liked it or not. Today, she most definitely was not in the mood.

Earbuds in her ears, head bowed down to better see her smartphone, Amber texted her twin-from-another-mother, Ashley.

"Sorry I didn't text before now, I had to stay late at school today," Amber typed with rapid-fire precision. She waited for a reply.

"What happened?" Ashley's text asked.

"I screwed up on the algebra test Monday and had to do study hall," Amber explained, "AND they confiscated my phone."

She brushed away the blond hair that the wind had blown into her face so that she could read Ashley's reply: "That was a killer test. I'm pretty sure I'll be spending my afternoons getting tutored."

"As if life wasn't boring enough already," texted Amber.

"Amber/Ashley" was how they were known in the halls of their middle school. After much deliberation and several promises made, the pair had been given permission to attend the K-pop band concert in August. Amber believed it was the most interesting thing that had ever happened in her entire life and she wanted more of it. Going back to the daily grind was annoying.

"I'm so bored," Amber texted. "I wish something interesting would happen."

They say "Be careful what you wish for" for a reason. A white panel van was keeping pace alongside the oblivious Amber as she bebopped down the sidewalk. In and of itself, a panel van in a neighborhood like hers wasn't an unusual sight, since many plumbers, roofers, and other professional caretakers were necessary for domestic perfection. This one, however, was worth noticing.

Suddenly, Amber felt a large arm go across her waist before she was lifted from the ground. She dropped her phone in surprise. There was no time to scream before another hand clamped some kind of cloth over her nose and mouth. The cloth smelled quite pleasant but made Amber feel odd and drowsy. She could no longer control her limbs very well. It struck her slowed mind that things were finally getting interesting, though not in the way she had anticipated.

Chapter Two

Callie

Calliope O'Callahan stared at the sparrow aggressively consuming the bits of french fry she had left on the picnic table. Its little black eye watched her warily, but hunger superseded its natural fear of people. The wind blew the maple leaves so that the sunbeams blinked into her face. The man sitting across from Callie was droning on about his financial woes, using terminology that a high school student such as herself wouldn't know. He wore a tailored blue-striped shirt with a power-red tie, his sleeves rolled up to his forearms as if he were about to dip them into a bowl of water. His hair was disheveled by the breeze, his face was puffy from lack of sleep, and his eyes had the terrified look of someone in really deep.

"Blah, blah, blah, merger," he droned on, "blah, blah, blah, should I invest?"

That was Calliope's cue to respond. She turned her attention to her client with a keen eye. This was the latest of several meetings she had had with Chris the Whale, so-called because he was obsessed with money and had a lot of it. Callie knew a great deal about him, from his professional life to his personal. He trusted her like no one else and paid well for her advice, so much so that he had her on retainer. She wasn't willing to hop the Amtrak to Charlotte for just any old client.

"You haven't been sleeping well, Chris," Callie said. "I'm glad you came to me or you might have made a stupid decision."

She made a show of placing the tarot cards on the table between them, asking Chris to make the cut. The bangles on her wrists made small tinkling sounds as she placed the cards in the Celtic cross spread. She turned each one over slowly and reverently, making little sounds or nodding her head. Chris watched her intently. He didn't have the time for or interest in explanations, so she didn't bother.

When she was done, she said, "I think you should invest. I see a decent return and very happy clients. Maybe even a promotion."

Chris let out a breath and drew a hand through his hair. "That's what I thought, too."

"Of course you did," Callie said. "You just needed the spirits to confirm it for you, Chris."

"Hey, you're the best," Chris said as he rose to leave.

"Let me know if you need to meet next week," Callie said.

"Will do."

The sparrow had flown off when Chris the Whale walked away, but then returned to its repast. Callie watched it for a while longer as she waited for her next client. In addition to paying her well, Chris was also good for referrals. Several of his friends, acquaintances, and clients visited Callie when she was in town. Checking her phone for the time, she noted she had at least twenty minutes until one of her new clients was due to show up, a Mrs. Jones. Callie had completed her trigonometry homework on the train ride, but she still needed to study for her Honors Biology test. She decided to pull out her notebook and go over plant respiration while she waited.

"Who the heck needs to know about plant respiration?" Callie said. Exasperated, she closed the book hard and shoved it back into her bag.

The sun had lowered so that it was peeking between the trunks of the maples; the sparrow, sated, was long gone. Finally, a woman who looked to be in her thirties sat down across from Calliope. She had her hair pulled back into a ponytail and was wearing yoga gear and a light jacket. She fidgeted nervously, unsure what to do with her hands.

"Are you Madam O'Callahan?" she asked.

"Yes. Mrs. Jones?"

"Yeah, I'm so glad you could fit me in today. I'm sorry I'm late, just, kids, you know?"

"Children can be a challenge," Callie said. At sixteen, she had very little if any experience with kids, but having some level of empathy with a client, especially a new one, was important. She then asked the question her mom had taught her to use with every client: "What question can I answer for you today?"

"I'm concerned about my husband, actually," Mrs. Jones said. "I'm a stay-at-home mother and he's been working lots of long hours lately."

Once again, Callie let her attention wander as Mrs. Jones related her marital issues.

Callie squirmed a bit. She had never gotten comfortable listening to a person's most intimate moments, since, so far, she hadn't had any intimate moments herself. Because clients were less likely to trust a teenager for advice, Callie always made herself up to look five years older. Finally, Mrs. Jones wound down.

"You are concerned about an affair?" Callie asked.

"Well, yes."

"It isn't an affair you should be concerned about, Mrs. Jones," Callie said, placing one of her hands over the woman's shaking one. "I see that your husband is suffering from a great deal of stress. Perhaps his job is in jeopardy and he doesn't want to admit this to you." Callie had actually asked Chris the Whale about Mr. Jones to feel comfortable with this assessment. It always paid to do a little work ahead of time in this business.

"Oh, I didn't even consider that," Mrs. Jones said.

"Your husband is working at a hedge fund?" Callie asked.

"That's right."

"It has taken on some toxic investments and may be in danger of going under," Callie said.

"What should I do?" Mrs. Jones asked, putting her other hand on her chest.

"You must be as supportive as you can. It is important at this point to allow him to talk to you about his concerns at work. Also, you may have to consider going back to work yourself."

"Okay," Mrs. Jones responded, contemplating Callie's pronouncement. "I appreciate your help, Madam O'Callahan. I can't tell you how much this has weighed on my mind."

"The spirits only wish to help, Mrs. Jones," Callie said. She waited a few moments, staring at the woman. A puzzled expression filled her face until light dawned. "Oh yes, I think Chris said it was a hundred and fifty dollars for the first session. Is cash okay?"

"Yes ma'am. I promise this will go to a good cause, Mrs. Jones," Callie said, carefully taking the small pile of folded bills from the woman's outstretched hand. "I truly am glad to help you through your difficulties."

"Thank you, that's very kind," Mrs. Jones said, standing and pulling her large purse up onto her shoulder. "Bye now."

Callie watched the woman leave and glanced at the time on her phone. Just fifteen minutes before the train left to head back north. She grabbed her own bag and rushed toward the station. The peasant skirt she had borrowed from her mom's costume closet wasn't as easy to rush around in compared to jeans. The sky had turned to shades of deep blue, with the hint of a blush of sunset behind the trees. She didn't know the sprawling city well, having visited only certain places within easy access to the train station and the annual Renaissance Faire, which was held outside the city limits.

Callie made it just in time to catch the Piedmont and hopped aboard for the two-hour trip home. Finding a pair of side-by-side seats, she stretched out across them and put her bookbag under her head. The rocking motion of the train lulled her to sleep in minutes as it left the sparkling city skyline behind.

Chapter Three

Callie

Callie awoke in her bed, silently cursing her phone as its alarm went off. Her eyes felt grainy and her head felt full of cotton as she groped for the offending phone. She had that biology test today and had promised her mother she would do well, and that would require caffeine and a hot shower. She pulled her legs over the edge of the bed and stretched her arms over her head as she yawned big and loudly. She meandered, half awake and eyes half open, down the hall toward the bathroom.

"Morning, Cal," a voice called from the kitchen.

"Morning, Peg," Callie croaked in response. "Can you pour me a Coke on ice? I'll be down after a shower."

"Sure thing, Cal," Peggy said.

Callie and her mother stayed with Peggy during the school year. More specifically, Callie stayed with Peggy while her mother did the Fair circuit. Peggy owned a three-bedroom house and a small shop near the university, where Callie worked weekends and some evenings to offset room and board, but she actually looked upon Peggy more as an aunt than a landlord and boss. It was simply in Peggy's nature to take in strays and make them part of her family.

Once Callie emerged from the shower into the steamy bathroom, she felt halfway human again. After caffeine, the transformation would be complete. Once she was dressed in her jeans, baby-doll T-shirt with a picture of an anime character on the front, and a blue hoodie, she headed down the hall to the kitchen.

Peggy would normally make a full-on lumberjack breakfast, but Callie never had the appetite for that much food on a school day. She opted for a bowl of cereal, a banana, and a soda.

Callie noticed the mail on the table. One letter was from the state and was addressed to Clair O'Callahan. She snagged it while Peggy had her back turned and shoved it into her bookbag to read later. When Peggy turned toward the table again, Callie shuffled through the remaining mail and said, "Nothing interesting."

"Glad you made it in okay," Peggy said. "How were the clients?"

"The usual." Callie shrugged.

"So, what's on the agenda for today?"

"Biology test," Callie said after chewing her cereal.

"Ready for it?"

"Hope so," Callie replied, her mouth full of banana. She looked at her phone. "Gotta go, Peg. See you later."

"Can I expect you for dinner?" Peggy called after her.

"I want to visit Mom after school, so can you make me a plate and I'll eat it when I get home?" Callie said, already half out the door.

"Okay. Give her hugs from me," Peggy said.

Callie headed down to the corner to catch the school bus. She had the uncanny ability to arrive just as it pulled up to the curb, and today was no exception. Most of the kids on the bus were freshmen and sophomores, but no one she knew, so Callie found a seat, shoved her bookbag under her legs, closed her eyes, and daydreamed, ignoring the noisy banter of her fellow passengers until they arrived at Burkinbridge High School. She opened her eyes just as the bus pulled into the bus lane, and filed out the door with the rest of the high school lemmings into the building, to her locker and then to first-period Honors English class. She enjoyed this class mostly because Ms. Poppins required ten minutes of journaling before she launched into a discourse on *The Old Man and the Sea*. Callie used the time to pour her heart, hopes, and fears onto the page. Much of the time, her journaling was about her mother.

Callie entered the lunch room right after her Honors Biology class was done. The test had gone well—she felt like she would get a low A or high B—so she could relax a bit with her friends at the Misfit Toy table. She grabbed a turkey sandwich, a bag of chips, an apple, and a bottle of water before she wandered over to the Misfits.

"Hiya, Callie O." Jonathan was a senior with aspirations of writing screenplays and directing movies. He was over six feet and so thin that his bones showed starkly and his clothes hung loosely on his frame, but he always had great hair, no matter what.

"Hey, Cal." Melinda was the anime freak of the group; she had colored her hair a shade of green at the top, fading into a shade of blue at the tips. Her fingernails were a matching green, her lipstick a matching blue, and her eyeliner was a bit thick for the daytime. Melinda had given Callie the anime shirt she was currently wearing under her hoodie.

Lastly, there was Grey. He was a quiet African American freshman who had simply sat down with them one day. Grey was a person of few words, but what he had to say was often hilarious. He looked up and inclined his head as a greeting as Callie sat down.

"Damn, I'm glad that's over," she said.

"What's that?" Melinda asked.

"Oh, the freaking bio test," Callie said.

"Wait till you get into physics," Jonathan said.

"I'm in no hurry," Callie told him.

"I have *got* to get my cosplay figured out soon," Melinda said.

"Dude, Animazement isn't until May, you got months," Callie said. "What's the emergency?"

"You know it's, like, four days long, right?" Melinda asked. "I've got to figure out four different costumes. It's, like, really freakin' expensive and I have to sew some of them. I gotta hit up the parents for the money over time or they'll get sticker shock."

"Sound logic," Grey said, then he went back to reading his comic book.

"Hey, there's an Orson Welles movie marathon at Grinder's this weekend," Jonathan said. "I don't want to go alone—please, please, someone go with me." He put on his cute poutie face and tilted it first toward Melinda, then toward Callie.

"I might could go after my shift at Peggy's on Saturday," Callie said, "but I'll need a ride."

"I don't have the funds, Jon, but if you're willing to pay my way..." Melinda said.

"Fine, if that's what I have to do," Jonathan said. "Jeez, great friends you are."

"You know you love us," Melinda said, giving him a hug around the neck and a kiss on the cheek.

"When's your shift over on Saturday?" Jonathan asked Callie.

"Um, I think five?" she said. "But I'll have to ask Peggy to be sure."

"All right, text me then," Jonathan said.

He looked at Grey. "Dude?"

Grey looked up. "Sure. When?"

"Starts at ten a.m. Saturday and goes all night," Jonathan said.

"Cool, yeah. Pick me up, okay?" Grey said, and went back to reading his comic book again.

The remainder of lunch period went by with the three of them discussing Orson Welles' films, anime, and whatnot, with occasional interjections from Grey, until the bell rang for afternoon classes.

The rest of the afternoon was uneventful, for which Callie was quite thankful since her caffeine buzz had burned off sometime shortly after lunch. She hauled her bookbag over her shoulder and joined Jonathan in the parking lot for a ride to visit her mom. She took that opportunity to pull out the letter from the state addressed to Clair O'Callahan. She only half understood the bureaucratic-speak from the Medicaid letter, but she saw something that concerned her, something about rejecting payment for therapy. She sighed heavily and jammed the letter back into its envelope. Callie had been working tirelessly to earn the money to offset the medical bills Medicaid wouldn't cover, especially the daily rent on the place where her mom currently resided. Now Medicaid was going to make that job even harder for her.

Once they were in the car and driving, Jonathan asked, "How has she been doing?"

"Good days and bad days," Callie said. "But I'm hoping for more good days soon."

"I hope so, too," he said as he squeezed Callie's knee. "You need her back to normal."

"Yup, I do." It was so hard to talk about her mom and not have tears well up. She didn't want to fall apart in front of her friends, so she kept much of what was going on to herself and Peggy.

They arrived at the Hillcrest long-term care facility a bit before three p.m. Callie thanked Jonathan for the ride, hitched up her bookbag, and arranged her face into an optimistic, carefree expression. She knew her mom wouldn't buy it, but she played this game anyway.

Chapter Four

Callie

"Hi, sweetheart." Callie's mom, Clair, stretched out her arms to receive a hug from her daughter. Callie dropped her bookbag in the chair next to the room's one window before carefully hugging her mom and giving her a gentle kiss on the cheek. Clair O'Callahan swept her daughter's auburn bangs away from her hazel eyes so she could see her face clearly. Callie held Clair's other hand, trying to avoid the IV cannula inserted on the back of it. A dialysis machine was whirring away on the opposite side of the bed, removing toxins from her body that the kidneys would normally handle. Callie's mom needed a new kidney, but she had an autoimmune disease called lupus that caused her body to attack itself. Being wanderers and working the Fair circuit may have given them enough to live on, but it didn't offer full medical benefits. Callie's mom had let the lupus go for far too long without treatment, and it had led to kidney failure.

"Hi, Mom," Callie said. "How are you today?"

"Today's been tough. I've got some edema that they're worried about, but nothing we can't handle," her mom replied.

"I'm sure. You'll outlive us all," Callie said, smiling.

"You know I'm gonna try to." Her mom smiled back.

"What do you feel up to doing tonight?"

"I think I'd like to watch a movie," her mom replied. "How about a rom-com?"

"Sounds good. Whatever you want." Callie left the room to check out a tablet computer from the facility's library. When she returned, she scooted the chair up to the head of her mom's bed, and they sat together to watch Katharine Hepburn and Cary Grant in *The Philadelphia Story*.

Once the movie was over, Callie's mom looked over at her daughter, who returned her gaze with a wan smile.

"What happened at school today?" her mom asked.

"Well, I had that biology test. I think I did pretty well."

"Good. I want you to do your best, Callie. I want you to graduate and go to college. Promise me."

"Momma, you know I'll do whatever you want me to," Callie said, "as long as you promise me you'll do what the doctors say."

"I'm doing my part," her mom said. "They want to try an experimental treatment to deal with my lupus so I can get on the kidney transplant list. I told them I would."

"That's good!" Callie sat up, finally feeling that small ray of hope again. Now the denial-of-service letter from Medicaid made more sense. They wouldn't pay for the experimental treatment. Well, come hell or high water, Callie would make sure the cost would be covered and her mom would get the treatment.

"It'll start next Monday," her mom said.

"Tell me about it," Callie said.

Her mom tried to describe the complicated procedure that would essentially re-engineer her immune system. Callie listened with rapt attention so that she could do some research on the new treatment. She liked to trust people, but that didn't mean she *did* trust people—and doctors even less.

"I'm gonna hang out with Jon, Mels, and Grey after work on Saturday," Callie said, "but I'll be back on Sunday after work, okay?"

"That's fine, just fine. I'm glad you and your friends can spend some time together. You're here way too much."

"It's just you and me, kid," Callie said, giving her mom a mock clip to the jaw with her fist. "I have to go for now. School tomorrow."

"I know. Go get some rest, your bags have bags." She indicated the dark circles under Callie's eyes.

"Let me know if you need me to bring anything on Sunday. Maybe they'll let me bring you a treat before you start the new therapy."

"I will, my love," her mom said. "Sleep well tonight. Dream of handsome princes."

Callie gave her a peck on the cheek and squeezed her hand. "Dream of slaying dragons."

She grabbed her bookbag and ordered an Uber to avoid bothering Peggy who was probably engrossed in a romance novel.

When she got to Peggy's, it was well past dark. She pulled out her books to do homework and nuked the plate of food Peggy had left in the fridge. She didn't even notice what she was eating and struggled with concentrating on her homework. Thoughts of her mother's new therapy battled for her attention and stoked her fears no matter what she tried to do to stave them off.

Chapter Five

Amber

Amber woke up, or at least she thought she had. She blinked her eyes a few times but couldn't see anything; her immediate world was pitch black. Her head hurt pretty badly, so she thought maybe she was in one of those coma thingies. She couldn't remember what had happened before, when she was walking home. Had she tripped and hit her head? Was that why she was in a coma? She tried to move a finger. That worked pretty well. She moved her hand and felt a soft sheet under it. *Do you feel sheets when you're in a coma?* She bent her knees, finding that her legs seemed to work as they usually did. Maybe sitting up would get her out of the coma. She gave that a try. The pain in her head became more like a migraine, but it eventually subsided to a dull ache after a minute. Still no light. She patted the sheet to see what she was lying on, then felt the edges and determined it was a twin-sized something or other. She turned to put her feet down on the floor and found that she was, indeed, on a cot in a very dark room. She felt her clothes but wasn't wearing the sweater-and-skirt uniform she had worn to school; instead, it felt like a cotton tunic or smock. This didn't seem like a hospital room unless they could make them completely lightless. She couldn't hear anything either. The room felt like a cube of trapped air with the only sounds the ones being made by her movements, her breath, and her heartbeat. *That is really weird*, she thought. Amber had visited people in the hospital before and had never been in a room like this. Maybe she should call out and let someone know she was awake.

"Hello?"

No response.

"Hey, I'm awake now, can I have a glass of water?"

She waited for another beat, listening for footfalls or a reply or anything.

"Is anyone there? I'm really freaked out now."

Still not a sound.

Amber decided to get up and find a door to this bizarre room. Besides, she really needed to pee. Gingerly, she rose from the bed, putting her arms out to feel for obstructions, shuffling her bare feet forward an inch at a time, her eyes open wide. Amber found her first obstruction about four feet from the side of the bed. She ran her hands along it and down to the floor and up as high as she could reach. The surface was cold and rough. She thought it might be made of concrete blocks because of the indentations every six inches or so. She leaned her body against the wall and moved slowly alongside it, once again stretching out her arms and shuffling her feet forward. She came into contact with a shelf about chest high. She felt nothing on the shelf, so she moved past it to the wall perpendicular to the one she was leaning against. It was the same kind of material, so she continued along it until her hand met the doorjamb. She stepped in front of it, feeling it all along the edge for a knob or handle. The door felt like solid metal; the only indication that it could be opened was a key lock, like on the front door of a house.

"Hey, I'm awake in here!" Amber yelled while banging on the door with her fist. The metal hurt her hand so she switched to a flat palm to smack the door. She paused briefly to put her ear to the door in hopes that she might hear something on the other side. She continued to pound and yell until her hands felt bruised and her voice hoarse. She turned her back to the door and slid down it until she was sitting on the carpeted floor, concerned that the staff or whoever had forgotten she was in the room.

Chapter Six

Callie

"Hi there, Callie, did you sleep well?" the bride-to-be, Alyssa, asked.

Alyssa Windermere was the daughter of the Raleigh Windermeres, who owned one of the historical mansions downtown and had some influence in the state legislature. She was tall, waif-thin, and beautiful. She also happened to be acquainted with Callie's newest client, Mrs. Jones from Charlotte, which was why Callie was working as a psychic medium at this bachelorette party. If everything went well, Callie expected to get paid enough to cover two more months of care for her mother at Hillcrest. She had learned at her mother's knee everything she knew about mediumship, and Clair was one of the best.

"Eventually," Callie replied. The bridesmaids and Alyssa had kept her up past two a.m. with their pre-wedding debauchery.

She and Alyssa were bundled up and seated on lounge chairs on a Bodie Island beach, along with Alyssa's bridesmaids, who weren't looking much better.

"We want to play a game with you," Alyssa said.

"Sure, what kind of game?" Callie asked. Her voice sounded more upbeat than she felt. This "game" was actually a test to see if she was what she claimed to be.

"It should be easy for you," Alyssa said. "We have a list here"—she handed it to Callie—"of different facts about each of us. You have to figure out which fact goes with which girl, okay?"

"I'll give it a try," Callie said. This wasn't that hard a test if you knew how to read people's expressions and body language. Of course, with the girls all bundled up like they were, it would be a bit harder. "Can we go in where it's warm, though?"

"I would like to go in for tea," the one named Jessica said, holding her blanket closer.

The others agreed with her.

"Fine, you lightweights, we'll go in," Alyssa said, pushing herself up out of the beach chair and stomping up to the house.

Once inside the Windermere beach house and sipping hot tea on the large and comfy sectional, the group stared up at Callie, who paced the floor in front of them. She read through the list of facts Alyssa had given to her and then looked carefully at each of the girls in turn. They began to giggle in anticipation and poked one another.

"First is 'I was born in Canada,'" Callie read. There was the mousy, introverted Barbara at the end, Jessica next to her, a statuesque beauty called Olivia, a ginger-haired girl with pixie-like features named Tosh, Alyssa next to her, and a dark-haired girl named Felicity, whom they called Flee. Callie looked for clues in their body language and found a tell in Barbara.

"I think it's Barbara," Callie said.

"Yes, it's me," Barbara said, raising her hand halfway.

"Second is 'I was born with a sixth toe on each foot,'" Callie read. *Who liked to hide their feet? Ah, Olivia.*

"Olivia," Callie said.

"Right-o," Olivia said.

Callie went down the list, missing only a couple, garnering enthusiastic applause after each correct answer and groans when she got it wrong.

"Very well done, Callie. Anyone else hungry?" Alyssa asked, clapping her hands together. "I'm famished."

Glynnis—the "help," as Alyssa put it—must have had radar or some sort of listening device in the room, because she chose that moment to announce, "Luncheon is ready, miss."

The party moved toward the dining room, talking animatedly with one another and Callie about the accuracy of her answers. The dining room was in a glassed-in enclosure with an incredible view of the beach and ocean beyond. A set of french doors led to a narrow deck that went along the outer wall of the house to allow access from bedrooms. Glynnis had laid out fruits, cheeses, bread, yogurt, and lunch meats for the girls to choose from. Callie got a bit of each item and ate them gingerly while being peppered with questions.

"How did you learn to be a psychic?" Jessica asked.

"My mom taught me from the time I was old enough to talk," Callie said.

"Your mom? What does she do?" Alyssa asked.

"She's a psychic medium who travels to shows around the country."

"So, you traveled with her?" Tosh asked.

"I did until I was old enough for school," Callie said. "Then I traveled with her in the summer."

"Did your dad travel with you?" Barbara asked.

"No, I don't know my dad," Callie said.

That last question brought a bit of awkward silence to the table until Alyssa broke the tension. "No worries, many of us come from divorced families."

Callie smiled but didn't reply. Instead, she ate a strawberry.

"So, what are we doing the rest of the day?" Felicity asked. "I don't want to stay cooped up in the house all weekend."

"Of course not!" Alyssa said, sounding almost offended. "I must take you all shopping in town. There are such cute shops on the island. Then we'll go to Lemon's for dinner and come home for a séance with Callie the Magnificent!"

All the girls responded with enthusiastic consent. Callie assumed she was not invited, which was fine with her. Her money needed to be spent elsewhere. Besides, it took time to set up a good séance.

Of the many rooms Glynnis had shown Callie for the séance, she decided on the game room for its large, circular table. She preferred to have people in a circle formation whenever possible so that she could see everyone easily. Callie laid out a dark blue cloth over the table and asked Glynnis for some candles to set around the room for "atmosphere." She then thanked Glynnis for her time but said she would need to perform the rest of the preparations privately. She shut the door on Glynnis, who looked a bit concerned about leaving a strange girl with odd proclivities alone in there, but she did not have a chance to argue.

Callie's preparations included a trick candle that would go out and relight when she pressed a wireless device adhered to the underside of the table within easy reach. She had also brought with her a small bell, which she placed in the center of the table. The bell would "ring" by having the wireless device turn on her MP3 player, which would then play a recording of the bell ringing. Callie was also well versed in fake knocks and having the wind blow through the room, all of which took time to set up. She took a peek out the door to make sure Glynnis wasn't eavesdropping before she sat down at her chair and performed a pre-check of all her devices and tricks. With that settled, she left the room and closed the door. She placed a "Do Not Enter" sign on the knob to keep everyone out until showtime, noticed she was hungry, and made her way to the kitchen for dinner.

"Hi, Glynnis," Callie said as she walked into the kitchen. Glynnis was reading a magazine at the kitchen table. "You don't get much downtime, do you?"

"No, but I love caring for Alyssa," Glynnis replied. "And soon, she'll be away and married."

Callie nodded and said, "What's available to eat for dinner?"

"There's a roast chicken in the fridge with some red potatoes and green beans," Glynnis told her. "Alyssa didn't let me know they wouldn't be staying for dinner, so there's plenty. Eat as much as you want."

Ah, to be wealthy enough not to care about your staff's hard work, Callie thought.

She finished up her meal and told Glynnis she would be in her room resting until the girls returned from their outing and were ready for the séance. With that, she went to her room, pulled off her boots, and fell fast asleep in her clothes.

The girls arrived back sometime after eight p.m. carrying shopping bags filled with clothes, shoes, jewelry, and other accessories, and they were none too quiet about it. Callie woke up when she heard their squeals and laughter and decided to get dressed in her mother's best psychic-medium garb. She started with a multicolored peasant skirt with a flouncy red blouse covered in ruffles. A wide piece of fabric, pinned in place by a large ouroboros brooch, encircled her waist. She wound her hair up with another piece of fabric and a dragon brooch. She placed several silver rings on her fingers, and necklaces with Celtic symbols around her neck. She then put on enough makeup to change her look from young and innocent to dark and mysterious. The transformation complete, Callie walked quietly down the hall to the séance room. She removed the sign before entering and then took her seat while she waited for the girls to arrive. It didn't take long before Callie heard them ask Glynnis where she was. Glynnis directed them to the game room while she said she would get Callie up from her nap. Having the girls see her already in place was another tactic she used for making herself seem prescient and mysterious. A successful séance was about the setting, the ambiance. Alyssa opened the game room door, laughing, but when she saw the transformed Callie in the dim, candlelit room,

Alyssa stopped in her tracks. The rest of the girls pushed her farther into the room so that they could get a look at Callie.

Callie's face was a mask of confidence and authority. She did not speak but merely indicated with her hand that the girls should sit. It didn't matter where, so she hadn't assigned them chairs. She figured that Alyssa would sit next to her anyway, and she was right. Barbara sat directly across from Callie, and Jessica to Callie's right. The others filled in the remaining chairs. When everyone was settled, Callie began the séance.

"We do not wish to anger the spirits who deign to visit us this night," she said. "To do so would invite strife to you and each of your families. Do precisely what I say when I say it."

The girls nodded, eyes wide.

"The spirits may speak through me or they may use something in the room to communicate," Callie continued, indicating the bell. "It is best if we join hands to complete the circle of protection and power."

Each girl took the hand of the one next to her, and Callie took Alyssa's and Jessica's. She could control the trick devices with her knees and feet.

"Each of you must think of a departed loved one whom you would like to have contact with tonight," Callie said. "Keep their names and faces in your mind, remove all other thoughts."

The girls all closed their eyes and concentrated hard.

"I feel a presence joining us," Callie said. "Spirit, identify yourself." She pressed the wireless device to cause the bell to ring. "You will have to ask the spirit questions that can be answered with a yes or no. Spirit, answer yes with one bell ring, and no with two." The bell rang once more. "Alyssa, I feel that this spirit is here for you."

Alyssa opened her eyes and looked around in hopes that she could catch a glimpse of the spirit. "Grandpa?" The bell rang once. "Oh, Grandpa, I've missed you so much! Please tell me you're okay?"

Again, the bell rang once. "Are you with Grandma?" And once again. "I wanted you to be here for my wedding, James is such a wonderful guy, I know you would love him." Another single ring. "You don't know how much that means to me." Alyssa's eyes filled with tears.

"Another spirit has come," Callie said. "Spirit, identify yourself. This spirit is communicating directly through me. She is a woman who died of cancer. Her name starts with a C."

"That's my aunt Cecilia," Tosh said, her eyes wide. "She passed only last year."

"Do you wish to ask her anything?" Callie asked.

"No, I just miss her," Tosh said.

"She is saying that she appreciated your visit before she died," Callie said, "and she is happy that you are doing well."

It was Tosh's turn to cry. Callie almost felt guilty. Almost.

She gave comfort to each and every girl through single and double bell rings. It was amazing how easy it was to ask just the right questions and provide just the right answers for these girls to believe they were having unearthly conversations with discarnate family members and friends. Callie felt pangs of guilt just a couple of times as she watched tears fall from the bride-to-be's eyes. She shook it off, remembering her mother's gaunt form and pained expression. These girls would be donating to a worthy charity whether they knew it or not. After exhausting all possible lines of spiritual inquiry, it was now time to show everyone the finale. Callie loved the finale.

"I feel another spirit," she said. "This one feels angry." She caused the wind to blow through the room the candles started to flicker. A loud, heavy knocking began to pound from the corner, and the stage candles' flames disappeared and reappeared.

Each of the girls jumped at the knocking sound and looked around at the flickering candles.

"We must send this spirit back from whence he came," Callie said loudly. "Help me send him back!"

The girls obviously had no idea how they should help, but they held hands as if their very lives depended on the protection they provided one another.

Callie swayed and groaned. Her eyes rolled back in her head, saliva dripped down her chin, and smoke snaked up from behind her. Finally, she dropped her head down onto her chest and sat still for a few seconds. Pretending to rouse herself, she said, "What happened?" She looked around at each of the girls, who in turn looked at her with saucer eyes.

"You dispelled an evil spirit," Tosh said. "Are you okay?"

"I—I think so," Callie stammered, looking a bit wan, her hand on her chest.

"That was incredible," Jessica said.

"I don't think I can do more tonight," Callie said. "Calling that many spirits requires a lot of energy. I will need to get some rest before I can do any more readings."

"Of course," Alyssa said, patting Callie's hand. "You have let me speak to my grandpa. I am so grateful!"

Chapter Seven

Callie

The bridesmaids had invited over a trio of young men who were also visiting the island for a weekend of carefree partying. Callie was in no mood for parties, so she changed into her usual jeans and T-shirt and pulled on her jacket, knit cap, and gloves to walk the beach for some communion time with nature's awesome force. The wind was strong, whipping the waves into froth and whistling past her ears. She smelled brine as the mist from the waves wafted ashore.

Callie decided to call Peggy to get an update about her mom. As far as Peggy knew, Callie was spending the weekend with Mels, who was aware of the duplicity and would cover for her if asked.

"She seems to be really upbeat today," Peggy said. "The therapy is still a go."

"Good," Callie replied with a sigh of relief. "I was worried they would cancel on her after the Medicaid rejection."

"How did you know about that?" Peggy asked.

"I have my witchy ways." Callie said.

"Just like Clair," Peggy said. "Are you having a good time at Melinda's?"

"Yeah, we're having a blast."

Callie had walked all the way down to Bodie Island's country club, where she sat on the beach in the glow of the lights emanating from the large ballroom and listened to the jazz music the band was playing, the wind pulling the sound to and fro, giving it a ghostly quality.

"Since when do you girls listen to jazz?" Peggy asked.

Callie realized that she had to come up with a quick response. "That isn't us, it's a bunch of old folks dancing to a live band." It wasn't a total lie.

"Oh. When are you coming home?"

"I should be back tomorrow evening unless something drastic happens," Callie said.

"I'll call you immediately if there's any news, I promise," Peggy said. "You try and have a good time, and don't worry."

"I'm keeping my mind on other stuff."

"Good, good," Peggy said. "Clair wouldn't want you to worry so much. I'll see you tomorrow night, then."

"Thanks, Peggy," Callie said, pressing the end button.

When she couldn't feel her nose and fingers from the cold, she decided to make her way back to the Windermere beach house. Perhaps things would be quiet enough for her to get some sleep since she had been kept up much of the night before. Fortunately, the girls had decided to play poker in the game room with the three visiting boys, keeping the noise down the hall and behind closed doors. Callie was able to get to sleep by midnight.

She woke up before her alarm, quietly showered and got dressed, then tiptoed down to the kitchen for some coffee and a bowl of cereal. Once she was done with breakfast, she patiently and quietly continued with her preparations for the day's psychic fun. It took a couple of hours before the earliest riser of the princess crew got up to join Callie in the common room. Of course it would be Barbara, who looked like she hadn't participated in the poker game; she appeared well rested and fresh from a shower.

"Good morning, Barbara," Callie said from her corner perch on the sectional sofa.

"Oh, I didn't see you there," Barbara said. "Good morning."

"How are you feeling today? It sounded like quite a fun night."

"I guess so." Barbara shrugged. "I went to bed early. It was a long day and the boys were paying more attention to the others anyway."

"They just don't appreciate us quiet types, do they?" Callie said. "Don't need them. Your prince will come sooner than you think."

"You think so?" Barbara asked.

"I know so, Barbara." Callie tapped her temple. "I am a psychic, after all."

"Oh, of course," Barbara said. "Sorry." She looked askance at Callie. "What did you see? I mean, what kind of guy? Is he someone I know?"

"It's someone who knows you," Callie said, "but he hasn't connected with you yet. He's afraid you'll reject him."

"I can't imagine doing that."

"He doesn't know that," Callie told her.

"Who is he? What does he do?" Barbara pressed.

"I have learned to keep such details to myself," Callie said. "Misinterpretations have occurred."

"Misinterpretations?"

"I may describe a person in a psychic way, which is knowing his spirit," Callie said, "but you may misinterpret that as being a different person than I would, since you wouldn't have the same type of connection."

Barbara nodded as she considered Callie's explanation. "What should I do to help him approach me?"

"Be open and kind, just like you are now," Callie told her. "You must walk your own path. Being with Alyssa and her friends is holding you back from your future."

"Are you saying I should give up my friends?"

"Of course not," Callie said. "Getting some distance from them for a while while you consider what you want for your life will help. After all, Alyssa is getting married soon and the group will organically change."

"So, this man won't approach me because of my friends?" Barbara asked.

"Together they are a strong force and he is just one man," Callie said.

"I hadn't thought of that," Barbara admitted.

"I see more if you want to know," Callie said.

"I would, actually."

The two of them talked for another hour before Tosh and Jessica joined them, each hanging on a boy. They all looked pretty rough in the rumpled clothing they had on the day before. One of the boys was suffering from major bed head.

"Coffee, please, Glynnis," Jessica yelled toward the kitchen.

"Yes, miss," Glynnis replied.

"Hiya Barbara, Callie," Tosh said as she plopped down on the couch.

"We've got to go," one of the boys said. "We're leaving on the noon ferry. It was a blast!"

"Cheers," Jessica said as she plopped down next to Tosh, waving a hand over her head.

"See you again sometime," Tosh said.

"Sure thing, you got my digits," the other boy said.

Barbara appeared to fold in on herself again just as Jessica and Tosh sprawled out on the couch next to her.

"What's going on here?" Jessica asked.

"Callie was just giving me a psychic reading when you came in," Barbara said.

"Really?" Tosh asked. "You do that, too?"

"That's my specialty," Callie said. "Would either of you like me to read you?"

"I don't know, I'm kind of a short book," Tosh said, giggling at her joke.

I haven't heard that one before, Callie thought sarcastically.

"Sure. That'll pass the time before we leave," Jessica said. "What do you know about me?"

"Well, I prefer to tell you in private," Callie said. "What I say is for your ears alone. You may tell anyone you want about it afterward, though."

"Fine, we can talk after coffee," Jessica said.

Callie took Jessica out on the expansive deck for her reading. They were sitting on deck chairs facing the ocean. The sky was filled with clouds, but the wind was quieter than it had been the night before. There was a small table between their chairs where Callie had placed a silver-wire-wrapped amethyst pendant attached to a black silk cord.

"What's that?" Jessica asked.

"It's a charm," Callie said. "You should have it."

"Why do I need a charm?" Jessica looked at Callie with distaste.

"Remember that I dispelled an angry spirit during the séance last night? I don't think I was able to make it go away completely," Callie said. "It can linger and attach itself to people."

"Is it here now?" Jessica looked around nervously. "Why would it attach to me?"

"It's hard to tell what angry spirits want to do until they do it," Callie said. "So I create these charms of protection as insurance."

"I didn't do anything! You're the one who brought it here." Jessica's voice was becoming strident.

"I did warn you that a séance could have consequences," Callie said. "This is simply a precaution. Take it or not, if you want, but if you take it, it would be more effective if you made a sacrifice."

"I'm not gonna have to cut up a chicken or something, am I?" Jessica asked.

"No, I mean a personal sacrifice. Think of it as an investment. This charm could protect you from more than just this one angry spirit," Callie said.

"I can give you money," Jessica said.

"If that's what you would like to do," Callie said. "Keep in mind, the more you sacrifice, the more faith you will have in the charm, and faith is what defeats evil."

"Okay, I'll get some funds together," Jessica said.

"Your donation will go to a worthy cause, I promise you," Callie said.

"You aren't keeping it for yourself?" Jessica asked.

"No, it would not be a proper sacrifice if I kept the money," Callie said. "Now that you have made the decision to protect yourself, I am able to see a much happier path open for you. Would you like me to tell you about your future?"

"Sure, of course," Jessica said.

Callie told her all about her successful career in law and a handsome husband with two gifted daughters. Satisfied with the result of the reading, Jessica went in to get her credit card while Callie "blessed" the crystal.

"Could you let Tosh know I'm ready to give her a reading if she wants one?" Callie said to a distracted Jessica. She got a thumbs-up in response. Tosh was a bit savvier than the others, so Callie opted to give her the reading first and then offer a smoky quartz crystal to her if she wanted one. Tosh would smell a rat with the type of hard sell she had made with Jessica.

"Jessica said I could come out now," Tosh said, poking her head through the open french doors.

"Only if you want a reading," Callie said. "What do you want to know?"

"I want to know what I'm going to die from," Tosh said.

"I see that you will live quite a long life and die from cancer," Callie told her. It was the most likely cause of death Callie had learned from Tosh's family history.

"That's not bad," Tosh said. "Okay...How about...Will I get married and who will it be?"

"You aren't the marrying kind," Callie said. Tosh had said as much herself on social media. "There may be a man you stay with for many years. He seems like someone who shares a love of profession with you and he holds you in high regard, but that path is not clear. All of this is dependent on your choices."

"That's true, I'm not interested in marrying," Tosh said. "I love what I do too much, but he sounds interesting."

"What do you do?" Callie asked.

"I'm a photojournalist," Tosh said.

"I did see many destinations in your future," Callie said. "I wondered what would cause you to travel so much."

"Where will I get a job?" Tosh asked.

"I see you as a freelancer. You don't want to be tied down," Callie said—also something Tosh had said about herself on social media. "If you choose to, you will be hired by one of the major news organizations." Which was a stretch of Callie's imagination, but made Tosh feel good.

"That would be awesome!" Tosh said.

The two spoke about Tosh's career path for a while longer. When the discussion started to ebb, Callie pulled out the smoky quartz pendant hanging from a deep blue silk necklace.

"What's that?" Tosh asked.

"I wanted to offer you something if you'd like it," Callie said. "I gave one to Jessica."

"Oh, that's lovely," Tosh said. "What's it for?"

"I offer crystals of protection to my special clients," Callie said.

"How much?" Tosh asked.

"As much as you feel it's worth," Callie said. "Many of my clients have been very pleased with my crystal charms."

"Okay, I'll be right back," Tosh said.

Callie didn't expect to get much from Tosh. She wasn't the kind of girl who felt like she needed much luck, instead using her ability and good looks to get what she wanted. However, the charm would be a fun story piece for her and if she had good luck while wearing it, she would believe in its nature as a protection charm. Sometimes that was all it took to get a repeat customer with referrals.

Since she was done with three of the clients, Callie decided to go inside, where she could get a hot tea and lunch and get warmed up. It was still pretty chilly outside even though it was near noon. She ran into Tosh, who handed her a credit card, which she took with her to the hallway to swipe on her Pay Square. She brought the card back to Tosh in time to see Felicity and Alyssa arrive in the common room.

"What's going on here?" Alyssa looked at the pensive faces of Barbara, Tosh, and Jessica as they stared out toward the ocean.

"We got read," Tosh said.

"What do you mean, red?" Felicity asked.

"No," Barbara said, "Callie gave us each a psychic reading."

"I want one!" Alyssa said, jumping up and down like a little girl at Christmas. "I want to know about my wedding!"

Felicity just sat down on the couch next to Jessica and stared at Callie.

"Sure, Alyssa," Callie said. "We can certainly do that, but I wanted to take a quick lunch break, if you don't mind."

"Fine," Alyssa said with a pout. "I guess I should eat something, too."

Callie went to the kitchen to grab the leftover roast chicken and put it between two pieces of wheat toast that she had spread mayonnaise on. Then she foraged for some of the fruit Glynnis had put out the day before. She sat down at the kitchen table to eat while the others made their way into the dining room for the luncheon Glynnis had set up for them. Callie didn't like Felicity's aggressive reaction just now. She had seemed to enjoy everything so far. Perhaps she was skeptical? Well, skeptics came with the territory. Callie had some weapons in her toolbox to counter any attack, as long as she was prepared for one.

Callie finished up her sandwich and wandered into the dining room, where the others were talking animatedly about the boys who had shown up the night before and comparing their hangovers.

"Alyssa, I'll meet you in the game room when you're ready," Callie said.

"I'll be there in a minute," Alyssa said.

Callie walked into a giant mess of bottles, playing cards, snack bags, and other trash. She cleaned up the table, putting what she could into a small trash can in the corner. She figured there was staff who would come on Monday to clean the house up. Well past a minute and more like fifteen, Alyssa finally opened the door to the game room and came in to sit by Callie, who was in the same chair she had used the night of the séance.

"Well, Miss Callie," Alyssa said. "What do the stars have in mind for me and my sweet James?"

Callie took Alyssa's hands and stared directly into her eyes. No one ever felt comfortable with that kind of close, direct eye contact, and Alyssa was no exception.

"What on earth are you doing?" Alyssa said, trying to pull away.

"Sorry," Callie said, "I should have warned you."

"I should say!" Alyssa said.

"Please let me try again?" Callie asked.

"If you must," Alyssa said, and moved back toward Callie. "Next time, warn a girl."

Callie didn't warn people specifically to unbalance them. It was more a form of power exchange, making her in charge of the reading instead of the client. She took Alyssa's hands once again and stared into her eyes. Alyssa started to giggle.

"I'm sorry," she said. "This is just too odd."

"I know," Callie said. "But it does help me read you better."

"Did you see anything?" Alyssa asked.

"I see that you are getting married at Duke Chapel," Callie said. She had looked that part up in the public wedding announcement.

"Yes," Alyssa said. "Two weeks from today."

"James is very much in love with you," Callie said.

"I should hope so!" Alyssa said.

"Your father didn't approve of him at first," Callie said. James had said as much in a social media post.

"My father had someone else in mind for me," Alyssa said.

"James took your father on a fishing trip in the mountains to change his mind," Callie said.

"That's right," Alyssa said.

"There was a bear encounter. James managed to scare the bear away, protecting your father." Callie had found a shaky video to prove this.

"Yes," Alyssa said, her voice quiet.

"You wanted your mother to visit you at the séance," Callie said. "She died in childbirth having your youngest brother."

"Yes," Alyssa whispered.

It might have seemed amazing to the layperson to know all that information, but Alyssa's family had a large social media footprint. All Callie had had to do was read a few interesting posts and backgrounds.

"What do you want to know?" Callie asked.

"Um, I want to know if I will have children," Alyssa said, "and if I will survive to see them grow up."

Callie wasn't prepared for that last request, so she closed her eyes for a while to think over the answer. Finally, she opened her eyes and looked at Alyssa.

"Medicine has come a long way since your mother's time," Callie said. "The doctors will be prepared to keep you safe during your delivery."

"That's a relief!" Alyssa said.

The reading went on to describe Alyssa's career and family life, what James's career would be like, and his potential for public office. Finally, Callie decided to bring up the charm she had for Alyssa.

"I offer my special clients charms for protection and luck. I have one here that I made for you," Callie said, pulling out a gold chain necklace with a ring dangling from it. The ring, which she had purchased from a pawn shop, had a square-cut diamond in an art deco setting.

"This special charm is a wedding ring from a woman who was happily married for fifty years before she passed away in her sleep. Her spirit will guide you when you need help," Callie said, holding up the ring for Alyssa to see. Callie didn't actually know the history behind the ring; it could have been hocked by a woman getting a divorce.

"This is incredible!" Alyssa said, taking the charm in her hand.

"This requires a sacrifice from you," Callie said, "in the form of a donation."

"How much of a donation?" Alyssa asked.

"A sacrifice means that you offer something of value to you, so please consider how much that would be for you," Callie said. "I won't be keeping it."

"I will apply that to your fee when we get back home," Alyssa said.

"As you wish."

The pair walked back to the common room where Felicity was sitting alone watching a football game.

"How'd it go?" Felicity asked when Alyssa sat down next to her on the couch.

"Callie has such insight!" Alyssa said. "You should get a reading too, Flee."

"Oh, I'm planning on it," Felicity said. Was it Callie's imagination, or did Felicity sound like she was planning to have a fight rather than a reading?

"Whenever you're ready," Callie said, "just let me know." She wasn't going to be intimidated that easily.

Chapter Eight

Callie

"You're a scam artist," Felicity said.

Callie and Felicity were back in the game room after Callie took a break from Alyssa's reading. *Oh, here we go*, she thought.

"What makes you say that?" Callie asked.

"I figured out your little tricks during the séance," Felicity said. "I looked it all up afterward and you didn't really say anything specific."

"What about Tosh's aunt?" Callie asked.

"That wasn't directed to her, she just piped up when you brought up a dead woman who had cancer."

"Fine, you got me there." Callie said.

"Look," Felicity said. "I love my friends, and Alyssa? She's not the shiniest knife in the silver drawer, so I don't want her scammed, you got that?" Her perfectly manicured finger was pointed directly at Callie's nose.

"I haven't run a scam here," Callie said, keeping her voice steady. "I may not be a real medium, you're right, and the séance was just for entertainment. If you'd like, I can perform a reading for you and you can judge."

"What the hell is the difference?" Felicity's tone was a mix of sarcasm and menace.

"I don't talk to the dead," Callie said. "I get impressions on live people."

"Fine—do your best damned reading right now or I'll let my friends know they've been conned, do you understand me?"

Callie simply sat there staring at Felicity, scrunching her eyes and tilting her head just a bit. She leaned into Felicity's space, which caused the woman to sit back into her chair, startled. What could she say to this woman to convince her? Callie had learned a few things from Felicity's social media posts but wasn't sure which one would do the trick. Skeptics' beliefs, once established, were hard to sway.

"What are you doing?" Felicity asked.

"Just what you demanded, my best damned reading," Callie said. "Now sit still, please."

Felicity sat still as directed, her menacing demeanor dissipating, but she kept her arms crossed and stared back at Callie in defiance. Callie let her mind wander while staring fixedly at Felicity's eyes, hoping for an epiphany. Finally, a vision flashed into her mind like scenes from a movie.

"There's a story you've never told anyone," Callie said, quietly. "You were raped by a basketball player in high school. He saw you at a party and came to talk to you. You talked for a while but then you started dancing with another guy. When you were heading to your car, he grabbed you and forced you into the back seat. He told you he wouldn't be rejected by some skank and he raped you. He said that if you told anyone he would kill you."

Felicity's eyes filled with tears; her mouth was wide open. When Callie finished speaking, the dam broke and Felicity put her hands over her face, sobbing. Callie came back from seeing the scene of Felicity's rape to seeing Felicity fall apart in front of her. She knelt on the floor in front of Felicity and held her as best she could.

"I'm so sorry, I shouldn't have done that to you," Callie said.

"Oh, my God!" Felicity said. "No one knows what happened. No one...How?"

"I saw it happen to you," Callie said, awestruck.

"Please don't tell anyone!" Felicity said between sobs.

"I would never, ever do that," Callie said. "I told you that everything I say is private and I mean it, especially this. But you shouldn't hold it in, Flee. You need to get counseling for what you've been through or you'll never be free."

"I know, I...just try to...forget about it," Felicity said. "I can't get intimate with anyone or it'll all come back."

Callie recalled the numerous times her mother had offered advice under similar circumstances and said, "Please promise me you'll get help. Your future will be so bleak if you don't resolve this. It'll be a lonely life. He's long gone and can't hurt you ever again."

"Thank you, Callie," Felicity said.

Felicity sat back up, rubbing the tears off her cheeks. After taking a few deep breaths, she said, "I need to go get packed."

As both girls stood up to leave the game room, Felicity grabbed Callie into a hug.

"I'm sorry I doubted you," Felicity said. "You're the real thing."

Callie had never had anything like that reading happen to her before. Reeling from the shock of it, she sagged against the doorjamb as she watched Felicity walk down the hall.

Chapter Nine

Amber

Amber was tired, thirsty, and still seated with her back to the metal door that had no handle. Still in pitch blackness, she heard nothing. Wasn't a hospital supposed to be noisier, and wasn't it really unsafe to put someone in a room with no lights? She decided to go back to the cot and lie down since there didn't seem to be anything else she could do. Using the door to guide her to a standing position, she walked forward in a shuffling gait until her right shin came into contact with the cot. She really needed to pee but didn't know where the bathroom was.

After what seemed like an hour, more or less, Amber heard someone put a key in the lock, the familiar crunch, and then the thunk of the lock as the tongue recessed into the door. Whoever was on the other side opened the door slowly, as if he or she thought Amber might still be asleep. She wasn't. She had been lying there, fear warring with hope as light began to filter into the room from the other side of the door.

"Hello?" Amber said. She shielded her night-blind eyes from the expanding shaft of light with her hand. No one answered. Instead, as her eyes adjusted to the light, she saw the silhouette of a body in the doorframe.

"Can I have some water? And where's the bathroom?" Amber sat up on the cot. "What am I doing here? Is this a hospital? Where are my parents?"

The body didn't move from the door. "Look in the corner, there's a place for you to pee," a man's baritone voice uttered. A shadowed arm pointed in the direction the voice indicated.

Amber looked around the room for the first time since she had been brought to it. There was the shelf she had run into, and a small set of cabinets across from the foot of the cot, and in the corner was a portable toilet like they used in old folks' homes. There was no window, and the walls, as she had suspected, were made of concrete blocks painted some institutional color like tan or gray; it was hard to tell which.

"I'll bring you water and some food," the person said, quickly pulling the door closed, leaving Amber once again in complete darkness.

"NO! WAIT!" Amber cried out. She lunged off the cot toward the door and stumbled into it as she heard the lock click. She smashed her ear against the cold surface. All she could hear were creaking sounds like heavy footfalls on wooden stairs and the sound of another door closing. She stood there dazed for a few minutes but then decided she really, really needed to pee.

Chapter Ten

Callie

"You are exhausted," Peggy said. "You can't keep this up or you'll be in a bed right next to your mom."

"I know," Callie said. "It's just hell week at school with exams and my English paper is due." True, she had a lot of school work, but the nights she said she was studying at a friend's house were actually spent in sessions with clients or as a party entertainer for bachelorettes or birthday girls. The Windermere party on Bodie Island alone had netted ten grand toward her mom's treatments. Frankly, she wasn't sure she'd pass this semester, but that would be a battle for another day. What was important was Clair's treatment.

"I've got to catch the bus," Callie said as she grabbed her bag and pushed open the door. "I'll make dinner tonight!"

"Okay, have a good day!" Peggy yelled from the kitchen just before the door slammed shut.

Callie sat in her first-period English class writing in her journal. *I wish I could give her my energy, my health, my power, but I am powerlessly watching her waste away into the shell of my mom, a chrysalis from which I hope she will arise one day, the mom I remember, strong, healthy, and beautiful.* It was then that a kid showed up to whisper something to Ms. Poppins and hand her a small piece of paper. Ms. Poppins put on her reading glasses, read the paper, frowned, and then looked up to see Callie returning her gaze.

"Callie, please go to the principal's office. You have a visitor," Ms. Poppins said.

The pain of dread spiking in her chest, Callie got up from her chair, collected her books and bag, and followed the kid. She felt like a dead girl walking as she made her way down the deserted hallway, the messenger's footsteps echoing along with hers down the corridor. When she arrived at the office, she saw Peggy there, speaking to the principal who had a look of commiseration on her face.

"Peggy, what's going on?" Callie asked.

Peggy turned around and took Callie's hands. "Sweetheart, your mom has been transferred to the hospital, to the ICU."

Callie felt like she had been punched in the face. "What? Why?"

"I'm here to take you to the hospital. We'll learn more when we get there." Peggy said as she steered Callie out of the office.

"I need to go to my locker first." Callie spoke automatically, her brain not registering things very well.

"Okay, I'll go with you," Peggy said, following Callie.

Once Callie got her books put away in her locker, she and Peggy walked to the car.

"What happened? Why did she need to go to the ICU?"

"The doctors were always afraid of infection, and since your mom was also on dialysis, there was a higher risk of one," Peggy said.

"There's an infection?" Callie said.

"That's all I know so far," Peggy said.

The car ride to the hospital was quiet with neither Peggy nor Callie interested in conversation. Once they arrived, they had to navigate the confusing hospital layout to find the ICU, then deal with the nurse at the nurses' station since visitors were restricted. Peggy pressed the button next to the double doors for the ICU and a woman's voice said, "How may I help you?"

"We're here to see Clair O'Callahan," Peggy said.

"Ms. O'Callahan is awake at the moment but the doctors are still assessing her. You'll need to wait until they let me know she can receive visitors," the woman said.

Peggy and Callie turned toward the chair-filled waiting area that had a coffeemaker and water dispenser on a small table. A flat-screen TV on the wall had a twenty-four-hour news station running on mute.

"I need to see my mother," Callie said as if she hadn't heard the nurse.

"Callie, we need to wait here for now. They'll let us in when they're done." Peggy gently pushed Callie into a chair, and then sat next to her, patting the hand she held in hers.

Callie pulled her hand from Peggy's grasp, wrapped her arms around her middle like a straitjacket, and began to rock back and forth. Peggy could do nothing more than gently rub her back and make soothing sounds.

"She'll get past this," Callie said. "She promised me she would."

"I know, sweetheart. She is very strong and she doesn't want to leave us."

Tears finally started falling down Callie's cheeks while she rocked back and forth. She thought the pain in her chest was what a heart attack might feel like; her intestines felt liquefied. Peggy found a box of tissues and held one out to Callie, who took it and angrily wiped the tears away before resuming her straitjacketed rocking pose.

They waited about a half hour before the ICU doors swung open automatically and a pair of lab-coated doctors walked into the waiting room. They noticed Callie and Peggy.

"Are you Miss O'Callahan?" the older doctor said.

Callie unfolded herself and stood up. "Yes, I'm Callie."

"I'm Dr. Leibowitz. Your mother is here as a precaution due to a high fever and possible pneumonia," he said. "Since she is immunocompromised, we need to have her on a strong set of antibiotics and give her breathing treatments to aid her recovery. I don't want you to worry too much, Callie, this isn't uncommon or unexpected. But we do need to be very careful."

Callie nodded, feeling a bit better with the news.

"We can let one visitor in at a time for a few minutes, and you'll need to wear a gown, gloves, and mask to protect her from your germs, okay?" the doctor said with a reassuring grin on his face.

"Callie, you go first—I'll talk to Dr. Leibowitz for a bit," Peggy said, nodding toward the double doors to the ICU.

The doors opened outward slowly and Callie passed through them, seeing a half wall where the nurses' station was located. She walked over to it.

"The gowns, masks, and gloves are right over there," a nurse said, indicating an alcove with a set of shelves.

"Thanks." Callie took a paper gown off the shelf and put it on, snapping the buttons closed, and grabbed a face mask from a box. It took her a minute to figure out how to tie the four strings together behind her head. She chose a set of gloves in her size and struggled to get them on over her sweaty hands. When she was properly covered, she walked back to the nurses' station.

"Ms. O'Callahan is in four," the nurse indicated with an outstretched finger. All the ICU rooms had only three walls with a wall-sized opening facing the nurses' station. There were curtains that could afford the occupants some level of privacy when needed. Callie walked over to room four, where her mother lay surrounded by pieces of medical equipment beeping at fixed intervals. One was the ever-present kidney dialysis machine that Callie had become familiar with; another was an IV machine that was pumping in fluids from three different bags. The other, Callie couldn't identify. Her mother was covered in a light blue blanket, the head of her bed raised to ease her labored, raspy breathing. She had a turban to cover her head since her hair had fallen out with her treatments, and her skin was papery and pale except for her cheeks, which were too red. She opened her eyes when Callie approached the bed.

"Callie, is that you?" she asked.

"Yes, Mom, I'm here," Callie said as she approached the side of the bed. She was too scared to touch or hug her mom, but she looked into her eyes.

"Shouldn't you be in school? It's a school day, isn't it?"

"No, I don't need to be in school, I'm here to see how you're doing," Callie replied.

"Oh, I just took a bit of a turn for the worse is all," her mom said. "I just need some strong antibiotics to kick this pneumonia and I'll be just fine."

"That's what Dr. Leibowitz said. He said this transfer was just a precaution," Callie said.

"That's right, no worries, my love." Then she closed her eyes and fell asleep.

"No worries, Mom. I love you." Callie kissed her gloved fingers with her masked lips and pressed the kiss to her mother's hot, ruddy cheek.

Callie tossed the gown, gloves, and mask into the trash by the nurses' station and hit the exit button to open the ICU doors. She saw Peggy sitting in the waiting area, a worried expression on her face.

"She fell asleep, Peg," Callie said, collapsing into the chair next to her.

"I'm sure they have her pretty doped up," Peggy said. "I can visit her later. You haven't had lunch yet—do you want to go down to the cafeteria with me?"

"Yeah, I could use some serious chocolate right about now."

After lunch, Callie insisted on sitting in the ICU waiting area, not wanting to leave Clair in case there were any developments.

"She's doing as well as can be expected," Peggy said. "It will be a while before there will be any change, so I think we should go home and get some rest."

Callie wanted to argue,Peggy but she was dog-tired and didn't want to sleep in the waiting room chairs, selfishly pining for the soft comfort of her bed. That, and knowing there wasn't a damn thing she could do for her mom, she caved in and left with Peggy. She just wished the pain in her chest would stop.

Chapter Eleven

Amber

"What does a girl have to do to get some water and food around here?" Amber yelled to where she thought the door was located. She was getting seriously pissed off at this jerk. The staff was really rude leaving a person, a minor no less, without access to water. Where were her parents? They should have been notified by now.

She was really and truly ready to punch this guy in the face. The next time she heard the door unlock, she was going through that door to find her parents. Her daddy was a lawyer who would make this guy regret the day he had messed with his daughter. She moved from the bed to sit cross-legged facing the door so she could spring up and dash out when it opened. It couldn't be much longer now.

As if on cue, Amber heard the sound of the key being inserted into the lock. Heart racing, she jumped at the sound and then got into a crouched position, ready to leap at the man. The lock thunked and the door swung slowly inward. Amber jumped forward, hitting the man's right leg as she dashed by him. She felt his hand barely miss her hair as he cussed at her. The glare from the overhead light blinded her, so she tripped when she came into contact with the bottom stair. The man was right behind her and managed to grab her ankle. She twisted her other leg over and kicked at what she thought was his face, making contact once, twice. He grunted and swore again as he tried to catch her other leg. She wrenched her ankle from his grip and turned to scramble up the stairs on all fours, causing nasty bruises and cuts on her legs as they smashed into the unfinished wood. Her eyes finally adapted to the light, so she stood and ran up the final set of steps toward the door at the top. Freedom and her parents were on the other side. Sure that the man was right behind her, she tried to turn the knob. She pushed but the door wouldn't open. She yanked back and forth on the knob, screaming with anger and fear. Then she heard a menacing chuckle coming from below.

"You stupid bitch, did you think it would be that easy?"

Amber didn't reply or move away from the door. It wasn't solid metal like the other one; it was a simple wooden door like the one to her bedroom at home. She pounded on it with both fists screaming, "*Help me!*" He didn't come up after her. She kicked the door a couple of times and then rammed her shoulder into it to dislodge it from the jamb, but she was simply too small and not strong enough to have any effect. She realized the futility of escaping and sat down on the landing, breathing hard. The realization that she wasn't in a hospital began to dawn on her.

"What do you want with me, you bastard?" she yelled.

"If you come down here on your own and get back into the room, I won't beat you," the man said.

"Screw you!" Amber yelled back.

"You give me no choice." He wiped blood from his face with the back of his hand and took each step deliberately, knowing that she had nowhere to go. He was very plain and slightly overweight, with a large nose and bushy black eyebrows in a round face. His eyes were squinty as he glowered at her. Amber shrank back until her back was to the door. He was only five steps away from her. She stood up and prepared herself for a fight. *I'll kick him again and make him fall down the stairs, then get his keys and run away.*

He was only two steps away now, his hands by his sides. She lifted her leg to kick at him but he snatched her ankle, whip quick. He pulled at her leg until she slipped onto the next step down. She tried to kick him with her free foot but he grabbed that one, too, and pulled her down the stairs. She struggled to grab at the edge of the steps to stop his progress. Instead, he lifted her up by her ankles until she was dangling from his hands, her back to his front. He released one of her legs to grab her around the waist but she was still upside down and backward to him. She couldn't get any of her blows to make contact. He turned and walked the rest of the way down the steps until he reached the dark room. He dumped her on the bed, headfirst. She turned over to face him and got backhanded right on the cheek. Amber saw stars. He didn't stop hitting her until she passed out.

Chapter Twelve

Callie

It had been a scary week, but Clair had recovered enough to return to Hillcrest and was back on track for a transplant. It meant that Callie had to double up on clients and whatever events she could book to cover the ever-increasing medical bills. This weekend's gig was a mini Ren Faire at the local park, where Melinda and Callie were munching on turkey legs during a lull in customers.

"Gotta love Faire food," Melinda said, her mouth full.

"There is something about it," Callie said. "It's the part I love best."

Her childhood memories surfaced with times spent in the tent watching her mother at her craft, helping the different vendors sell their wares, learning sword fighting and horseback riding from the "knights," and her favorite: learning to play the hammered dulcimer. She got good enough at it that she received one as a birthday present and gave solo concerts during the season. She had learned so much from her Rennie family.

"Something I said?" Melinda asked.

"Hmm? Oh, no. Just thinking about the past," Callie said. "Missing Mom."

"Yeah, I can imagine. You guys had such a cool life always traveling around. I'm so jealous."

"Don't knock your comfortable life, Mels," Callie said. "It wasn't all turkey legs and funnel cake. We were always together, though. Taking care of each other."

Melinda didn't know what to say, so she ripped another bite out of the turkey leg, velociraptor-like. Another client stopped by so Callie put down her turkey leg to meet with her.

"Thank you for coming," Callie said to the client, another college student. "Please come in and have a seat over here." She indicated a small camp chair on the other side of a small, cloth-covered table. Melinda smiled, gave a thumbs-up, and stepped outside the tent to give them some privacy.

"What question can I answer for you today?" Callie asked the young woman.

"I'm trying to decide on my major," she said. "What do you see me doing in my future, and will I be happy doing it?"

Callie closed her eyes to consider the question. It seemed that answers came to her like short bursts from a movie ever since her encounter with Felicity on Bodie Island a couple of months back. She found that she didn't need to weave her way through vague responses any longer.

"You are drawn to animals and have wanted to be a veterinarian since you were very young, but your parents are both lawyers and want you to join them in their law practice," Callie said.

"Yes, that's so amazing!" the college girl said. "What should I do?"

"You will be successful along either path. You will be fulfilling your parents' dream for you if you go into law, but you will follow your own natural desire if you choose to work as a vet," Callie said. "You have the inclination to make anything you do meaningful."

"So, that doesn't clear it up much," the girl said, pouting.

"I'm sorry I couldn't identify which was the better choice, but it does mean you won't make a wrong one whatever you decide to do," Callie said.

"That's true," she said.

"Is there anything else you want to know?" Callie asked.

"Yeah, I'm with someone right now, but I don't know if they're right for me," she said.

Once again, Callie closed her eyes. She saw another young woman but then saw a man, older than college age. "I think this relationship is what you need now, but your future shows another."

"Okay, just a phase then," the girl said. "Thanks." She put money in the money jar, which had a sign that said "Suggested donation per reading: $20" in front of it. She smiled at Callie before she left through the flap in the tent. Melinda came back inside.

"She looked happy," she said.

"This is getting easier the more I do it," Callie said. "It's like I'm seeing little bits of their lives."

"Really?" Melinda asked. "What do you see about mine?"

"Mels, I don't really want to look at your privates," Callie said.

"Come on. It's not like you don't have my permission," Melinda said.

"I really, really don't want to, Mels." Callie waved her hands as Melinda began to protest. "I promise if you need to know something, I'll tell you, okay?"

"Fine," Melinda said. "You owe me a funnel cake with cherries and whipped cream."

"You drive a hard bargain, girl," Callie said. "You have a deal."

The Faire closed for the day at five p.m., so Callie grabbed the money out of the donation jar and put it in a bank envelope, which she then put in her bag. She stowed away anything that could be stolen. Even though the Faire had a security group keeping an eye on things overnight, items could still wander off. The sun was already setting when Callie arrived at Peggy's shop. She parked and went to the back door, knocking to get her attention.

Peggy opened the door for Callie. "Hey there, how was the Faire today? Did you get a lot of business?"

"Not bad—I haven't counted it yet. I wanted to come in to do that." Callie moved past Peggy into the storeroom. She pulled out the bank bag and began separating the bills on the table.

"The clients are pretty happy with the readings," Callie said. "Some of them gave me more than twenty dollars."

"Great!" Peggy said. "Your mom will be pleased that you've developed your skill."

"I wonder if it's what she sees when she reads clients," Callie said.

"What do you mean?"

"I see little bits of their lives, like a preview of a film," Callie said. "It zones in on certain parts when they ask specific questions. It's so weird."

"I don't know much about that," Peggy said. "You should talk to your mom about it tonight."

"Yup, I'm almost done with the count and then I'll be ready to leave."

Peggy always took the money Callie earned and put it in the shop's bank account, then made a donation from the account to Clair's medical fund—all to avoid the tax man, one of Peggy's least favorite people.

The medical bills coming to Peggy's house were of a staggering amount, into the hundred-thousand-dollar range. Contemplating one plan after another to help pay down the debt distracted her from the movie she and her mom were watching.

"Don't worry, baby," her mom said. "We're still working on my immune system, it's just taking a bit more time to kick in."

"What?" Callie realized that her mother was watching her.

"You aren't watching the movie," Clair said. "I know you're worried when you get that groove over your nose." She reached out to smooth the wrinkle.

"Oh, yeah. I just want you to get better," Callie said, instead of what was truly going through her mind at the moment.

"So do I, trust me."

Clair had lost so much weight that she almost resembled a skeleton covered in papery skin, mottled with purplish bruises where IV lines had been removed. Her hair was coming back in, but it was wispy and gray instead of the reddish blond it had been before the illness. She was supposed to be getting better, but she seemed to get worse every week.

"We had a good show today," Callie said, changing the subject. "I had Melinda with me and she was a peach, as usual."

"You have such good friends to lean on. I'm so grateful to them," her mom said. "Keep them close to you, no matter what happens."

"I don't think I have a choice, they're like fleas on a dog. Can't get rid of them," Callie said, smiling. "Mom, I wanted to ask you about how you read for your clients."

"What do you mean?"

"Well, what do you see? Anything?"

"What I see when I look at anyone: whatever they show me," Clair said.

"I've been seeing more things when I focus," Callie said. "It's like I'm zeroing in on their inner thoughts."

"That can happen when you work on it," her mom said. "Practice makes it better, just like anything else."

"Have you ever seen pictures in your mind? I mean, like you're watching a movie?" Callie asked.

"No, I've only ever had impressions or symbols popping into my head," her mom said. "When that doesn't work, I give them something that I hope will help."

Before Callie could ask Clair to elaborate, Peggy came into the room with a takeaway container in her hand.

"Anything good in the cafeteria?" Callie asked.

"Brisket night," Peggy said. "Get it while they still have some left."

"On it," Callie said, giving her mother's hand a squeeze. She left Peggy with her mom so they could talk in private for a while.

Callie was taking her time picking at her dinner, texting her friends and setting up appointments with clients, when she heard the announcement that visiting hours were ending in ten minutes. She dumped what was left of her food in the trash and took the tray up to the conveyor belt. Callie had just reached the edge of the open door to her mom's room when she overheard her and Peggy talking quietly.

"You know I will take care of her," Peggy said.

"I know you will, you always have," her mom said. "You've been my sister in all of this and more like an aunt to Callie all these years. She's just going to need you a lot more."

"Hey Peggy, visiting hours are over," Callie said when she finally stepped inside the room. "Everything okay?"

The two women quickly masked their serious expressions with forced smiles.

Clair wiped her eyes with a tissue. "Just being maudlin. I'm allowed."

"You get only five minutes of that per day. You know the rules," Callie said, wagging her finger in mock admonition.

"That's my fault," Peggy said. "I got her started."

"Well then, that goes for you, too," Callie told her.

"Yes, ma'am," both women said in unison.

"Visiting hours will end in five minutes," a disembodied voice said over the loudspeaker.

"That's our cue," Peggy said, giving Clair a hug. "Good night, sister."

Callie took her place. "Night, Mom. I love you. Focus on getting better."

"I will always watch over you, my daughter. Always."

Callie felt an odd pull. She couldn't help feeling that those would be the last words that her mother would say to her.

Chapter Thirteen

Amber

Amber felt as if pain had taken up permanent residence in her body. The only time she could remember pain even close to this level was when she had sprained her ankle in dance class. Her mom had wrapped the ankle with an Ace bandage and given her some medicine. It had been more like a vacation than anything else, because she was allowed to watch TV on the couch.

She didn't know how long she'd been in the room, but the SOB had made her life miserable since she attempted to escape, giving her just a small cup of water and a couple of slices of bread now and again. She couldn't depend on the feeding intervals to determine the elapsed time, and her stomach felt hollow and growled constantly. He would beat her if she didn't move fast enough or just for kicks, she wasn't sure. Any time she had the temerity to ask the man a question, he answered her with a smack to the face and "you talk too much."

She was covered in dried blood and her body was painful from bruises and cuts. The smock she was wearing was stained with her blood and sweat to the point of stiffness. Everything in her little dungeon stank, from the toilet that hadn't been emptied to the sheets on the bed to her own body. It was all so foreign to her. At no time that she could remember had she ever been denied basic necessities. Not only that, but at home she always got what food she wanted when she wanted, and she could spend ages in a bath frothy with bubbles, at least when her schedule permitted it.

The key turned in the lock. Amber pulled her knees up to her chin and made herself as small as she could. The man's silhouette formed in the lighted doorframe, and he appeared to be carrying something. *Oh good, more bread and water*, Amber thought, *my favorite*.

"Are you going to behave?" the man asked.

Amber thought, *Yeah, I'll behave, you waste product*. She said "yes" out loud instead, keeping her eyes downcast.

"Good," he said, and walked into the room. "Put out your hands."

She did as she was told. He connected the bracelets to her wrists, each ratcheting into place; a foot-long chain connected them. He did the same to her ankles.

"Ouch!" she said. The ankle cuffs pinched her. She shrank back, expecting his response to be a backhand to her face. She wondered what fresh hell was on the agenda for today.

"I'm going to let you come upstairs to get cleaned up," he said. "So come on, get moving."

Amber straightened up and slowly slid off the cot, her injuries making her move like an old woman. The chains weren't heavy but they were cumbersome and noisy. The sound reminded her of a dog she used to pass in her neighborhood that would come at her as far as his chain would allow, barking and lunging for all he was worth. At first that dog had frightened her, until she realized he could get only a few feet from his doghouse. The neighborhood kids would taunt the poor creature until he nearly lost his mind, barking wildly and frothing at the mouth. When no one was watching, Amber would toss him treats. She saw herself in that dog sometimes, able to go only as far as her parents would allow and no farther. Now she was literally chained like that dog and going nowhere.

The man shoved Amber toward the stairs. She was apparently moving too slowly for him, but she hurt everywhere; the sharp pain in her side made it hard to breathe. The chains clanked and dragged on the wooden stairs as she made slow progress toward the door at the top. A brief moment of hope that her escape was on the other side of that door was dashed by how impeded she was by her injuries and her shackles. It amazed Amber how her desires had distilled down to nothing but food, water, cleanliness, and the absence of pain.

The man unlocked the door and grabbed the chain at Amber's wrists, then pulled her into his living room. A bookcase was askew on the left, apparently made with hinges to swing shut and hide the door to her prison. There was a dark green couch with a coffee table in front of it and a large-screen TV attached to the wall with a cabinet below it. The cheap carpet was the usual beige color that contractors installed, expecting buyers to change it when they moved in. There were no tchotchkes, curios, trinkets, or trophies anywhere. No pictures, art, or posters adorned the walls. The place was boring except for the giant picture window next to the front door. She could see at least three other houses across the street and a bit of the man's front lawn and driveway. There were no leaves on the trees and the sky was overcast, but it was the most beautiful view Amber could ever remember caring about.

The man pulled the distracted Amber forward toward another set of stairs, which she gingerly navigated, holding on to the handrail to pull herself up. At the top was a hallway with two doorways on each side, one of which opened to the bathroom. Like the living room, there was nothing personal in it. There was a towel, washcloth, toothpaste, and a toothbrush still in its packaging on the counter.

"Take a shower and get all that mess off yourself," the man said. He took out the manacle keys and undid the wrist bracelets, but left the ones on her ankles attached. He leaned over to turn on the shower. "I'll be right outside this door. Don't take all day." He turned around and pulled the door closed, locking it behind him. Amber saw some clothes that appeared to be her size hanging on the door hook. She turned to look at herself in the mirror over the sink. Her cheeks were so bruised they looked like twin plums, and there was a cut on her lip. Her nose was no longer straight, and there was another bruise across her chin. Dried blood was all over her face, and her hair, usually a bright golden blond, was now mousy-colored and had become thin and flat. But what disturbed Amber the most was her eyes. The person she saw in those eyes was unrecognizable.

Chapter Fourteen

Callie

C allie awoke shivering and sweating all over, her heart racing. She sat up and clutched at her chest, taking great gulps of air to calm herself. Once her galloping heart was beating more like a canter and she could breathe normally again, she glanced at her cell phone and noted the time: 2:17 a.m. A panic attack, it had to be, but what had caused it? She got up shakily and walked quietly down to the bathroom and then to the kitchen for a mug full of milk warmed from the microwave. She sat at the kitchen table contemplating the cause of her attack. No tests at school and she hadn't forgotten to write a paper or turn in any work that she could think of. Her mom's health seemed to be improving, even if it was at a snail's pace. There were no notifications on her phone, so she put her rinsed mug in the dishwasher and decided to check on Peggy. She crept up to her door and carefully turned the knob, opening the door far enough to see Peggy's form tucked under the comforter and hear the sound of rhythmic snoring. She closed the door carefully. *It must be the hospital bills giving me fits*, she thought. She returned to her bed, yawning now that the milk was taking effect, and fell into a fitful sleep.

The next morning, as Callie was having her usual breakfast of cereal, banana, and soda, her phone rang. Once she saw that the call was coming from Hillcrest, she answered it immediately.

"Is everything okay?" Callie asked.

"Is this Calliope O'Callahan?" a male voice said.

"Yes, is my mom okay?"

"This is Sean Steadman of the Hillcrest long-term care facility," he said. "I'm calling about your mother, Clair O'Callahan."

"I know, I saw the caller ID. Please, is she okay?" Callie asked again.

"I'm sorry to have to tell you that your mother passed away last night," he said.

"No, she didn't. I think you have the wrong person," Callie said. "She's been doing better. She was about to get on the kidney transplant list."

"I'm sorry, Miss O'Callahan, but we haven't made a mistake."

"I don't believe you," Callie said. "I'm going to be there as soon as I can to prove that you have the wrong person." She hung up.

"Peggy!" Callie yelled.

"What's the matter?" Peggy called back from her bedroom. She was getting dressed for her day at the shop.

"We have to get to Mom!"

"Why? What's wrong?" Peggy poked her head through her bedroom doorway.

"Some guy called and said she was dead," Callie said. "I think he's wrong."

"Oh my God," Peggy said. "I'll be done in a minute and we'll go."

Once they arrived at Hillcrest, Callie and Peggy all but ran to Clair's room. Callie saw that the bed was empty and cleared of the sheets and blankets. Clair's belongings were nowhere to be found. It seemed to Callie as if they had erased her mother's existence. She turned and ran to the attendant's station.

"Where did she go?" Callie demanded.

The person at the attendant's station did not recognize Callie. "Which resident are you looking for?"

"Clair O'Callahan in room three-oh-two," Callie said. "Where is she? Did they have to transfer her to the ICU?"

"Let me check, miss," the attendant said. He typed on the computer's keyboard. "I'm sorry, miss. The status says that Clair O'Callahan is deceased."

"No, that isn't what happened," Callie said. "She's been transferred. I want to speak to Sean Steadman. Now."

"I'll page him for you," the attendant said. "Please have a seat in the waiting area."

Peggy put her arm around Callie's shoulders and pulled her toward the waiting area. They sat silently for a few minutes until a man in a suit walked in.

"Miss O'Callahan?" he said, standing in front of Callie's chair. "I spoke to you on the phone about your mother?"

Callie stood up. "There's been some sort of mix-up. Hasn't my mom been transferred to the ICU?"

"No, unfortunately. I checked myself. There is no mix-up," Sean Steadman said. "Your mother passed away early this morning."

Callie suddenly lost the ability to stand, all but falling into the chair behind her. She felt the universe shift ever so slightly out of phase with reality, like she had just joined Rod Serling in the Twilight Zone. Her mom could not be gone. She had promised she wouldn't leave Callie alone. Callie had kept her end of the bargain by working hard in school and taking every client she could to pay the medical bills.

"But she promised me," Callie said, voicing the thought that repeated itself in her mind.

"She tried to hold on, Callie," Peggy said. "She really tried."

"What do you mean? Did you know this was going to happen?" She stared at Peggy, anger starting to overtake shock.

"She told me what the doctors said about her progress," Peggy said. "The prognosis was poor—she wasn't responding to the immunotherapy."

"Why didn't she tell me?"

"She was hoping for another miracle." Peggy started to cry.

"She was a coward, you mean," Callie said.

"Don't say that! Don't ever say that about your mother!"

Sean Steadman took that moment to interject, "Ma'am, are you Peggy Boyle?"

"Yes." Her voice was shaking.

"We have been given permission for you to take possession of Ms. O'Callahan's personal items and we'll need your signature on a few legal documents. Are you able to do that now?"

"I guess it's better to take care of it now," Peggy said. "Callie, let's go, dear."

Callie worked on autopilot, standing up like a robot. Shock had overwhelmed her brain and nothing was making sense. They went with Sean Steadman to his office and sat in a pair of chairs in front of his desk. He had two bags with the Hillcrest logo next to his desk and showed them to Peggy.

"This is what was in her room. If you would please check to see that all is present, we'll have you sign off on having picked them up," Sean said.

Peggy took the bags and looked through them, tears glistening on her cheeks.

"Everything's here," she said, her voice cracking.

"I will need to have you sign this document"—he handed her a piece of paper—"for the disposition of Ms. O'Callahan's body. She had already made arrangements, I understand?"

"Yes, I was given instructions," Peggy said quietly. She signed the document and handed it back to Steadman.

"The last documents will be sent to your home; please verify the address," he said.

"That's correct," Peggy said, and signed that document as well.

Steadman placed the documents into a folder that was at least an inch thick and had "Clair O'Callahan" on the tab.

"Once again, we are so very sorry for your loss," he said, extending his hand to Peggy. "Please let us know if there are any questions or issues."

"We will," Peggy said, taking his hand. "Thank you for your help today. I'm sorry for the drama earlier."

"Please don't worry about it. Grief strikes us all differently."

Peggy stood up and put her hand on Callie's shoulder. Callie looked up dazedly and stood up to leave. She thought for a moment how odd it was that her chest wasn't hurting anymore.

Chapter Fifteen

Callie

Damn the sun for shining and the birds for singing. Damn the laughter and the joy, for all of it is dead to me today, Callie thought. *She has left me with no family, to face the world alone with only the vagaries of human kindness to aid me. I truly hate her.* She stood in the tiny living room of Peggy's house, made even smaller as people in somber outfits milled about eating finger foods, drinking soda or tea, and talking to one another in hushed tones about Clair O'Callahan's too-soon death.

"Man, I'm gonna miss her," a burly man with a long dark beard said to his companion.

"That's her daughter over there, right? I wonder what will happen to her?" she replied in a hushed tone, indicating Callie with a glance.

"I suppose the CPS will have to put her in foster care," the man said.

"Doesn't she have any family somewhere?"

"Not that Clair ever mentioned."

"I don't know what I'm going to do," another woman said to a friend whose hand was on her shoulder, comforting her. "Clair was the only person I could talk to about, you know…"

"I understand," replied the friend. "This is hard on us all. She was such a gifted person."

A woman in a simple black dress approached Callie. "You must be Callie," she said, taking her hand. "You look so much like your mother."

Callie pulled herself out of her reverie to answer, "Yeah, I guess so."

"I'm so sorry for your loss," the woman went on. "I really appreciated her help. She was a gifted medium."

"I'm glad for you," Callie said flatly.

As the woman moved on to speak to Peggy, others approached Callie to pay their respects. She heard only snippets of what her Rennie acquaintances and Clair's clients said to her, replying with "thank you" and "I appreciate that." It was almost too much to bear when all she wanted to do was be alone with her grief, but she stood there nonetheless.

It had been only a week since her mother had died. The instructions for Clair's memorial were prearranged, so Peggy and Callie had had to do very little to set things in motion. Callie had barely spoken to Peggy that entire week, feeling betrayed by how much she had kept from her about how ill her mother really was. She had declined requests from her clients, citing a loss in the family. Besides, she didn't really need the money anymore, except to pay an outstanding balance or two after the life insurance policy paid out, nor did she need the pain and angst that reading people could generate on top of what she was already dealing with. She did decide to go to school to keep some semblance of normalcy to her life. What else did she have left, after all? Melinda, Jonathan, and Grey would talk about mundane issues during lunch, trying to distract her from her pain, but one day she had had enough of that and decided to eat alone. Fortunately, the Misfits respected her space and just texted her with "We love you. Come back when you feel up to it, we'll be here." The teachers wouldn't engage with her in class, probably to avoid any awkwardness; she wasn't sure. She wasn't sure about much these days, especially about what would happen next.

Callie glanced at the brushed-copper urn containing Clair O'Callahan's ashes. It was sitting on a table, illuminated by sun from the front window and surrounded by vases full of flowers. Various other objects and cards had been placed on the table as mourners passed by it to pay their respects. She couldn't seem to get any closer to the table for fear that her own body would simply disintegrate, that her corporeal form would not be able to contain the sheer amount of pain and anger that being close to what remained of her mother would cause.

She heard Jonathan's voice emerge from the back door. *Finally, a friend*, she thought. She turned to see him come toward the living room with the rest of the Misfits in tow. As they approached, Callie was able to see only their wobbly forms as the unshed tears in her eyes made her vision waver. Melinda didn't say a word, but simply came up to Callie and wrapped her arms around her tightly. Jonathan then embraced them both, and Grey gently put one arm around Callie's back and awkwardly patted her shoulder. Callie's tears flowed freely down her face, their embrace preventing her body from flying apart as it had threatened to do all day. There they stood, the Misfit tangle of comfort letting all the rest of the world flow around them as it would, protecting Callie through the onslaught of her grief.

Chapter Sixteen

Callie

Sometime after the memorial, Callie walked into the house from the bus stop to find Peggy and a strange woman sitting at the kitchen table, legal-looking documents spread out on its surface between them. The conversation stopped as she walked in, and both Peggy and the woman stood up to face her.

"Callie, this is Maureen Johnson from the Child Protective Services department," Peggy said.

"Hi, Callie," Maureen said. She was a Black woman who looked to be around forty, dressed professionally if not expensively in a dark pantsuit. She held out her hand to Callie, who shook it.

"Why are you here?" Callie asked, trepidation rising. Was this woman about to take her away to some stranger's house?

"Please, sit down with us so we can talk about it," Maureen said. Callie sat down and put her bookbag next to her chair.

"I want you to understand your rights as a minor of the state. Since your mother was the only family of record we have, the state is required to find a suitable family member to take custody of you or, in lieu of that, a home considered to be suitable for you," Maureen continued.

"So, you're here to take me away. Is that it?" Callie asked.

"No, not at this time."

"Your mom and I talked about this at length," Peggy said. "We went through the legal channels as far as we could to make this happen."

"Make what happen exactly?"

"You've been living here for most of your life when you weren't traveling with your mom," Peggy said. "Clair and I talked about it. I wanted to make our arrangement permanent so you wouldn't be put in the foster care program."

"We will abide by the wishes of the decedent within the provisions of the law," Maureen said. "If we find no other family member who would be willing to become your legal guardian until you turn eighteen, you may stay with Ms. Boyle. She has petitioned for and been granted foster parent status."

"Since you are over the age of thirteen, you do have a say in this," Peggy added.

"That's nice," Callie said, sarcasm drenching her words. "I have no other family and I would like to continue to live here until I graduate from high school, so don't waste the state's money."

"I'm glad you said that," Peggy said, "because I've already begun legal procedures for adoption."

Callie's jaw dropped. She had thought of herself as an orphan, and it hadn't dawned on her that she could ever have any other true family until she started one of her own. Despite her attempt at being stoic, Callie began to cry. She rose up from the chair and turned her back on the two women so they wouldn't see the tears escaping down her cheeks. Peggy came up behind her and placed a hand on her shoulder, and Callie turned around and let the older woman wrap her in a loving embrace. "Shhhh, I know, Callie, it's okay." At that moment, Callie forgave her, suddenly appreciating the immense sacrifices Peggy had made to have Callie live here all these years. And now, Callie had no one else.

Once their emotional union was done, they both sat back down and wiped the tears away. Maureen Johnson wiped at her own cheeks, having become emotional herself.

"I'll take that as a yes," Peggy said, smiling.

"Hell yes!" Callie said. "Now let's get down to business."

Maureen Johnson completed the first of several interviews with Peggy and Callie and left with signed documents. The two decided on a celebratory meal of pizza delivered from their favorite pizza joint and half a gallon of chocolate Moose Tracks ice cream, to be devoured while watching Godzilla destroy Tokyo on the TV. After the final credits of the movie ran, Peggy told Callie she had something for her from her mother.

"What is it?" Callie asked.

"Just wait." Peggy went into her bedroom and came back with an envelope in her hand.

"Your mom had a lot of time to think and a lot of time to write while she was sick," Peggy said. "She didn't want to say any of this to you while she was alive, in case she recovered. I know it seems to you like a cop-out, but she really didn't want you to lose hope. She couldn't bear it."

She handed the envelope to Callie. "This is the first of dozens of letters to you."

The envelope was a simple one, the kind business letters came in. It had "To Callie, letter #1" on the front in her mom's handwriting. Callie carefully opened the flap and pulled out a piece of white copy paper her mom had probably gotten from Hillcrest. She opened the folded paper and read:

My dear Callie,

I imagine that you're feeling like I betrayed you by leaving you when you thought I was getting better. It's okay to be angry with me for that. I feel betrayed, too, by my body, which isn't as strong as my spirit and won't do what I desperately need it to do. All I can do now is watch over you from the other side and have Peggy continue to take care of you until you're ready to go out on your own.

Please don't give up on school. You are so clever and intelligent, I know you'll go as far as you want to. But don't do it for me anymore, do it for yourself—follow your own path and make your mark on the world.

I've never met anyone as brave as you are. No other child would have been able to endure what you have, even before I became sick. You took care of me and the medical bills and stayed in school on top of that. That bravery will serve you better than any other trait you have.

You asked me recently about how I developed my psychic ability. I didn't want to tell you more, because everyone develops differently. I have noticed your psychic skill growing over these last few months and I didn't want to interfere. Don't be afraid of it, it's just another sense you have that others don't have as much of. You will find guidance when you need it most, just like I did.

I hope that someday soon, we'll be able to talk to each other again, Your loving mom

Callie stopped reading. "Do you know what this says?" she asked Peggy.

"No, these are private. I have my own letters from your mom, plus we talked over much of what would happen when she passed."

Callie sat with the letter on her lap contemplating its contents. *What does that mean, "soon we'll be able to talk to each other again"?* She couldn't wrap her brain around that one. Maybe her mom had been delirious when she wrote that part.

"Do you want to talk about it?" Peggy asked.

"No, it was beautiful." Callie's tears dripped onto the letter. She brushed them away and put the letter back into the envelope.

"I'm sure she would rather have said this to you in person someday," Peggy said, "but she didn't get her wish."

"We rarely do," Callie replied.

Chapter Seventeen

Amber

It was a beautiful autumn day. Amber and her parents were at the park having a picnic next to the concrete pond where ducks and geese would gather, competing over morsels of bread that she would throw out to them. Squirrels chased one another in spirals up and down the trunks of the oak trees, which would drop the occasional acorn and leaf when a breeze rustled their branches. Mom had packed fried chicken, potato salad, macaroni salad, and chocolate chip cookies. The blue sky was marred only by the rare fluffy cloud, and Amber lifted her face to the sun's warmth like a worshiper.

"Would you like some more potato salad?" Mom asked.

"I wish I could, but I'm bursting already."

"Just so you know, there's plenty here if you change your mind. I know it's your favorite," Mom said. She had made the Southern-style potato salad herself, using extra pickle relish. She rarely had time to cook like that anymore.

Amber lay on the plaid blanket with her head resting on her folded arms.

"We got your midterm grades," Dad said. His basso voice was filled with what sounded like disappointment.

Amber tilted her head toward him to look at his expression. She knew he was just pulling her chain. "Exceptional, weren't they?"

"Quite," Dad said. "Probably the best you've done so far. And you sounded like a professional pianist at your recital."

"I do love Mozart," Amber said. She really didn't care for classical music that much, but she knew how to play her dad like a fiddle.

"Given that you're finally applying yourself, young lady," Dad said as he went for something in the interior pocket of his jacket, "we thought you deserved a treat."

He held what looked like a pair of concert tickets splayed like playing cards in his hand.

Amber jumped up from her relaxed position and went for the tickets. She held them like the precious things they were, trying to read which concert they were for.

"Amalia?" she said, her voice squeaky with a combination of excitement and amazement. "These are, like, impossible to get!"

She held the tickets to her chest as if to keep him from taking them back in a "just kidding" maneuver. "How?"

"You remember one of my law partners has a daughter about your age, right? You met at the family party last year. I think her name is Sylvie or something. Anyway, they can't make the concert, so Nat sent me an email asking if you'd be interested. I said sure, so I got them for what she paid for them."

"I can't believe it!" She jumped at her father and wrapped her arms around him like a boa constrictor. He smelled of the outdoors and chicken grease. He held her firmly and for a long, long time. "I love you, Squishy."

Then everything went black. She was floating in nothingness, seeing nothing and feeling pain. The thunk of the lock had brought Amber back from her perfect dream where her parents still loved her to the hole where she was kept like a caged animal by an evil zookeeper.

"I guess I'm not going to the Amalia concert, am I," she said under her breath.

"What?" the man asked.

Amber didn't reply, just stuck out her feet so the man could apply the ankle cuffs. He didn't use the wrist cuffs anymore since she didn't have the energy or will to fight him. They were cumbersome and noisy anyway. She had been allowed to come upstairs at irregular intervals, not only to get a shower but also to clean the man's house and prepare his meals. He had had to teach Amber how to do both, since people had been cooking and cleaning for her all her life. He was not a patient teacher. One time she had scrubbed the toilet until she thought it sparkled, but he had grabbed her by the neck, putting her face a mere inch from the water, and said, "See that spot? Do a better job or I'll make you drink from the toilet!"

Cooking was a whole new level of abuse. Amber had speckles of healing burns from grease thrown at her when she had accidentally burned the pork chops.

"Tonight I want you to make meatloaf," he said as he pushed her up the stairs. "Do you know how to make meatloaf?"

"No," she whispered.

"What was that?" he asked, pulling her around to face him. He was paranoid that she was mocking him when he couldn't hear her.

"No, I don't know how to make meatloaf," she replied, her eyes avoiding his.

"You are such a useless piece of crap," he said. "I should just kill you now and start with a new girl. You're lucky I don't want to waste the time."

Amber had heard this enough not to react to it anymore, but it had terrified her the first few times he had said it.

"Get to cleaning the bathrooms and dusting, then I'll show you what to do," he said.

"Yes, sir."

After finishing the upstairs bathroom, Amber came downstairs to where the man was watching television. It was still football season, she noted. She was walking into the kitchen to get a dust rag from under the sink when she saw mail sitting on the kitchen table. He had never left anything out that could identify him or his address before. She stood there for a minute trying to decide what to do. Finally, she went under the sink to get the dust rag and started wiping down surfaces in the kitchen until she got to the table. As she made lazy circles with the rag with one hand, she turned an envelope over with the other so she could see his name. *Gary Smith, 19 Markham Place, Wendell.* That's where she was. The address was instantly seared into her memory.

"What are you doing?" Gary was standing there leaning against the wall, staring at her. Had he seen her looking at his mail?

"Dusting, sir," Amber said, continuing to make the lazy circles with her left hand. Her heart was banging in her chest. She kept her eyes down and pretended to be calm. If he saw her with the mail, it would be a very bad day.

"It's clean enough in here. Go do the living room while it's halftime," he said.

Her eyes were trained on the floor but she had recently learned to see well with her peripheral vision. As she shuffled her chained feet into the living room, she watched this man, Gary Smith, follow closely behind her.

Chapter Eighteen

Callie

November went from warm and sultry to wet and cold, which suited Callie's mood. After the initial shock had worn off, Callie was slowly accustoming herself to orphanhood. It didn't hit her all the time, since Clair had traveled frequently and spent the last months of her life in care. But the pain sucker-punched her whenever she thought *Oh, I need to work out a ride to see Mom* or *I wonder which Faire Mom is at right now*. Memories were all she had left, and she clung to them while running her hands down the fine silk scarves Clair loved so much and covering her face with blouses that still held Clair's scent of patchouli and pine. Some days were easier than others, but those that weren't had Callie lying on Clair's old bed, crying gut-twisting sobs into her pillow so Peggy wouldn't hear. She didn't want anyone pushing into her grief to lie and say that everything would be okay.

"Hey Callie, can you eat anything?" Peggy would ask.

"I'm good," Callie would say.

"Try to eat some soup at least," Peggy would cajole, pushing Callie by the shoulders to the kitchen table. She would eat dutifully, staring at the table so she wouldn't have to make eye contact.

Then the terrors would hit. *What happens now? I don't have anybody but Peggy. Will they take me away from her and put me with some family member I've never met?* She would melt into the corner of the couch, shaking violently, pale and soggy from tears. Peggy would try to soothe her, saying, "Callie, your mom and I worked this out before she passed. You'll be okay until you graduate from high school. You'll stay with me until then."

"But you're not my mom!" Callie would scream. "You aren't family! They'll take me away from here!" And then she'd run up the stairs and slam the door to her room. Peggy would hear Callie play a mournful tune on the hammered dulcimer until quite late into the night.

School let her take a few days off when she needed to, but all the students and some of her teachers either avoided her or gave her the dreaded look of sympathy. Callie mostly ignored the platitudes, and tried every day to remember her promise to Clair to do well and go off to college. She would follow through with her commitment to her mom, even though Clair hadn't kept her half of the bargain. Mels thought a sleepover at her house would rouse Callie out of her funk, but it only served to remind Callie that Mels had parents when she had none. Thoughts of her absent, faceless so-called father came to her with greater frequency, sometimes accusing him of being an evil, soulless creature who would abandon his daughter to this fate and sometimes being the innocent, ignorant fool who knew nothing about his daughter's existence. What if he did know? Would she have to move away to be with him in a new state, at a new school, with new friends?

She was sometimes full of hatred for her mother. Clair had promised she would live, lying to her only daughter's face, but had died rather than push through the pain. Then Callie's guilt would kick in and she would say "I'm sorry, I'm sorry" over and over.

The school counselor insisted she visit after school to assess her state of mind. "I want to give you these pamphlets so you can choose from some options to help you through this trying time." She pressed them into Callie's hand the way Melinda's grandma did with hard candies. "There are so many choices, from group therapy to individual counseling. Just give them a call." As if Callie could even begin to make a decision one way or the other.

Eventually, Peggy had had enough. "You are going to this counselor I know. She's available tomorrow. No, you are going," she said, when Callie argued against it. "I cannot handle this behavior from you. Frankly, it's frightening."

Peggy's counselor friend was of the transpersonal therapist variety. She was cool with Clair's being a spiritual medium and provided Callie with some nonpharmaceutical options to help with depression and anxiety. Still, it was a long, arduous, Sisyphean battle. Peggy hated leaving Callie at home alone, so she dragged her to the shop to "help" at the register. It was during one of those evenings while Callie was moping at the front counter, intimidating anyone who would approach to pay for items, when Jonathan and Melinda appeared in front of her. She pulled herself up, noticing their bright expressions.

"What?" she asked with a guarded tone.

"Did you notice they finished that café down the street?" Melinda asked.

"Didn't know they were building anything."

"Yeah," Jonathan said.

"And it's your kind of place," Melinda said.

"What kind of place is that?" Callie asked, less curious than annoyed.

"You'll see," Jonathan said, coming around the counter. He grabbed Callie's hand and pulled her toward the shop door. "We're stealing Callie away, Peggy," he called out.

"Fine, just bring her back in one piece, please," Peggy called back.

Melinda grabbed Callie's backpack and Jonathan helped her put on her coat as they passed through the door. They walked down the street arm in arm, *Wizard of Oz*-style, for a few blocks, Melinda squealing when the cold wind bit, until they arrived at the Bent Spoon.

The door was made of a hefty wood, with a spoon bent at a ninety-degree angle carved into its middle. Jonathan tugged at the large brass handle, and warmth met them as they walked in. Chai and coffee smells hit them, along with the noise of excited college students. It was the grand opening with free coffee, tea, and small plates of appetizers. Jonathan pulled Melinda and Callie into the line for beverages, and Callie looked around while they waited. The walls were painted black except for one that had a huge mural of mystical plants, chakra symbols, and birds in bright colors over a raised dais peppered with plush pillows and barefooted students. Sheer wall hangings draped from trapezes provided separations for tables if the occupants desired a bit of privacy. Callie then noticed pieces of bent cutlery affixed to the walls and hanging in intricate shapes throughout the establishment.

"This is my kind of place, huh? You think I'm bent out of shape or something?" Callie asked Jonathan.

"What? No, that's not what I meant," he said. "It's a psychic place. You know, like Uri Geller? The Israeli who could bend spoons?"

"Never heard of him," Melinda said.

"He's the guy who went on talk shows back in the seventies saying he could bend metal with his mind," Jonathan said. "That's him." He indicated a photograph over the coffee bar. "He made spoon bending so popular that people were having parties to try it out themselves."

When they arrived at the coffee bar, Callie and Melinda each ordered cinnamon hot cocoa while Jonathan requested the chai.

"Welcome to the Bent Spoon," a bespectacled girl with several piercings and shades of purple in her hair said. "Here are some upcoming events." She handed each of them a flier. "We also have an arcade upstairs." She indicated the sign that spelled out "Psy-cade" in bright neon pink over another spoon-bedecked door. "It's really fun!" Then she moved on to the next group in line.

Melinda managed to muscle through the throng to a table for three that had just become available. She stared down a pretender for the chair until the hopeful usurper raised his hands in surrender and slinked away. Callie and Jonathan joined her, though Callie almost spilled the hot cocoa down her front when a young man made an attempt to pass behind her. She read over the flier for a few seconds.

"Looks like they're going to have a party for New Year's Eve." She had to yell to be heard.

"Yeah, and a competition in the Psy-cade," Jonathan said.

"You should do that, Callie," Melinda said. "I think you'll win it." Melinda looked at Jonathan in a meaningful way as if they'd planned this beforehand.

"Hmph," Callie said. She tipped the last sip of cocoa into her mouth and stood up. "Let's take a look at this Psy-cade."

She maneuvered through the crowd, assuming that Melinda and Jonathan were following, and went through the heavy door under the neon sign. She nearly walked into the back of a person just inside the dark staircase. Melinda and Jonathan crowded in behind her as they slowly stepped up the stairs, avoiding those who were trying to exit by squishing against the right-hand wall. Eventually, they made it to the desk, where a series of signs with a notice and instructions written in a large font were prominently displayed: "Welcome to the Psy-cade, an experience unlike any other arcade in the world!"

The remaining signs provided information on registering and basic gameplay: "Each player starts with fifty credits. Each game costs credits to play but more credits are rewarded in proportion to the wins. Losers get nothing but can purchase more credits." They waited their turn to register at the kiosks just past the desk. Callie put in her name and cell phone number, which she was required to confirm before continuing, and then received a user number that she would need to remember if she wanted the system to keep track of her scores.

After they registered, they followed others into a space filled with games and interfaces, but nothing flashed or made those annoying electronic noises that other arcades always had. Instead, calm ambient music played in the background and noise-canceling materials lined the walls. Even so, there was an underlying buzz of voices with the occasional cheer or sound of defeat.

Callie saw an unoccupied pinball game called Mind over Matter. "I want to try this one."

Input your player number or press Start to begin.

Callie pressed 77705 into the number pad.

"There are no buttons for the flippers," Jonathan noted.

This game will test your psychokinetic ability. Using the power of your mind, can you move the ball where you want it?

"Here goes nothing," Callie said. She focused hard on the ball as it was released from the top of the game. Then she tried to get the flippers to move. Nothing seemed to work.

"I think I understand why this game was available," Callie said. "This is really hard."

"Yeah, but if you can win it, look at the credits it'll give you," Jonathan said. "It's like a credit for every point you make."

"Here's something for two people," Melinda said, indicating two adjacent booths with "Mind Reader" over the top.

"Come on, Callie, I know you can do this one," Melinda said. "I'll be your test subject." She squeezed into the booth and sat down. Callie went into the next booth and read the instructions: *You will see 25 sets with 3 pictures per set. Visualize which of the 3 pictures your partner is viewing. Press Ready to begin.*

This should be easy, Callie said to herself. She pressed the ready button and pretended she was doing a reading for a client. Taking her time, she pressed only the button under the picture she was sure of. The computer calculated her score as "extremely telepathic." She emerged from the booth to the sound of applause. Apparently, spectators could watch the session and see the points racking up on a screen above the booths.

"Just as I thought," Melinda said with a satisfied grin.

Jonathan gave Callie a big hug. "Awesome job! You got a hundred and fifty more credits to play with."

They walked through the Psy-cade watching the other games in session. One girl was playing Circle of Lights, trying to get the lights to go around as directed; another was playing Whac-A-Mole. There were also video dice games, a robot maze, and a claw game with no joystick.

"This is really cool," Callie said. "A place for psychics."

"Seriously consider this competition on New Year's Eve," Melinda said, pressing the point. "The winner gets ten thousand dollars."

"Wow," Callie said. "I do have more free time now since, you know, Mom died."

"Yeah," Melinda said, squeezing Callie's shoulders. "It might help get your mind off it. She wouldn't want you to be sad all the time."

Callie sighed. "I know what you're saying is true, I just can't seem to get past it."

"Well, here's a place custom-built for Callie," Jonathan said. "It would be a shame for you to blow it off."

"All right already," she said, "I get the point! Let's get back to Peggy's, though. I've got a lot of homework to do tonight."

"Welcome to the Psy-cade's first annual Psychic Tournament!" said the emcee into a microphone. "To participate, you should have been given a number at registration—don't forget that number! You'll be entering it at each station."

The Bent Spoon was filled to capacity. All the chairs had been removed and tall tables placed along the walls, leaving the first floor standing room only. There was a line of people that stretched outside the café and down the block. Callie was one of the first to register, having arrived to wait in line early that morning. She had been in nearly every day of her winter break and most evenings and weekends after the cafe's grand opening. At times, Melinda or Jonathan would join her, but for the most part she showed up alone. It beat having to deal with real life, and the ten grand for the winner was an additional draw. She had practiced like a mental athlete, finding the games she was good at and avoiding the others, like the Mind over Matter one. Her clients had started to ask when she'd be doing readings again, and she had promised them that after the New Year she would be scheduling them. It had been impossible to wear her mother's garb or even go into her mother's room without falling into a spiraling depression, much less being in the right mental state for a psychic reading. Now she stood under the neon Psy-cade sign, bouncing on her toes with pregame jitters.

"All right," the emcee said, "here are the rules: those of you participating in the games will play one round on the game of your choice. Those with high scores will go on to the next round. Those who do not score will be disqualified from the tournament. "*But*"—he paused here for emphasis—"you may participate in the Psy Games on this floor for floor prizes. Is the first round ready?" A roar erupted that hurt Callie's ears. "Let's get started!"

The door to the Psy-cade opened and Callie was all but pushed up the stairs. She ran up and beelined to the Mind Reader game, sliding into the second booth. She inputted 77705 and waited for someone to occupy the sender booth. It gave her time to take long, slow breaths to get herself calm and focused. The computer screen dinged: *Press Ready to begin.* She felt the familiar change in her head, like her brain was shifting gears into a special awareness. Taking her time, she chose the picture only when she was sure which one the sender had picked. *Congratulations! You are extremely telepathic* appeared on the screen. Callie hoped it would be high enough to make the second round.

Just then her phone dinged with a text: "How'd you do?" It was Melinda checking on her progress. Melinda had been forced to stay home for her family's white elephant party since her grades had been less than stellar lately. Jonathan was out with the other seniors but promised to text when he could. With a mug of hot cocoa in hand, Callie found a spot at one of the tall tables in the café so she could text Melinda back: "Went ok. Stiff competition. Will know about the next round soon."

"How d'you think you did?" said a male voice.

Callie looked up from her phone. She had been so focused on replying to Melinda that she hadn't noticed someone already seated at the table. He was dark-skinned with a straight nose and jet-black hair. He smiled as he waited for her reply, showing neon-white teeth.

"I did my best, I hope it's good enough. Sorry, did I take your table?"

"It would be impossible to call dibs tonight." He laughed and held out a hand. "I'm Sahil."

Callie shook it and said, "I'm Callie."

"Are you a student here?"

"I'm still in high school," she replied. "How about you?"

"I'm in the psychology graduate program at the university," Sahil said.

"Are you competing tonight?"

"No." He laughed again. "I'm working."

"Oh. I've been here a lot and haven't seen you before," Callie said.

"It's just for tonight," Sahil said.

"All right, everyone! Can I have your attention," the emcee said over the din. Once the crowd quieted down he said, "If I call your number, you have qualified for round two. All others are welcome to stay for the Psy Games and door prizes."

Callie listened while the numbers were listed. She began to despair until finally 77705 was called. She pumped the air and said, "Yes!"

"Good luck," Sahil said.

"Thanks!" Callie gulped the last of her cocoa. "Made it to 2nd round," she texted to Melinda and Jonathan. Melinda replied with a string of emojis.

Callie followed the others back to the second floor. Most of the group stayed on the first floor for the Psy Games, but there were enough people left in the Psy-cade competition to keep the second floor full. Once again, Callie played Mind Reader with a grade of "very telepathic," netting two hundred points toward her total. However, she needed more points, so she found another game that wasn't occupied. Her skills at mind-over-matter games never increased beyond the beginner level, so she found the Remote Viewer game. It was similar enough to Mind Reader to net her more points. She had to describe a picture that she would see after answering questions about it. Closing her eyes, she let her mind go blank. An impression of "fuzzy animal" and the color white came to her. She answered questions about the scene, such as whether it was outdoors in a natural area or inside a structure. Once she completed the questions, a picture of a white rabbit filled the screen, netting her fifty points. She went through more sessions until a buzzer sounded, followed by the announcement "End of round two." She accumulated four hundred more points. As she made her way downstairs, she felt really good about her standing.

It was getting late and Callie was exhausted. December thirty-first had become January first, and her head hurt. The crowd had thinned to just the final players and their friends. She saw Sahil in a huddle with some others, apparently going over the final scores so the prizes could be distributed. They must have come to a conclusion, because they split up, sending a representative to the emcee with the results.

"Thank you all for staying into the wee hours," the emcee said. "We have the final results!"

The small crowd applauded and cheered halfheartedly.

"Okay, we've obviously been here long enough. For the runner-up, we have number 104956."

A tall girl clapped for herself and launched toward the emcee with a squeal of joy.

"Third place goes to 11998, with a cash prize of one thousand dollars."

Another girl ran up, shaking her hands hallelujah-style, to receive her prize.

"Wonderful. Now I need 89238 and 77705 to come up, please."

Callie and a guy who could have been on the cover of a magazine for billionaire sailors went up to stand on either side of the emcee. Callie had seen 89238 competing in Remote Viewer.

"All right, we're going to have one last door prize for the night. Whoever guesses the first-place winner gets a coupon for a Bent Spoon beverage. Those who think 77705 won, move to the left. For 89238, move to the right." He waited for the crowd to settle before saying, "Second place goes to...77705, for a cash prize of five thousand dollars, which means 89238 is our first Psy-cade champion, with a cash prize of ten thousand dollars!"

The winner, who looked like he had expected to win all along, took center stage with a haughty smirk and then bowed to the crowd with a flourish like a stage actor. He accepted his award without acknowledging the emcee. Callie was disappointed in her second-place showing only because this smug jerk had won instead. She accepted her prize with grace, thanking the judges and the emcee, and then she and the winner were herded under the Psy-cade sign to be photographed. He put his arm around her shoulders, leaning into her as if he knew her personally, and she just about sneezed from the strong, spicy cologne that assaulted her nostrils. She stiffened from his touch but smiled as best she could for the camera before extricating herself from his hug.

"Congratulations, Callie," Sahil said, patting her shoulder.

"Thanks," Callie said with a grin. "I see you were one of the judges."

"Yes, I am here as a representative of the Psy Syndicate. They sponsored this event. Forgive me for asking, but are you under eighteen?"

"I'm sixteen," Callie said. "Why?" She was concerned that she had broken a rule and would have to forfeit the prize money.

"We need to have an adult sign some documents for you. Can you have your guardian sign this for us?" Sahil handed Callie an official-looking document printed in a very small font.

"Oh, if that's all you need," Callie said, "I'll get her to sign it right away."

"Great!" Sahil said.

She was done in and just wanted to get a ride home and go to bed. "Oh crap!" she said.

"What's the matter?"

"Buses aren't running this late. I need to find a ride home."

"I was heading out myself—can I give you a ride?" Sahil said.

"That's very kind but I have a friend I can text," she said, pulling out her phone.

"Jonathan! I got second place!" she texted. "Can u pick me up? I didn't realize how late it was and I don't have a ride. Don't want to wake Peggy."

A full minute went by, making Callie think she would have to wake Peggy after all, when the reply came through. "Sure, be there in fifteen. Gratz on the win!" A GIF of a dancing trophy followed.

"I don't want to leave you on your own," Sahil said from behind her. She jumped and then turned to face him.

"Whoa, sorry about that."

"No worries, just focused," Callie said. "I don't mind the company." Trying to fill the uncomfortable silence, she asked, "So what else do you do for this Psy whatchacallit?"

"Psy Syndicate," Sahil said. "It's an organization where psychics are welcome to work and help researchers study the phenomenon. I'm a research assistant there working on my dissertation."

"Sounds fascinating."

"They offer all kinds of opportunities for people with psychic talent," he went on. "It's why they sponsor stuff like the Psy-cade tournament. You and your guardian could come by there with the waiver if you're interested in checking it out."

"Hmm, maybe. Well, my ride's here," Callie said. "Thanks for hanging out with me."

"It was a pleasure," Sahil said.

Chapter Nineteen

Amber

Gary Smith. What a boring name for a monster. A name like that made him seem almost human—almost. Amber rolled over on her cot and stared into the darkness. What could she do with this information? *19 Markham Place*, she reminded herself. It wouldn't do to forget it when it mattered. She would have only seconds to make a call if she ever found a phone in the house. Maybe she could slip something in the mailbox for the delivery person. Amber's mind was going through the hamster wheel of possibilities when she heard the lock disengage. She covered her eyes as the door swung open and the glaring light poured through.

"I want to clean the car today," Gary said. "You're going to vacuum it and wipe the interior for me."

Amber couldn't believe it. First she got this golden information, and now she might actually have the opportunity to use it. She put her feet out for the shackles.

"I'm not going to put them on today," Gary said. "I don't want the neighbors to see you in chains or they'll call the cops."

Even better. She could run the first chance she got, right out of the garage and to one of the houses next door. She tried to keep her face passive while she did a little happy dance of hope in her head.

This would be the first time Amber had been let outside since her capture. Gary must have thought she was too cowed to try an escape. They arrived at the locked door, which apparently led to the garage.

With the key in the lock, Gary turned to her and said, "Don't do anything stupid or I'll kill you, do you understand?"

"Yes, sir," Amber replied. As usual, she spoke without any inflection.

He looked at her carefully and then went through the door first. It was a single-car garage just as sparsely populated with stuff as his house was. There was a set of shelves with just a few items, which included the little hand-held vacuum cleaner and a toolbox in the corner. He had a small gray two-door sedan with both doors open already. What compelled Amber most was the garage door: it was open too. After so much time in captivity, Amber was blinded by the bright sunny day, so she breathed in deeply through her nose to get all the smells, like a dog in a fast-moving car with the window down.

"Remember what I said," Gary warned her.

She quickly turned her gaze to the garage floor. Gary riffled through a box on one of the shelves and produced a bright orange cloth. He grabbed a spray bottle that sat next to the box.

"Here." He handed them to Amber. "Use these to wipe down the dash and all the surfaces. Read the instructions first. You don't want to screw up my car."

She dutifully read the instructions on the back. "It says to wipe down with a damp cloth after application."

With a huff, he found another cloth and went through the kitchen door to moisten it. Amber felt a strong desire to run, but he didn't take long enough for her to move even one step toward her freedom.

She wiped down the surfaces in the car's interior while Gary stood near the trunk looking at a cell phone. It was the first time Amber had ever seen him with one and he was quite distracted by it, tapping out texts and then swiping screens. He was so caught up in the phone that she could have walked outside, right past him, if he hadn't been between her and the garage door. After wiping everything with the cleanser, Amber got the moistened cloth and wiped each surface again, paying special attention to detail. She was in no mood for a beating.

Gary grabbed the small vacuum and plugged it into the wall outlet. He handed it to her and she began to vacuum under the steering wheel. She tried to find every speck of dirt on the floor and around the seat. When she stopped to move over to the passenger side, Gary got a phone call. Rather than having Amber stop vacuuming, he tried to walk out to the lawn to listen to the caller. He couldn't hear because one of the neighbors was mowing, so he went back into the garage and into the house, closing the door. Amber couldn't believe her luck: for the first time in her memory, Gary wasn't watching her. She held the vacuum in her hand, unable to move for a moment. He could come out at any second.

"Just go," she said out loud to herself. "Just go, just go, just go."

She put the vacuum down on the passenger seat, leaving it on so Gary wouldn't peek out to see what she was up to. She took a few steps toward the open garage door, looking back toward the closed door to the house. A few more steps and she was out on the driveway, looking back once more. She turned to see a hedgerow between her and the neighbor who was mowing the lawn. He couldn't see her. She took a few more steps out onto the driveway. It was really uncomfortable to walk on it, so she tiptoed until she got to the small patch of grass along the hedges. *Which way should I go?* she thought. The only person visible to her was the man mowing his lawn, but his back was to her and the mower was loud. She ran along the hedgerow until she could go around it. She was only ten feet away from the neighbor, her hand reaching out to touch his shoulder, when she was wrenched up off the ground.

Gary was carrying her over his shoulder as quickly as he could, with one hand pressed tightly over her mouth. She screamed against his hand and kicked just like she had the first time he'd carried her, but she didn't have the strength to do any damage. He held her like that until he got her into her basement prison, then his fists rained down on her like rocks spewed from an erupting volcano.

Chapter Twenty

Callie

"**I** am so proud of you!" Peggy said. "Clair would be too." It was New Year's Day and they were settling in on the couch to watch the Rose Bowl Parade. Peggy had awakened Callie with the smell of bacon and french toast, which was about the only thing that would get her out of bed. Callie pushed her bed-head hair from her eyes and nursed a mug of hot cocoa while cuddling under Clair's favorite knitted afghan. She felt the loss of her mother most acutely on days when she would have normally been around. Fairs were never scheduled during the holidays, and her mom would have been the one cooking breakfast and watching the parade on the couch with Callie. Christmas had just been a cry-fest, to the point that Callie had given up and gone to Clair's old room to read her Christmas letter.

Happy Winter Solstice, my dear girl,

We have had so many wonderful times during the winter season, haven't we? I'm remembering the first one we had at Peggy's. You were so little and you worried that Santa wouldn't find you. We didn't even have all our boxes unpacked and you insisted that a letter must go to the North Pole at once! We had to go through everything to find your crayons and construction paper. We even went directly to the post office to put it in the slot.

Do you remember when you got your very own dulcimer? Franz made it for you himself. He was so proud of your progress with it. I think you hugged him so hard that he couldn't breathe! I hope you won't give up playing just because it might remind you of your losses. Franz passed far too early and so have I. I think we'll both be there to listen to you play, in spirit if not in the flesh.

Now you will be making your own memories with other people. Try not to be sad about that—it's the way life is. If I had lived, you would have gone off on your own eventually and spent time with your new family. Now Peggy is more than just a friend you live with, she is family. I suppose you've felt that way before, but now, it's official.

You know that I believe we'll see each other again. Life doesn't end with death, it just changes. If you ever need me, just think about me and I'll be there.

Love always,

Mom

Callie had clutched that letter for hours while lying on Clair's old bed wrapped in Clair's favorite blanket, wishing that her mother was there. She hadn't come downstairs until she could no longer ignore her growling stomach. She got out the plate of Christmas dinner Peggy had saved for her and heated it up. The house had been silent and the night dark and cloudy, just like her mood.

She dashed a tear away before Peggy noticed. Her New Year's resolution was to stop pining for Clair and do what her mother wanted: get on with her own life.

"Yeah, Mom probably would have won last night, hands down. I only got second place," Callie said.

"You're just starting out," Peggy said. "Give yourself a break."

"They gave me a waiver for you to sign. I'm too young to legally receive the cash prize." Callie got up to get the waiver from her bag and then handed it to Peggy before leaping back under the warm afghan.

Peggy looked it over and said, "I don't mind signing this, but it requires a witness."

"There's no hurry," Callie told her. "Or we could just go there and they could witness your signature."

"Oh, the Bent Spoon?" Peggy asked. "That's just down the street from the shop, isn't it? I could do that."

"No, it's the Psy Syndicate that's giving away the money. One of the judges was telling me about it. He invited you and me to visit."

"What's a Psy Syndicate?"

"He said it's a place for psychics to learn and work, and for researchers to study them," Callie said.

"Is it something you want to do?"

"I guess. I mean, I would meet people who can do what I can, right?"

"Honey, whatever will make you happy," Peggy said. "I would love to see you smile for real again. Let's make an appointment next week while you're still out of school."

The following Monday, they were driving up a partially hidden, semicircular driveway paved with red bricks. Peggy parked in front of the converted garage that was set aside for visitors. The house was made of dark flagstone and had peaked gables that reminded Callie of a fantasy cottage on steroids. The only indication that they were at the right place was a brass plate by the door that read "Psy Syndicate" in scrolled letters.

"All it's missing are a few well-placed gargoyles and a massive door knocker," Peggy said.

She pressed the button on the modern electronic panel and waited for a reply.

"Welcome to the Psy Syndicate, how may I help you?" said a voice from the speaker.

"Hi, I'm Peggy Boyle, here with Callie O'Callahan. We have an appointment."

"I'll be there in a moment."

Callie ran her hand over the branch of a giant plant in a huge stone pot on the porch while they waited.

The door opened to a thin, professional-looking woman with shoulder-length dark blond hair. "Thank you for your patience. My name is Kristin. I understand you're here to fill out some documentation."

"Yes, we need a witness for my signature," Peggy said.

Kristin moved to one side to allow Peggy and Callie to pass through into the foyer. It was no less impressive than the outside. A central large staircase with a burgundy runner went up to the second floor. Kristin took them into a sitting room just off the entrance. None of the furniture looked like it was from this century. Callie thought it was all probably old before TVs had even been invented. A fireplace half her height took up most of the wall across from an ornate sofa. An ancient-looking mirror hung above the mantelpiece.

"Please take a seat," Kristin said. "Do you have any questions about the form?"

Peggy pulled it from her bag. "Callie was interested in taking some courses here." She pointed to a section at the bottom of the page. "It appears there is a waiver to do that instead of receiving the prize money."

"Oh, yes," Kristin said. "Are you interested in the training program?"

"I don't know exactly," Callie said. "I mean, you have some information on your website, but I'd like a chance to check it out first."

"Of course," Kristin said. "We'll be having an open house in a few days. It's our annual fundraiser and tour for prospective donors and students. Would you like me to put you on the list?"

"Yes, please," Callie said. "Do we still have to sign the document?"

"You can wait until after the open house to make a decision. You have a year to take possession of the prize money."

Callie had begun the second half of her sophomore year, which was, frankly, a relief. She felt that the rhythm of school life would help her move the grieving process forward.

"I wish I had been at the Psy Games," Melinda said. "I think you would have won if I had been there."

Callie was blowing on a spoonful of soup. Winter weather was visiting, cold enough for soup but not for snow. "I think you're right, Mels. You've always been my good-luck charm."

"How much did you get?" Grey asked. He plopped a tater tot into his mouth.

"Second place got five grand," Jonathan said.

"If you weren't already my best friend, you'd be my best friend," Melinda said. "Can I hit you up for a loan? I have this cool cosplay but I need some EVA foam and the parents aren't budging. The grades weren't good last semester."

"I didn't get the money yet," Callie said. "I'm thinking of using it as tuition for classes they offer."

"They offer classes at the Bent Spoon?" Jonathan asked.

"Not there. The sponsor is the Psy Syndicate," Callie said. "It's a place where they work with psychics. They teach people how to use it, and they study it and stuff."

"I think I'd rather have the cash," Melinda said. "I don't want to take any more classes than I have to."

"I bet you'd take classes on makeup and costuming if you could," Callie said. "It's like that for me."

"You have a point," Melinda said.

"I'm going to their open-house fundraiser this weekend," Callie said. "So if I don't think it would do me any good to take the classes, I will definitely hook you up, Mels."

"Oh, a party?" Melinda perked up. "Can you take a plus-one?"

"I wish I could, but my plus-one will have to be Peggy," Callie said. "She has to sign off on the waiver and whatever paperwork they need."

"I never get to have any fun," Melinda said, pretending to wipe away tears.

"You can help me with makeup this weekend," Jonathan told her. "I have to submit a film project with my college application. Grey is helping with sets and sound."

"Will there be pizza?" Melinda asked.

"Of course," Jonathan said.

"Then I will bring my kit," Melinda said.

Grey and Melinda talked with Jonathan about his film project while Callie drifted off in thought. Five grand would go a long way toward real college tuition or even helping Peggy with bills. She could help Jonathan with his film project and Melinda with her cosplay. Why was she even considering psychic classes? Whatever. She would go back to the Psy Syndicate for their fundraiser and then have Peggy sign the waiver for the money.

The Psy Syndicate's front entrance was decked out in fairy lights, preserving Callie's first impression that it was a set for a fantasy film. A liveried attendant took Peggy's keys to park the car while another attendant stood at the doorway with an electronic pad and stylus to check them in. Callie wore one of her mother's black formal dresses and high heels, while Peggy was dressed in a slightly more upscale bohemian blouse and skirt. They gave their names and were escorted in by yet another uniformed staffer. Small tables were set up in corners with hors d'oeuvres and various beverages. A massive chandelier that Callie had not noticed during their first visit cast sparkles over the foyer walls, and more fairy lights lit the banisters on the staircase. Small groups of people were speaking with Psy Syndicate staff.

"The next tour will begin in five minutes. Please gather at the foot of the staircase," a man said. Callie recognized him as Sahil from the Psy Games.

"Let's do the tour," Peggy said. "I've been really curious about this house." She took Callie's arm and all but dragged her to the staircase. Unaccustomed to wearing heels, Callie tripped over the carpeting and came up short right in front of Sahil, who smiled at her. "Callie O'Callahan. Good to see you again."

"Yeah, same here." Callie smoothed her dress and cleared her hair from her face. "Do you teach any of the classes?"

"No, I'm strictly research at the moment," Sahil said. "Why? Are you thinking about taking some courses here?"

"I might."

"If I can stick my nose in, I think it would be smart of you to take them up on that offer," Sahil said. He turned to the small group at the foot of the stairs. "Ladies and gentlemen, last call for the house tour."

Once everyone had gathered, Sahil said, "Welcome to the Psy Syndicate's southeast branch, dedicated to furthering research into psychic abilities, also known by the Greek letter Ψ for short. This is one of the newest locations in our worldwide organization and was recently donated to us by the Forsythe Foundation. The Forsythe house is old by American standards, having been built in 1870; it's been in use by the university since 1925. Please follow me."

Sahil led the murmuring group to the left side of the staircase.

"This floor has been dedicated to classrooms and administration." Sahil indicated the rooms off to his left as he walked down the hallway. They didn't look like any classrooms that Callie was familiar with, but more like old-fashioned libraries. Comfortable chairs and a few small tables were set in no particular pattern and the decor was calming. There were instructors in some of the rooms having discussions with other small groups of prospective donors and students.

"The Psy Syndicate is looking for potentially ψ-talented people to hone their skills and perhaps learn new abilities. Once trained, the ψ-talented are asked to participate in research programs, which we hope will provide us with knowledge about how ψ works and how to make it work more reliably," Sahil said. He continued down the hallway to the back of the house. He stopped at a kitchen that looked part industrial and part domestic. A woman was directing waitstaff to take trays out to the visitors. She wore a dove-gray chef's smock with sleeves rolled up to her elbows and a surgeon's cap to keep her hair at bay. Her arms were covered from the wrists up in vividly colored tattoos, and she was too focused on piping something onto small pieces of bread to take notice of the people staring into her workspace. Callie's experience with chefs was solely from the Food Network on TV, so she expected some shouted demands. But this woman smiled at her staff and made it seemed as though cooking for the event were no different from taking a walk by the pond.

"We have a permanent kitchen staff for those students and visitors who decide to stay here," Sahil said. "Chef Lucia has kindly offered her services tonight for the event, but she normally provides the daily menus."

Sahil guided the small group to the back door and opened it for them to file out onto a porch with thick flagstone balusters supporting a filigreed iron railing. Large stone pots held evergreens suffused with more fairy lights, lending an unearthly air to the evening. A set of flagstone steps led through a fantasy garden of natural stone and metal sculptures in organic shapes. A small stream wound its way beneath small bridges in the walkway, which led to a Japanese-style building fronted by a sand and stone meditation garden. Callie wrapped her arms around herself, shivering from the cold.

"This is our meditation and meeting center," Sahil said. "Our students and guests may participate in different forms of meditation and martial arts here. Later this evening, our director, Cyril Rhys-Doyle, will be giving an illusion show in the auditorium."

Peggy turned to Callie and whispered, "Does that name sound familiar to you?"

"Kinda, yeah," Callie whispered back.

The double doors were made almost completely of glass, with dark wooden shapes like bowed bamboo making up the frames and handles. The room Sahil led them into had a floor that had a spongy quality to it, but the walls were a golden pine that shone in the light. The window took up the entire back wall, making it seem as though the room were part of the garden. A dais with a gong was on the opposite wall, and mats and yoga equipment were stored neatly in the corner. Through the next door, a series of unfurnished rooms with more mats led to a couple of corporate-type meeting rooms farther down the hall. The hall ended in a set of double doors like those found in a theater.

"If you would please follow me back to the house," Sahil said, turning to lead the group back down the hall and through the garden.

Once inside the main house, Sahil had the group go up a set of narrow stairs. "When the house was built, these rooms were the servants' quarters, but they have since been converted to testing rooms."

At the top of the stairs, Callie noted a long, hotel-like hallway with doors down the length of it.

"Each room tests for different aspects of ψ," Sahil said. "Each ψ-talented candidate will be tested in these rooms to find out what they excel at and what needs work. The more technical testing occurs at the psychology department at the university."

The group made its way down the hall, peering into each room. Callie saw that many of the rooms had computers and games like those at the Psy-cade.

"If you will follow me back to the foyer, we'll conclude our formal tour," Sahil said. "You are welcome to visit any room on the main floor, but the rooms up this main staircase are for private use by our staff and guests."

The group followed Sahil back to the foyer, where he stood waiting to give another tour. Callie and Peggy decided to get a few of the hors d'oeuvres and drinks before looking around. But when Peggy started talking in detail about the mushroom tarts with one of the waitstaff, Callie wandered off without her. Munching on a canape, she poked her head into the nearest classroom. A woman with long gray hair and a light puckered scar down her cheek looked up and smiled at her.

"Hello there," the woman said. "Welcome to the mediumship classroom." She had a bit of an Irish brogue to her speech.

Callie put her hand to her mouth as she mumbled, "'Scuse me."

"Sorry, I caught you with your mouth full." The woman held out a hand. "I'm Dorcas. Are you a prospective student?"

After swallowing her mouthful, Callie took Dorcas's hand. "I may be. I want to know more about this place before I decide."

"It's always good to be cautious," Dorcas said. "Maybe you could tell me a little about yourself and what you want to accomplish."

Callie told Dorcas about growing up with a carnival medium and how she had taken up her mother's mantle when Clair got sick. "I went to the Psy-cade a lot after that. I managed to take second place at the Psy Games on New Year's Eve. That's the money I could use for classes."

"Wow! Congratulations, Callie," Dorcas said. "That's no small achievement. And you have had such an interesting life, though not without some tragedy."

"Lately, my life has been all about taking care of my mom, going to school, and seeing my clients. My mom would say the responsible thing to do is put my winnings aside for college, but I'm really curious about the psychic skills I could hone."

"Let me just say that your skills may increase with training and an understanding of what we know so far about how ψ works," Dorcas said. "We have a long way to go before we truly grasp it, that much I know, but if you increase your skill set, you could increase your client list as well."

"I definitely thought of that," Callie said.

"We could also help you with your future endeavors. You say you want to go to college—do you know what you want to study?"

Callie shook her head.

"Several people who were simply searching for why they are the way they are found answers far and above their original questions. Some have joined the Psy Syndicate to help, not only with research but with aiding the police or helping to find lost items and so forth," Dorcas said.

"Really?" Callie said. This part sounded fascinating to her. She had never contemplated doing anything with her skills other than readings.

"It's true," Dorcas said, "but the police don't like to admit they use psychics to solve their cases. You might have noticed how some people think psychics are frauds."

Callie blushed a little. She thought about all she had done to manipulate certain clients to part with their money. When Clair was ill, Callie was willing to do almost anything to save her life. Now, charging for the fake séances and useless charms would only be lining her own pockets and bilking innocent, albeit gullible, clients of their cash.

"Attention, please!"

Callie and Dorcas were both startled by the loud voice coming from the back door.

"The illusion show will begin in the auditorium in ten minutes."

"Have you seen Cyril's show before?" Dorcas asked.

"I don't think so, but his name sounds familiar."

"It is a treat. You should go and watch," Dorcas said.

At that moment, Peggy reappeared next to Callie. "I've been searching all over for you. Let's go quick to get good seats," she said, taking Callie by the hand and pulling her to the back door. Callie waved to Dorcas, who smiled and finger-waved in reply.

They didn't get the best seats in the house, but the auditorium was small enough that no seat was bad. The plain walls mirrored the Japanese minimalism of the rest of the building, and the acoustic engineering muffled the audience while projecting the speaker on the thrust-style stage.

"I saw a picture of Cyril Rhys-Doyle," Peggy said. "I think I've seen him on TV before."

"Maybe," Callie said. "I don't generally watch magicians anymore."

Callie had always spent her summers traveling the Renaissance Faire circuit with her mom, but while her mom was working, Callie earned a little extra money by assisting with some of the stage productions. One of them was Manny the Magnificent, comedic magician. She had to check all his magic props to make sure they worked, and had learned the names of all the sleight-of-hand tricks. She eventually graduated from stagehand to magician's assistant or audience confederate—the "random" person the magician chooses from the audience.

The conversations quieted as music was piped through the auditorium speakers and the house lights dimmed. Cyril Rhys-Doyle entered from stage right wearing a tailored black suit with a red satin lining and an ornately embroidered golden vest. His white shirt was open at the collar, and his pants had matching red satin piping down the outer seams. His hair was the kind of curly mess that made women want to run their hands through it, and he had a closely cropped beard as neat as bird plumage. His eyes were hooded as he affected the mysterious-magician stance on the stage.

Without saying a word, he produced a deck of cards, fanned them out, and had an audience member choose the jack of spades, which he himself was not allowed to see. He had them sign their initials on the card and then replace the card in the deck. In a series of mind-boggling prestidigitation, Rhys-Doyle continually hid and recovered the signed card from several locations, including the auditorium's rafters. Finally, the deck solidified into a block of plastic with the signed card visible on top.

He then produced a blank set of cards and asked a different audience member to draw a picture on one without allowing him to see it. He had them return the card to the blank deck, then he drew a picture on an easel that had been brought onto the stage. He asked the audience member to check under their seat for the card. Amazed, the audience member showed it to the audience: the picture on the card was an exact replica of the one drawn on the easel. Finally, a pile of balls and cloth was brought onstage. Rhys-Doyle covered each ball with the cloth and they began to levitate like ghosts, which he made dance to the tune of "When You Wish upon a Star." He then made each ball return to the floor, whereupon he stomped on each piece of cloth to show that the balls underneath had disappeared. The show completed, Rhys-Doyle bowed to enthusiastic applause. Callie nodded her head as she clapped, impressed by his ability, which far outshone that of Manny the Magnificent.

"I hope you have enjoyed your evening so far," Rhys-Doyle said. His voice had a chocolatey timbre, and he spoke with a proper BBC British accent. "We appreciate your generosity to the Psy Syndicate. Without your support, we could not continue our vital work into extrasensory perception and manipulation. I know you were amazed by my simple tricks on the stage just now, but that was an illusion—a trick of the mind and eye. I would like to introduce a true magician who can manipulate a machine using only his energy and without any physical touch whatsoever. Please welcome Malcolm Edwards!"

A willowish man with a stoop, who seemed disheveled compared to Rhys-Doyle, strode onto the stage and grasped his hand, pumping it heartily.

"Malcolm's particular psychic skill is the manipulation of objects, otherwise known as psychokinesis," Rhys-Doyle said. "We have here an electronic device that we call a random number generator. It will rotate lights in either direction without any pattern. Malcolm will ask the lights to move in the direction of his choosing." A giant board with light bulbs arrayed in a circle with a five-foot diameter was rolled onto the stage. Callie had played this game in a smaller format at the Psy-cade but had had very little luck controlling the lights.

"Thank you, Mr. Rhys-Doyle," Malcolm said with a heavy Southern accent. "I will need a minute to get squared away here." He stood on the stage breathing in and exhaling forcefully a few times, his eyes closed and his head bowed. With a deep inhalation of breath, Malcolm spread his arms wide, his hands like quivering blades as he concentrated. "The lights will move clockwise for three rotations." As he said it, the lights lit up in the clockwise direction. Callie counted once the top light was illuminated, and again for two more rotations. The lights flickered between the top few, back and forth without direction.

"Now the same in the counterclockwise direction," Malcolm said.

The lights did precisely the same thing in the opposite direction.

"They will alternate back and forth, one rotation each," Malcolm said, and they did.

He brought his hands down and turned to face the audience, bowing to generous applause. He grasped Rhys-Doyle's hand again before he exited the stage.

"I know some of you may believe that his skill was simply more stage magic, but I promise you it was not," Rhys-Doyle said. "Our next guest will identify the location of one of our volunteers using a skill known as remote viewing. Your government hired him during the Cold War to spy on the Soviet Union using only his far-sight. Please welcome Theodore 'Teddy' Smith!" He clapped his hands as a square-shouldered man who might have been a boxer in his younger days came onstage with the aid of a walking stick.

"Teddy will use his ability to see where our volunteer is located right now. No one knows where she has gone. Once Teddy describes the location, we will call our volunteer and compare the description to the actual location."

Teddy closed his eyes and then began to describe what he was seeing in his mind's eye. "It's very large, in a circle or maybe oval shape. I hear a lot of people there, like a celebration or maybe a sporting event. I see the colors red, white, and black. I see a lot of white. It feels cold."

As Teddy was speaking, Rhys-Doyle was writing the information in bullet form on the easel. "Anything more you want to add, Teddy?"

"No, that should do," Teddy said.

"All right, let's dial up our volunteer," Rhys-Doyle said. A projection screen scrolled down from the rafters, and the sound of a ringing phone pervaded the auditorium. A young Asian woman with a knitted cap and mittens answered her phone using its camera feature. "Hi, this is Christine Wong."

"Christine, this is Cyril Rhys-Doyle. Could you show us where you are right now?"

Christine panned her cell phone around. The audience could see tiered seats filled with fans dressed in red and black. She then focused the camera onto a skating rink: there were two teams playing hockey. Applause erupted from the audience.

"How was that, sir?" Christine asked.

"Quite good. Thank you, Christine," Rhys-Doyle said. "Thank you for coming tonight, Teddy. Stellar work as usual." Teddy exited the stage, carefully navigating the stairs.

"This concludes our show, everyone!" Rhys-Doyle said with a flourish. "Please continue to enjoy the canapes and drinks. If you have any further questions, I will be happy to answer them for you in the main house."

The theater doors opened and people began filing out of their seats.

"That was just mind-blowing!" Peggy said, waving her hands for emphasis.

"I have to say, Rhys-Doyle sure has some skills," Callie said. "I only figured out how he did about a third of his tricks."

"Yeah, yeah, I'm not talking about him, though he is a fine and talented male specimen," Peggy said, "but how do you think the other two did it?"

"I have no clue," Callie said. "I guess they're the real deal. I mean, I saw some people do some of the same stuff at the Psy-cade, but they weren't as good at it."

"Are you kidding me?" Peggy asked. They were walking along the fairy-lighted garden path. "That can't possibly be for real."

"Rhys-Doyle is saying that it is, and they teach that stuff here," Callie said.

"If you can learn to do that, it'd be worth every penny."

The rest of the crowd seemed to be just as amazed, since their conversations pretty much echoed what Peggy was saying. They saw Rhys-Doyle in the main foyer surrounded by potential patrons and students, deftly handling the barrage of questions being fired at him.

"Callie, you should come meet Mr. Rhys-Doyle," said Sahil, who had walked over to Callie at the canape table. Grabbing her elbow, he steered her toward the crowd.

"Wait a second!" she said. The canapes were delicious, and she was famished.

Sahil waved his hand to get Rhys-Doyle's attention, which embarrassed Callie even further. Rhys-Doyle turned to him and said, "Yes, Sahil, what do you need?" in an annoyed tone. But then he saw Callie, and in the span of a moment his face changed from the master of illusion to a man utterly confused. "Clair?" he said. He began pushing his way through the throng, saying, "I'll be just a moment, please." He grasped Callie's free hand and looked carefully into her face.

She swallowed hard and said, "Clair's my mother."

"She had a...? She never told me," he said. "You are the spitting image of her. Is she here tonight?" He began to look around the room. "Where is she?"

"She died last year," Callie told him.

"No! She was far too young, far too good."

Callie thought he wanted to say more but couldn't. "I know," she said. "It isn't fair."

The three stood in awkward silence. Rhys-Doyle produced a silk handkerchief from his breast pocket and dabbed just below his eyes. Was he crying?

Sahil said, "Callie placed second in the Psy Games."

Rhys-Doyle looked at Sahil as if he'd just remembered he was there, then looked back at Callie. "I'm not at all surprised." With that, he squeezed Callie's hand one more time and went back to the group of patrons.

Callie gazed after him. This man knew her mother. Moreover, was he crying over the news that she had died? Had her mother ever mentioned this man to her before? Was that why she recognized his name? She searched for Peggy in the crowd, finding her surrounded by women of her age and mode of dress.

Callie said, "Peggy, I've decided to use my winnings to take classes here." *And to find out who this Rhys-Doyle person was to my mother.*

Chapter Twenty-One

Amber

Amber didn't know how long she had been lying on the cot recovering from her beating. Gary hadn't killed her, but she hurt so much that she wanted to die. Delirium had set in, either from her injuries, dehydration, or fever. She vaguely remembered Gary trying to force water into her mouth, but she didn't have much recollection of anything else.

Momma? she thought. *It's me, Amber. I miss you so much. Please get me out of here! I hurt so bad and I want you to hug me...*

Suddenly, Amber had a sensation of being in the kitchen, not at Gary's house but at her own. It looked different from when she had seen it last. It seemed less like a magazine picture and more like her friend Ashley's lived-in kitchen. Mom normally never left a plate in the sink, but there were a lot stacked in there now, along with wine glasses and coffee cups. Amber looked at the kitchen table, the place where she did her homework after school and before dinner. It was covered with unopened letters and papers. She glanced down at one of them; it had her school photo on it, along with "Have You Seen Her?" printed in large letters.

Amber then found herself in the living room, where her mother was on the couch covered with a blanket her grandmother's grandmother had knitted. She was a hot mess—her hair looked like it hadn't been cut for weeks and her face had lines that hadn't been there before, especially between her eyebrows. There was an empty bottle and wine glass on the coffee table. Looking around the living room, Amber saw more of the same clutter: shoes left on the floor, mail flotsam left wherever it was laid, and take-out food containers left for the flies. This was not the mom Amber remembered, so why was she fantasizing about this other woman who looked like an unkempt version of her?

Movement on the couch caught Amber's attention. Her mother's eyes were open, bleary and bloodshot, but also wide with astonishment.

"Amber?" she croaked. "Sweetie? Have you come home?"

Amber snapped back to her aching body. She realized that during her vision, she had felt clear-minded and unharmed. She rolled over onto her left side. The pain from her broken ribs had been so severe that she was unable to sleep on her right, and she still couldn't breathe out of her nose. At best she could handle only shallow breaths through her mouth. Her eyes had been swollen shut but she could see a bit more each day—not that it mattered in her darkened hole. She hadn't tried to chew food or speak, since her jaw felt unmoored and her teeth felt cracked.

The vision of her home had been so very real, as if she had left her body and visited her mom just by sheer will. Now that she considered it, she *had* left her body, she was sure of it. She had felt a sensation similar to floating upward, and then she was suddenly where she wanted to be: home. The shock of seeing her distraught mother snapped her back to her cell. *Wait just a minute, didn't Mom say something to me?* It seemed as though she was focusing right where Amber was and had said, "Have you come home?" Tears welled up in Amber's swollen eyes and slipped down her cheeks to further moisten her sweat-soaked pillow.

Chapter Twenty-Two

Callie

It was a bitterly cold Saturday morning. Callie was all but running down the garden path to the meditation center, late for the Psy Syndicate's orientation for new students. A tai chi class was in session, and some of the practitioners stared at her as she hurried past them as quietly as her shoes would allow. She looked at each closed door along the hallway until she found the one with "Orientation" on a sheet tacked to the door. She opened it slowly, peering in to find the conference room full with only one unoccupied chair—near the podium, of course. The wondrous smell of pastries that were piled up on another table made Callie's stomach growl audibly. One of the teachers she had met during the open house stood at the podium.

"Hi, can I help you?" Dorcas said. "Oh, it's Callie, isn't it? Come in, dear, take a seat. We were just introducing ourselves." She indicated the chair next to her. "Everyone, this is Callie."

Callie nodded toward the group and sat down.

"Let's go around the table one more time and introduce yourselves."

The woman next to her was middle-aged and had shoulder-length salt-and-pepper hair. Callie thought she might be a teacher. "Hi, my name is Faye. Nice to meet you, Callie."

An elvish-looking girl with long hair who looked younger than Callie said, "I'm Siobhan."

Next to Siobhan was a strikingly beautiful girl with dark skin and hair in long braids. She said, "I'm Chillian."

And then there was winner 89238, the sailor boy with the self-satisfied smirk. "Well, if it isn't second-place girl. My name is Winston."

Callie, in an effort to be the better person, simply nodded in acknowledgment, turning her attention to the next few people at the table as they introduced themselves. Each of them had a plate of food and a beverage in front of them. Callie berated herself for being late as her stomach continued to growl its displeasure.

"Lovely. I'm sure we will all get better acquainted later, but we must stay on schedule," Dorcas said. "First on the agenda is the video, so let me get that started for you."

She fiddled with the control panel until she got the projection screen lowered, and then touched a few more buttons to lower the lights in the room and get the video started.

"Welcome to the Psy Syndicate," a pleasant-sounding male narrator said. There was drone-generated video footage of a stately, ivy-covered English manor. "We are a worldwide organization of parapsychological researchers who are endeavoring to unlock the secrets of psychic ability. The Syndicate began in 1892 when a pair of American psychologists came to Oxford to study the phenomenon with the aid of our illustrious founder, Dr. Regis Smythe." An ancient black-and-white photo of several unsmiling men and a couple of corseted women in long dark dresses took the place of the manor. "We have completed over a thousand studies on the existence of telepathy, clairvoyance, mediumship, precognition, and remote-viewing ability. Now, with your help, we hope to delve into the origin of these psychic abilities through fMRI, EEG, and other medical tests developed by neuroscientists from around the world." Various pictures of medical equipment and testing rooms with candidates flashed on the screen. "You will be tested first to see which of these abilities you possess, and then you will be given an opportunity to take classes to develop your psychic skills further.

Once you have completed the classes, you will be asked to take the psychic skills test again. If you wish to participate in the study on the origins of psychic ability, please notify the director of your facility. We appreciate your interest in the Psy Syndicate."

Dorcas manipulated the control panel to resume normal lighting. "I believe you have all had a tour of the facility during the open house, but we will take you around again so you can find your way when you take your tests and classes."

Kristin was placing forms, pens, and binders in front of everyone at the table. Callie saw her own name printed on the binder's cover and the spine. She opened it up to see a few sections that were empty. The forms were the standard legal types she had seen throughout her schooling and with the Ren Faires.

"Each of you has received some documentation to fill out before you begin at Psy Syndicate," Dorcas said. "You have also received binders to store your information as you go through your programs. After you are tested, you will be assigned some core classwork but will also have electives to choose from. Let's go through the documents first and then we'll take a break."

After the onerous task of filling out legal documents was done and break time was called, Callie made a beeline for the food table, piling one mouth-watering treat after another onto a plate she considered much too small. She noticed Chillian was doing much the same. They made eye contact.

"If they feed us like this all the time, I'm going to need stretch pants," Chillian said.

"I know, right?" Callie said. "They have a full-time chef here. I saw her working during the open house."

"Yeah, she even does requests," Chillian said.

"Oh, you know Lucia?"

"Only since I moved in," Chillian said.

"You live here? At the Psy Syndicate?" Callie asked.

"Yeah, that Rhys-Doyle guy brought me here from Philedelphia," Chillian said. "I thought I won the lottery."

"No kidding," Callie said. "Why did he move you down here?"

"Because I've got skills," Chillian said, flinging her braided hair back and putting her hand on her hip. "No, for real, he thinks I can help make money for this place."

"You do, like, readings or something? Are you famous in Philadelphia?"

"In a way," Chillian replied.

Before she could say more, Dorcas called them back from the break. A bunch of people had entered the room wearing deep blue knit shirts with "Psy Syndicate" embroidered over the left pocket. One of them was Sahil.

"We have assigned a guide to each of you," Dorcas said. "They will take you through some basic tests in the upper wing of the main house and show you around. Feel free to ask them questions. Don't forget to take your notebooks, you'll be needing them."

Sahil made his way through the suddenly cramped room to Callie, who was trying to get back to the table for her bag and binder.

"We have to stop meeting like this, people will talk," Callie said as Sahil approached.

His smile increased the wattage in the room. "This time it's on purpose. I wanted to work with you."

"Really?" Callie said. "Why's that?"

They managed to get her items through the door, carried along by the small tide of students and guides as they headed to the main house. Sahil leaned in to Callie so she could hear him better.

"Your skill rates quite highly among those tested. I wanted to work with the best."

"Then why not work with the guy who won first place?"

"He may have won the Psy Games but I think you have more innate ability in the other areas I'm interested in."

"I'll try not to disappoint."

The group was squeezed as they walked carefully up the narrow staircase to the testing level.

"Today is just preliminary testing so you can get used to the way things work," Sahil said. "Let's see"—he regarded his clipboard—"we're in room eight down the way here."

Callie followed him to a room with nothing more than a table, two chairs, and a wooden partition that split the table in two.

"We have the forced-choice telepathy test here. Go ahead and take a seat," Sahil said.

Callie put her bag on the back of a chair and placed her binder on the table. "So, the mind-reading test?"

"That's the easy explanation, yes," Sahil said. "Are you familiar with Zener cards?"

"I've heard of them but I'm not sure what they look like."

"Since you're so good at telepathy already, I'm not going to show them to you. I will concentrate on one card at a time for thirty seconds apiece, and you write down your best impression of what I'm seeing, okay?" Sahil placed several pieces of paper and a pen in front of Callie. "Just put the number of the card next to your answer. Do you need to do anything to help your concentration? Some people have a ritual or require some meditation time."

"Nope, I'm good."

"All right, let's begin."

He sat down across from Callie with only his deep blue-black hair showing above the wooden partition. Callie could hear him shuffling some cards.

"Ready?"

"Yes, I'm ready," Callie said, her eyes on the paper in front of her, her head perched in her hand while the other held the pen at the ready.

"Go," Sahil said.

She took a deep breath as she looked for the vision of the card through Sahil's eyes. She saw waves in a brief moment of clarity. She quickly drew a *1* and wavy lines next to it.

"Next," Sahil said.

She wrote a *2* and the word *green* next to that.

Sahil continued to view the cards as Callie scribbled her answers on the sheets, quickly filling in the blank spaces until they reached twenty-five cards.

"That's all of them," Sahil said. "Let's see how you scored."

He took the paper from in front of Callie and began reviewing her answers.

"You scored way above chance here," he said, "just as I thought you would, and without knowing what the cards look like."

"Can I see them?" Callie asked.

Sahil handed the deck to her. There were five cards each of five shapes, each in a different major color. "Besides the shape and the color, they each represent a number," he said. "The circle is one line, the plus is two, the wavy lines are three, the box is four, and the star is five."

"So that's why I got a number or a color sometimes," Callie said.

"That's what gets through," Sahil said. "We still don't know why it's like that, but we hope to learn."

They had time to go through the test once more before a general buzzer sounded.

"That's our cue to move on." Sahil looked at his clipboard for the next room number. "We're in room ten, the PK room."

"PK?" Callie asked.

"Sorry, we use a lot of abbreviations here—you'll get used to it. PK is psychokinesis. It means moving things psychically," he said. "This room is for electronic PK."

Inside, on a table with a chair in front of it, was a computer with white noise on its screen. There was no keyboard or mouse or any other interface she could see.

"Just have a seat here," he said. "The idea is to see the actual picture behind the interference. Do whatever feels comfortable to clear the picture, then we'll move on to the next one."

Nothing was happening on the screen. Callie was a bit mystified about how to manipulate electronics. It wasn't something she worked with much, having had a pretty analog upbringing.

"Some people have mentally 'talked' to the computer to get it to clear. Try that, maybe," Sahil said.

Callie felt pretty silly talking to an inanimate object, but she gave it a try anyway. Only a mild change occurred on the screen. She could barely see a large palm tree on the left, maybe a canoe down at the bottom. Then the screen went fuzzy again.

"That's not bad," Sahil said. "Let's move to the next picture. I'm sure you'll get the hang of it."

Although Callie never got complete clarity with any of the pictures, they were discernible enough to identify what was in them. Sahil wrote some notes in her binder and then announced that they could go down for lunch. She was more than ready for the break.

"You're really working those psychic muscles today," he said. "Are you up to more?"

"I think I can try some more after lunch. I'm used to performing all day when I'm at Ren Faires."

"I've never been to a Ren Faire. What's it like?" Sahil asked.

"It's basically an outdoor re-creation of the European Renaissance time period," Callie said. "Local people pay to come watch shows, listen to music, eat food, and buy stuff. My mom was one of the entertainers, so to speak. She had a small tent or some other shelter where she did psychic readings for the visitors. We would travel around during the summer with the different Rennies, but mostly we stayed with the same troupe."

"That sounds like a really idyllic childhood," Sahil said. "A whole lot more amusing than what my parents had me do."

"It was pretty fun except when I had to muck horse stables or deal with hundred-degree heat and thunderstorms," Callie said. "I also didn't have access to Wi-Fi, TV, or any other device for the summer. Plus, I wasn't around many people my own age until I started school. I would go help other Rennies when I got bored, so I learned a lot of skills."

"What else did you learn besides doing readings?" Sahil asked.

"I learned how to do stage magic, for one," Callie said. "I recognized some of what your director was doing the other night but not all of it. He's pretty talented."

"He really is, but he retired from stage magic to work for the Psy Syndicate," Sahil said. "He told us that he saw real magic a long time ago and wanted to learn how it worked."

"He seemed to know my mom," Callie said. "I don't remember ever seeing him before."

"He said he was inspired by a talented person he met years ago. Maybe it was your mom."

"That would explain his reaction when he met me," Callie said. "But I wonder why he never came to visit her, since she was here the whole time."

"He hasn't been at this location very long," Sahil said. "He transferred from the Oxford branch to run this one. This place is relatively new."

"It doesn't look that new," Callie said.

"Oh, the house? It's almost a historic landmark. It was given to the university and they let the Psy Syndicate use it. They got it fixed up and added a couple of buildings to the property so they could use it as one of their research locations. And they can hire college students like me."

Once they arrived at the dining room, they lined up for the buffet of Southwestern-style foods. Since she had eaten so much at the orientation meeting and didn't want to look like a glutton in front of Sahil, Callie was modest in her selections. The dining room had similar seating to her high school cafeteria but was much smaller. After she and Sahil sat down at a round table that seated six, Callie saw Chillian enter the room and waved to get her attention. Chillian lifted her chin in acknowledgment and then turned to the buffet. While Callie's attention was on Chillian, Winston had sat down right next to her.

"Ah, Second-place girl," he said.

Callie turned to face him. "My name's Callie."

Sahil stared at Winston while slowly chewing a bite of enchilada.

"You really shouldn't be upset by that second-place showing at the Psy Games," Winston said. "It's hard for girls to be competitive, you know."

Callie blinked but kept her cool. Working among the public for so long had taught her to stay calm under duress. Sahil just raised his right eyebrow.

"Quite honestly, I was surprised that your strategy of playing the low-point games worked at all. But this place, it's a different animal, Second-place. You can't play it safe like you did during the games. If you think you're going to make it here, you might just want to pack it in. I mean, you're just a pretty carnival hack, after all."

"And what the hell are you, Prep boy?" Chillian asked, having joined them at the table.

Winston sneered at her. "Ah, it's the Deathwatch Beetle. What a fascinating skill you have. Maybe we could talk about it over, say, dinner?"

"In your dreams," Chillian said.

"That could be arranged, too," Winston said. "If you'll excuse me, I need to go speak with my research guide about my exclusive contract. TTFN."

"If this was Philly..." Chillian said, not finishing her sentence, but the look on her face made her meaning clear.

"What's a deathwatch beetle?" Callie asked.

"It's a kind of wood-boring beetle," Sahil said. "Legend says that one would start to make clicking noises in the walls when someone in the house was about to die."

"So you know when—" Callie started.

"People are going to die, yeah," Chillian finished.

"That's a bummer," Callie said. "I mean, it's amazing, but it must be really hard to see that."

Chillian didn't reply, just stared down at her plate and pushed the food around with her fork. "You know, I'm just not that hungry. I'll see you later, Callie?"

"Um, sure, yeah," Callie said. But Chillian was already walking out of the dining room.

After the awkward lunch, Sahil and Callie returned upstairs to the next testing room.

"Are you still feeling up to it?" Sahil asked.

"Even more than I was before," Callie said. "I'm going to show that jerk just what a girl can do."

"That's the attitude," Sahil said, clapping Callie on the shoulder. "Let's kick his butt."

They entered the remote viewing room. It had a computer, just as the PK room did, but this one had a different screen, which she recognized from the Psy Games.

"This is pretty similar to clairvoyance except you're going to describe a target picture that has been randomly selected. What's important here is to keep your mind clear and simply tell me the impressions you're getting. Feel all the senses, not just the visual.

Don't try to identify what you're targeting, just keep your mind open to impressions. Got it?"

"Okay, I'll try," Callie said.

"Try to enjoy this—it works better than thinking like it's a test," Sahil said. "If you're having trouble, try visualizing a bowl of rice and repeat some numbers over and over."

She cleared her mind of the usual clutter, allowing thoughts of friends, her deceased mother, and Winston the Clod to simply pass through her mind without consideration. Eventually blips interrupted her mental whiteboard.

"I'm seeing a lot of circles...and the color black...some rectangles. It feels like it's outside, not inside. I'm smelling something weird, I just can't figure out what it is," Callie said.

"Don't dwell on that, just move on," Sahil said.

She got her mind whitewashed again before receiving more information, which she shared with Sahil. "That's it."

"Ready to see the photo?" Sahil said after he completed writing. He clicked on the screen, which showed a Civil War–era brick house with white trim in the background and a pyramidic pile of cannonballs sitting by a small black cannon on an immaculate green lawn.

"Not bad," Sahil said. "I think you described the location quite well, just a few unrelated impressions."

"These tests feel kind of the same to me," Callie said, "except for the PK computer."

"That's something we're looking at," Sahil said. "What part of the brain is working when you do each activity." He looked over the schedule. "We're done with testing for the day, but we have about a half hour before you need to go back to the conference room. Do you want to tour some more or do something?"

"I think I'd like a snack and something to drink," Callie said.

"Let's go raid the kitchen."

They went down the narrow hallway to the stairs, making a sharp turn left to get to the kitchen. The staff was between prep for lunch and dinner, so Callie and Sahil had free rein.

"The drinks are over here." Sahil showed Callie a glass-front refrigerator filled with bottles, canned sodas, and milk. "And you can help yourself to these snacks over here." He indicated a table with baskets of fruit, trays of vegetables with ramekins of dips, granola bars, and small bags of popcorn. It looked like junk food was not on the menu. Callie grabbed a banana and a bottle of sparkling water.

"I'm going to eat this in the conference room," Callie said. "Will I see you later?"

"I'll be around today, otherwise I won't see you until you're scheduled to test again," Sahil said.

"I don't know what the rest of the schedule looks like, but maybe we could meet for dinner?" Callie asked.

"I have plans this evening," Sahil said, "but I will see you for testing. You did really well." He clapped her on the back. "Take care." Callie watched him go, glad he couldn't see the disappointed look on her face.

The winter day was clear but cold and a bit breezy, so Callie rushed through the garden to the meditation center and got to the conference room in plenty of time. Her intention was to eat her snack while going over some of the Psy Syndicate literature, but she stopped short at the doorway. Cyril Rhys-Doyle was standing at the podium with Dorcas, shuffling through papers and speaking quietly with her.

"I'm sorry, is it okay for me to be in here?" Callie asked them.

The fellow conspirators looked up simultaneously. "That's fine, Callie, we're just discussing the afternoon program. Mr. Rhys-Doyle needs to leave this afternoon so we're adjusting the schedule to suit," Dorcas said.

Rhys-Doyle didn't speak, but he stared at Callie with an odd intensity. He returned his attention to Dorcas when she asked him a question. Callie did her level best to ignore the pair, who were speaking in low tones. She read through the first paragraph three times without retaining a thing. She felt self-conscious about eating the banana, so she left it, unpeeled, on the table. This was not like her. Rhys-Doyle was freaking her out.

The new recruits began filing in for the afternoon orientation session. Chillian seemed just as she had that morning, as if the lunchtime run-in with Winston hadn't happened. Winston had his usual haughty smirk as he made eye contact with every young woman in the room. Callie denied him the satisfaction of giving him any notice. Once everyone was accounted for and seated, Dorcas brought the room to attention with a knock on her podium.

"I hope everyone had a productive time with testing and an opportunity to eat some of the magnificent food Chef Lucia prepared for us today. For those of you who were unable to attend our fundraising event, I would like to introduce you to our director, Cyril Rhys-Doyle." Dorcas stepped aside and put her hand out to indicate the director, who stood up and straightened his suit jacket as he stepped to the podium.

"Thank you, Dorcas," he said. He looked along the table. "I do see some familiar faces from the fundraiser, as well as our Psy Games winners, but I would be grateful if you'd introduce yourselves once more." Everyone responded, not only to his voice but also to his stage presence, by sitting up a bit straighter and leaning toward him. As each person introduced themselves, he asked them some basic questions. He skipped Callie, Winston and Chillian.

"Welcome, all of you, to this newest branch of the Psy Syndicate." He extended his arms to encompass the room. "There are several other branches around the world. As you saw on the video, the original location is in Oxford, but we also have facilities in Brazil,

Spain, and India, and one other location in the United States in Los Angeles. The sweeping goal of the Syndicate is lofty but difficult. I'm certain you have all had your run-ins with doubters."

Many heads nodded, some vigorously.

"Imagine the derision amongst those who claim they are scientists." He shook his head slowly, looking down at the podium, his hand to his heart. "They say what you can do is impossible, that it doesn't fit the standard model of physics, that you and I and all the others who study these phenomena are simply delusional or, even worse, evil."

He paused while his audience stewed over the last statement.

He placed his hand on his chest. "I know otherwise, as do you. You all have your reasons for being here—many are personal, some are altruistic, and some are for financial gain. All of those are quite understandable, as you each have a skill you wish to further, and I want to help you with that. By achieving your best, you provide the Psy Syndicate with valuable information." He struck the podium firmly, punctuating every statement. "We will find out what psi is, how it works, where it comes from, all because you are willing to help us research it." He spread his arms wide again. "With all the data we have collected—and will continue to collect—we will prove to the doubters that there is more to their lauded standard model than they were previously aware of."

Some of the people in the room actually cheered in agreement.

"If you remain with us, you will find a supportive environment. No one will deride you; instead, you will be celebrated for your talent." He swept his hands to indicate all who sat at the table. "If you apply yourselves to the best of your ability, you will reach the pinnacle of your skill set to utilize as you desire."

Callie glanced around to see the shining faces eager to please this man as if he were the psychic messiah. Even she could feel the pull of his significant stage presence.

"To that end, we have a comprehensive list of courses available to you. They are listed in the literature," Rhys-Doyle said, indicating the handouts Dorcas had given them earlier.

"We have asked you here specifically because you show a great deal of promise," he said now adopting a more serious demeanor. Leaning forward he said, "Yet promise is only part of what we're looking for. It takes more than innate ability to become a successful psychic, just as it takes more than skill to become a successful ball player. Those of you who dedicate the time and energy to your ability will be rewarded with more than just being better psychics."

He stood up straighter. "The Psy Syndicate is more than simply a research facility—we have opportunities for you to apply your abilities." He glanced at Chillian, who looked down at the table rather than meet his eye. "Though we are a new location, there are already several talented psychics under contract with us."

That must be what Winston was talking about at lunch, Callie thought, *and why Chillian was brought all the way from Philadelphia by Rhys-Doyle himself.*

"Imagine what you can do under the aegis of the Psy Syndicate." He paused to allow them time with their respective imaginations. Callie considered it along with all the others. She had made not a small amount of money to help with her mother's medical bills. Could she make more through a relationship with the Psy Syndicate? It would certainly help with college tuition.

Dorcas appeared at Rhys-Doyle's side, touching him lightly on the forearm and whispering close to his ear. He nodded and said, "I'm so sorry, ladies and gentlemen, but I do have a plane to catch. Thank you for your time." He bowed slightly and then headed for the door.

Callie was disappointed that she wouldn't have a chance to speak to him privately at some point during the day. She really wanted to know the details of his relationship to her mother.

"Well then, everyone, shall we go over the classes?" Dorcas asked.

Chapter Twenty-Three

Amber

"Why did you make me do it?" Gary asked her. His hands were clasping her shoulders, shaking her violently with each word. "I told you I would kill you if you ran. Why did you run?"

Amber simply stared at the space between his eyes, blinking slowly as if she were drugged. She knew it drove him nuts, but it was a small thing she could do, some semblance of control in this screwed-up situation.

"*Why!*" he roared, with one last shake of her small frame.

Amber felt like her brain was a Ping-Pong ball being whacked around in her skull. There was going to be a brutal headache later. "I don't know. I guess I'm just stupid."

"Yes, you are," Gary said, removing his hands from her shoulders. "I guess you need more lessons." He grabbed her feet and put on the shackles, but also put the manacles on her wrists as well. This time, the handcuffs had a chain only a few inches in length.

He waited impatiently for her to get up off the cot and cuffed her head when he felt she was taking too long. Her legs were wobbly and her head swam with the effort of standing. Gary grabbed the chain between her wrists and tugged her to the base of the stairs. He took them at his usual pace, dragging Amber behind him. She was going to have a few more bruises on her shins and toes from being too slow to lift her feet onto each step. He dragged her up the next flight of stairs into the bathroom.

"Take a bath. You're a stinking mess," he said, shoving her in and slamming the door.

"I can't take off my clothes with these on my wrists," she said to the door.

He wrenched open the door, making Amber take a step back. He produced the shackle key and removed the wrist manacles, but he left those around her ankles intact.

"Don't even think about opening this door," Gary said, shaking a finger in her face. He slammed it once again, leaving Amber alone.

The bruised tissue surrounding her eyes had abated enough for her to see her reflection in the large mirror over the sink. Tears started to flood her eyes and roll down her cheeks. This reflection wasn't her. It was a torn-up, abused, emaciated girl with thinning hair and multicolored skin where fresh and old bruises ran the color spectrum. Unwilling to see this wraith any longer, she went to the bathtub to turn on the hot tap and plug the drain. She knew there would be a bar of soap in the holder and nothing else. No razors or poisons to end her life or to use against her jailer. The steam rose from the hot water, turning the bathroom into a sauna. She gently lowered herself into the tub, wincing over every new and healing wound.

Gary's loud voice interrupted Amber's reverie. "Hurry up in there!"

She had been soaking in the hot water for what felt like a very short time, but got to scrubbing immediately. Her hair was tangled and took a lot of brushing through with her fingers. More hanks of hair came away from her scalp, so she tossed them into the trash can. Scrubbing her face was so painful that she gave up and put her face in the water, which was turning gray from the dirt, grime, and dried blood washing off her body.

Gary pounded on the bathroom door, making Amber work even faster. When she could see no more blood or dirt anywhere, she pulled the plug and watched the water drain from the tub as she dried off with the large towel. She looked around but couldn't see any change of clothes. "Do you have something for me to change into?"

There was a pause before the door opened just enough for Gary to toss in a clean tunic and underwear. Once she was done drying her hair, she got dressed. "I'm done," she said.

The door swung open. Gary grabbed her by her left wrist and dragged her into his bedroom. He sat on the edge of his bed. "Do you know what I could do to you right now?" he said.

Amber felt a terrifying new panic. Was he going to molest her? He was leering at her, looking her up and down, and she felt sure that was the next indignity. She wrapped her arms around her middle and began to shake.

"I warned you that I would kill you if you ran," he said, "but I didn't because I have already spent too much time getting you trained up." He threw his hands up in exasperation. "I really thought I could trust you but you defied me!"

"I won't run, I promise!" Amber said, her voice shaking with fear.

"I can't trust you!" Gary said. "I have to do something about this."

He reached out to her and pulled her close then reached behind to grab something. She closed her eyes and began to whimper. She didn't want this to happen. She would just die if it did. Gary put something around her throat. He was tugging it to be snug but not to choke her.

"There," he said, and let go of her. She opened her eyes and reached up to touch what he'd put around her throat. It was made of plastic and had a box attached. There were little metal circles on the inside.

"That's a shock collar. If you try to leave this house, you will regret it. If you defy me ever again, you will regret it. Do you understand? I will know where you are every second, and I will use it if you even look out the window. If you try to get someone's attention, I'll use it. As a matter of fact, you won't even know *when* I'll use it." He brought his wrist up so she could see the black band with a small LCD on it.

She began to calm down. That was it? A dog collar? How bad could a shock be compared to the beatings or rape? Amber was relieved.

Chapter Twenty-Four

Callie

"So, how was your first day as a psychic guinea pig?" Melinda asked.

Melinda had convinced Callie to join her and Grey at the local anime and science fiction fan convention. She was dressed like a curvy version of Sayaka Miki from *Madoka Magica*. Callie went in her usual costume of jeans, T-shirt, and jacket, making her essentially invisible next to Melinda, who was stopped frequently to pose for pictures taken by adoring fans of the show. They were sitting on the floor waiting for the next event, munching on hot dogs they had purchased from a street vendor outside the convention hall.

"I just went through an orientation and had some baseline tests done," Callie said. "I did meet some other people there."

"Huh," Melinda responded. "What were they like?"

"They all seemed pretty normal except for this one guy called Winston. He's a complete jerk. Calls me Second-place girl and a carnival hack." Callie said.

"I hate guys like that," Melinda said, wiping mustard from her chin.

"He's also really shady," Callie said. "Makes my skin crawl."

"Anyone there cute?" Melinda asked.

"Yeah, the guy who tested me, Sahil," Callie said.

"Ooooh, tell me more," Melinda said.

"I met him on New Year's at the Psy-cade during the Psy Games. He was one of the judges. Then he was at orientation and told me he wanted to work with me because I was really talented," Callie said. "He's got this gorgeous smile, and his hair is so dark it has these blue highlights when light shines on it. He's been really nice to me."

"Did he ask you out?" Melinda asked.

"Nope," Callie said. "He shut me down when I asked *him* out."

"Ouch," Melinda said.

"He's in college doing his dissertation work. I think I'm too young for him," Callie said.

Grey came over and sat down with them. He was dressed as Omoi from *Naruto*. His cosplay sword was so large he had to lay it across his lap to keep it from protruding into the crowd walking by. He was munching on potato chips.

"Hi, Grey," Callie said. "Enjoying the con?"

"Yup." Grey lifted a bag of swag to show Callie.

"Great," she said.

The doors to the event room opened, and the costumed and uncostumed alike poured out through the double doors. Callie, Melinda, and Grey waited until the human deluge ended before filing in with the large crowd that had been waiting outside the room. Callie didn't know who the speaker was that Melinda and Grey had come to see, but he was there to talk about upcoming anime releases in the US. The three were able to find seats together in the center of the third row. Callie was focused on Melinda, who was talking to her excitedly about the potential new releases, so she hadn't really noticed the person next to her until she heard her name.

"Callie?" the voice asked.

Callie turned to acknowledge the speaker only to see that it was Winston.

"I thought that was you," he said. "What a small world."

"Some would say too small," Callie said, instinctively shrinking away from him.

"Hi, I'm Winston," he said, extending his hand across Callie's lap to Melinda. Melinda grasped it distractedly.

"This is Grey and Melinda," Callie said, making an attempt at being courteous.

"Hey," Grey said, and then turned his attention to the table at the front of the room where the guest speaker would be sitting.

"Hi," Melinda said. "Where do you know Callie from?"

"I was the winner at the Psy Games. Callie here placed a distant second," Winston said.

Callie nudged Melinda's side and said, "He's the one I told you about, remember?" *Get a clue, Mels.*

"Ohhh, that's right," Melinda said.

"I didn't know you enjoyed anime," Winston said to Callie.

"You don't know me at all," Callie said.

"That's true, I don't," Winston said, "but I look forward to getting to know you better."

"I thought you considered me a carnival hack who won't be staying long at the Psy Syndicate. Why would you want to know me better?" Callie asked.

"I suppose I spoke too soon at the orientation luncheon. I actually find you fascinating. A fun diversion," Winston said.

Callie felt a frisson of fear climb up her spine and raise the hair on the back of her neck. It was fortunate that someone came to the microphone at that moment to introduce the guest speaker, because Callie really didn't want this conversation with Winston to continue. She felt a wrongness about him, confirmed by the sinister subtext to what he had said.

When the speaker finally answered the last question from the audience, Callie stood up to leave, but Winston blocked her exit.

"See you later, Callie," he said, smiling up at her.

"Yeah, later, Winston." She turned to exit the row in the other direction, knowing that his eyes were on her the whole time.

Melinda dropped Callie off well past midnight. Peggy was already asleep and had left a small light on in the kitchen, but the rest of the house was dark. Callie felt like the main character in a horror film, with all the shadowed places harboring something undead and evil. She climbed the stairs as quickly as she could and rapidly but quietly shut her bedroom door. She flicked the switch to turn on the overhead light and stood there giving her room a quick inspection. It was the comfortable and safe bedroom it had always been, the evil undead existing only in her imagination. How many times had she walked into this dark house without any ill effect? Something had her jumping at shadows. Maybe it was a subconscious effect of seeing Winston at the convention, she decided.

She took off her clothes, threw them into the hamper, and put on the shirt and pajama pants she slept in. She set her phone on the bedside table with the face illuminated so that she could still see after she turned out the overhead light. Once she flipped the switch, she leaped into her bed and pulled the covers up to her chin, just like a child afraid of the bogeyman in her closet. She was too wired to sleep, so she read texts and surfed social media until she was calm and her eyelids were drooping. She returned her phone to her bedside table just before she passed out.

Suddenly, there was a sound like someone whispering her name. She opened her eyes to the dark and searched her room but couldn't see anything. The sound seemed to be coming from outside so she got up and looked through her window, but she couldn't see anything unusual. She went downstairs, following the whisper; it seemed to get louder as she approached the front door. She opened it and saw a form across the street wearing a white fedora and a white duster coat. She couldn't make out if it was a man or a woman, but she knew it was the source of the whisper. She caught a whiff of cologne on the light breeze but couldn't place where she had smelled it before. The figure gave Callie a two-fingered salute before it crossed its arms and leaned against the light pole.

Just as suddenly, Callie awoke in her bed, realizing that what she had just experienced was a lucid dream. She looked at the time on her phone: 3:30 a.m. She told herself that she was still jumpy from earlier and covered her head with her extra pillow. She fell back to sleep and dreamed normal dreams until Peggy woke her up several hours later. The memory of the figure in white would not leave her any time soon.

Chapter Twenty-Five

Callie

Callie hitched her bag up onto her shoulder, waved to Peggy as she drove away, and then typed the entrance code on the security panel under the Psy Syndicate plaque. The lock clicked and Callie walked through the main foyer into the dining room, where Lucia had laid quite the breakfast spread. Once Callie had piled her plate with food, she glanced around the room for somewhere to sit. Winston was at a table with some of the instructors, kissing up, no doubt, and gave her a little finger wave. She couldn't stifle the goose bumps that gesture caused, so she turned away from him and looked around some more. She noticed Chillian's long braided hair and went toward her table.

"Hi again," Callie said. "Mind if I sit here?"

Chillian looked up and said, "Yeah, sure."

Callie placed her plate on the table and let her bag drop to the floor. She nodded to the others seated across from her, people she had seen at the orientation but hadn't really spoken to yet. They continued their conversations once they acknowledged Callie.

"You are so lucky to get this awesome food every day," she said, tasting the first bite of her blueberry pancakes.

"Lucia is the best!" Chillian said. "But now I'm gonna need stretch pants." She indicated her middle, which looked just as taut as it had on orientation day two weeks ago.

"I can imagine," Callie said.

"Are you here for the classes?" Chillian asked, chewing on a piece of bacon.

"Yeah," Callie said. "Sahil went over my test scores with me and said I should concentrate on telepathy and mediumship. They seem to be my strongest psychic abilities. Are you taking some courses?"

"I think I'm in your telepathy class," Chillian said. "The one this morning, right?"

"That's it," Callie said, "and it's starting soon. We'd better get going."

After gathering their dirty dishes and placing them in the designated bins, Callie and Chillian entered one of the first-floor rooms situated behind the main flight of stairs. It had obviously been a sitting room once, with a huge marble fireplace as the centerpiece. About a dozen students were sitting in comfortable-looking chairs, and a slim woman with wavy salt-and-pepper hair stood leaning against a desk. She nodded to Chillian and Callie as they found a couple of chairs in close proximity to each other.

"Good morning, everyone," the woman said. "I hope y'all are here for 'Telepathy, an Introduction.'" When no one got up to leave, she said, "Good, I'm glad to have you here today. My name is Sherrill." She pronounced this with the emphasis on the second syllable. "This is my first class for the Psy Syndicate, though I have taught many others how to work with their special gifts over the years. As such, I hope to have your input for what works well for you and what doesn't."

She moved around the desk to pick up a sheet of paper. "I will be calling your name from the roster here; just let me know who you are so I can put a face to your name." She went down the list, looking at each person who said "here."

"Fantastic, we have everyone who signed up." She clapped her hands together with infectious glee. Callie immediately liked this gentle woman with a Southern accent and felt her tension and nerves begin to slip away...until Sherrill said, "Now, it's important not to be shy in this room. We all need to open up to one another in order to build trust. Trust begets success in this class. That being said, we'll start out by talking about our experiences with our special gifts. I'll go first so you know what I'm looking for."

Sherrill began her tale at her childhood. She would say things to her parents that made them upset with her. They would shake her by the shoulders and tell her not to say things like that, meaning things she shouldn't know about but did. Early on, she learned to distinguish the acceptable things from the spirit things, and reacted appropriately so that her parents would be calm and love her. As she grew, her talent did as well, especially when she was among children her own age, who were frequently cruel in their thoughts toward her. She began to resent that she could hear them and worked to wall off the intrusions into the secrets she shouldn't and didn't want to know—until one day, when the town pond's ice was melting away. She heard the yelp and then the bubbles as a boy named Jeffrey began to drown. She screamed and screamed, "Jeffie is in the pond! Jeffie needs help!" and her father, knowing her as he did, heeded the warning and ran. That day, her parents hugged her, as did little Jeffrey's parents. That day, she realized she had a gift, not a curse, and that day, Sherrill dedicated herself to learning and refining the special gift for what good it could bring to the world.

"I began to work with the police on certain difficult cases, though they would never admit that to you," Sherrill said. "It can be difficult and painful, but rewarding in the end. Anyway, that's my story. Which of you wants to tell us yours?"

The woman named Faye whom Callie had met at the orientation raised her hand. She was a plump woman, all circles and ovals, with large brown eyes. Sherrill came over to her and grasped her hands.

"Faye Matthews and I have known each other since dirt. We go to the same spiritualist church," Sherrill said. "Go ahead, love."

"Maybe it's in the water where we live," Faye began, "but I grew up with visions, too. Mine weren't about other people—living ones, anyway. I would wake up in the middle of the night and see these 'people' walking around my bedroom or standing at the foot of my bed just staring at me, sometimes trying to speak, but nothing would come out of their mouths. I would see flashes of images that would make my head hurt. My parents were also very upset when I told them what I saw, so I kept it to myself. I did have a couple of dead folks I would talk to when I was playing alone. Mother and Dad were upset about that, too. I learned to talk to them through my mind so my parents wouldn't be bothered. When I started school, I just wanted to fit in, so I began blocking my spirit friends in order to get along with my living ones. Eventually, all those dead folk just stopped visiting. I felt pretty normal after that and would just get flashes of information here and there. Now I'm on my own, and I want to learn how to get that all back."

Sherrill gave Faye's hand a reassuring pat. "Thank you, Faye, for your courage in sharing that with us today. I'm sure we can get your gift up and running again. Anyone else want to volunteer?"

One student after another related their own fantastical stories. Some had had the gift first appear during childhood; others had had it come in bits and pieces, the way Callie's experience had been so far. Some had a family history of psychic ability, and others had experiences similar to Faye's and Sherrill's, with parents frightened by what their children could do.

Chillian glanced at Callie, who glanced back. In that briefest of moments, they shared a connection. Callie felt a kinship with this young woman similar to the one she had shared with her mother. It was deeper in that small moment than had been accomplished through years of familiarity between herself and Jonathan, Melinda, and, more recently, Grey. Even her relationship with Peggy didn't go this deep, though she'd known the woman for most of her life. It was disorienting and then comforting in a way. Up until this moment, Callie had been nervous, trying to form coherent thoughts that she could translate into speech, fighting the tightness in her throat that would make her voice squeak, she just knew. But that moment of understanding gave her the courage to raise her hand.

"Hi, I'm Callie," she said. "My mom was a carnival medium who did the circuits of Renaissance Faires and state fairs all over the place. I used to travel with her when I wasn't in school, so I learned how she did readings. I didn't think anything about it at the time, but when she got sick, I took over her client list so we could pay the medical bills. I didn't think there was any special ability to it until I started seeing things I couldn't possibly know. It's been getting stronger and clearer since she died."

Callie didn't look around; she didn't want to see how people reacted to her confession. But she looked directly at Chillian, who gave her a smile and a thumbs-up with both hands before sharing her own story.

"I'm Chillian," she said, meeting Sherrill's gaze, "and I'm from Philadelphia. Mr. Rhys-Doyle found me at my grandma's house and asked if I wanted to come down here to work with him. You see, I've been seeing the future all my life, but not just any future. I see people's deaths. I remember freaking this one guy out so bad when I told him he'd be shot to death just down the street at that corner with the fence, he threw down his drugs and his gun and just walked away. He didn't end up dying, so I knew I could change the future if I just told people to avoid certain things. I got a reputation with the gangs there, so they left me and Grandma alone."

Chillian paused to take a breath before continuing. "My family consisted of my mom and my grandma. Mom got pregnant with me when she was about my age so I was pretty much raised by my grandma. She was weird like me, able to see the future, but more than I could. She always knew who was coming and what they needed, so she would have it on hand when they arrived. Mom didn't have any kind of ability like that, so she felt left out and we didn't get along as well. My sperm donor died when I was two so I was dadless."

"It does seem like tragedy and trauma can activate these senses in people," Sherrill noted. "We're still not sure why, but it may be a survival skill." She clapped her hands together as if to awaken the room from a reverie. "I think it's time for a break, don't y'all?" Murmurs of agreement met her statement and people began to rise from their comfy chairs.

"Well, that wasn't fun," Callie said as Chillian joined her. They were all queued up at the door.

"Yeah, and I really needed to pee," Chillian said, grinning as she rushed toward the bathroom. Callie followed her.

"So, no dad, huh?" Callie said. She was washing her hands while staring at Chillian in the mirror. Chillian was wiping stray mascara from under her eyes.

"No dad," she confirmed, looking through her purse for lip gloss and then applying it.

"Same here," Callie said.

"Hmph. I didn't miss mine. He wasn't worth missing from what Mom told me. Like I said, he was just a sperm donor."

"I guess mine was, too," Callie said. "He hasn't come forward to claim me now that my mom is gone."

Chillian turned to face Callie and held her by the shoulders. "Don't spend too much brain space worrying about him. Just get on with your life with the people who give enough of a damn to stay with you." She let go of Callie, who swayed a bit from the force of the encounter. "We should get back to class." She turned and left, Callie following in her wake.

"One thing you need to know about telepathy that we've found through research is that it's a passive experience," Sherrill said. "By 'passive,' I mean that you just let information come to you—you don't go in search of it. What I'm going to have you do first is quiet your pesky thoughts so that the telepathic signals can come through."

Sherrill had everyone sit upright in their chairs and place their feet directly on the floor and their arms on the armrests. "It's really important that you leave your body free-flowing, no kinks or constrictions," she said.

Next, she had everyone concentrate on one part of their body. "It's really hard to get that brain to stop thinking altogether, so let's give it something to focus on."

Callie concentrated on her right big toe. It was stuck inside her heavy winter socks and boots so she gave it a wiggle. It felt warm and cozy in its dark home.

"Okay, now that you've become bored with that part of your body, move up to another part. Keep moving up your body until you've got to the top of your head—just be sure to keep your concentration on that body part and don't let your mind contemplate what Chef Lucia is making for lunch."

The room was quiet as the class meditated for the next few minutes.

"Okay, how did that feel?" Sherrill asked.

"I'm feeling like I just woke up," Chillian said, "but I feel light and refreshed rather than groggy."

"Excellent!" Sherrill said. "Anyone else feel something like that?"

Others in the class, including Callie, nodded in agreement.

"Focus on that state of mind; it's perfect for letting information flow into your conscious thoughts. So much of telepathy is subconscious and very quiet for many people. For others, it's as easy as thought."

Sherrill then had the class choose partners, with one person focusing on an object she handed out to them. Their partner had to try to "pick up on" what the object was. They worked like this, switching roles partway through, until the lunch break.

"We're not meeting again until next weekend, which is a lot of time in between classes, so much of your work will be done at home," Sherrill told them. "Practicing telepathy is just like practicing piano—you won't get better without putting in the work. I will be sending your assignments via email, and I want you to write up a daily log of your experiences and how your practice is going."

Callie was accustomed to a homework announcement being greeted with groans and curses, but this group was actually excited about it. Even with regular schoolwork and clients to visit, she was looking forward to what she could accomplish at the Syndicate.

Chapter Twenty-Six

Callie

Callie said her farewells to Chillian as she left the dining room after lunch to attend her mediumship class. Chillian was assigned a precognition course for the afternoon. Callie remembered which room she was going to since she'd met Dorcas during the open house, but it had been changed, resembling the setup her mother had usually preferred for her readings, albeit much larger. A giant Arthurian-style round table surrounded by a dozen high-backed chairs took up most of the room. The table lamp was covered with a red cloth that cast everything in a soft scarlet hue. Callie felt a pang of loss as volumes of memories flooded her mind. Tears welled in her eyes.

"Good afternoon, Callie," Dorcas said. "You can choose any place around the table you feel comfortable with."

Callie swiped away the tears she hoped no one would notice and found a chair opposite the door while other students filed in and took their seats. Dorcas took a roll call. Faye Matthews was sitting at Callie's three o'clock but she didn't recognize any of the others seated around her. Worse, she was far younger than anyone else there. *Great.*

"I am so pleased to see everyone here today," Dorcas said with her lilting accent. "I know this room is a bit over the top, but it may help set the mood, as it were." She indicated the decor with a sweep of both hands. "Mr. Rhys-Doyle found this table at an estate sale in England. He says it was once used by Leonora Piper, who worked with the Society for Psychical Research at the beginning of the twentieth century."

Callie looked down at the table, as did everyone else, and noticed that it did seem very old, covered in nicks and discolored in places.

"I know that many of you have not had communion with the discarnate but might benefit from the experience of lending your considerable energies to those who have." She gestured to Callie and said, "Miss O'Callahan's departed mother worked as a medium. Do you have any special abilities in that area?"

"Not yet," Callie said, unhappy to be singled out in front of the class, especially considering her current emotional state.

"Not to worry, love," Dorcas said. "It can take time to manifest, especially with someone so young. Who among us has had experience with discarnates?" Faye Matthews tentatively raised her hand; another woman raised hers as well.

"This is quite promising," Dorcas said. "Ms. Matthews, is it?"

"Yes, but Faye is fine."

"And Ms. Singh." Dorcas nodded to the other woman who had raised her hand.

"You may call me Mari."

Dorcas had the two women describe how they contacted the discarnates. Did they have spirit guides? Were they in a trance during the contact or did they remember it? Did they manifest any physical items or sounds? It was fascinating for Callie to hear people discuss attributes of their experiences that she had thought were merely special effects she and her mother used to employ for entertainment. She was having a hard time believing that these women were sane and not suffering from delusions. However, Dorcas and the other students seemed to believe everything the two women were reporting, so Callie kept her skepticism to herself. She and Mels would have a good laugh about it later.

"I know the rest of you do not have any history of discarnate communication. You may develop it in time, but you are also valuable participants in this endeavor," Dorcas said. "As a group, you increase the possibility of discarnate participation and can aid Mari and Faye in developing their abilities further."

Not exactly what Callie had signed up for, to be sure. Maybe it was selfish of her, but she wanted to develop her own abilities, not be a conduit for someone else's. Perhaps she could get into Chillian's precognition class if it wasn't too late.

"I know you're thinking 'What's in it for me?' right now, I can tell," Dorcas said, looking directly at Callie. "What we've found is that people exposed to certain types of psychic ability tend to develop them, if they're predisposed. Perhaps it's a matter of belief, but who knows? What we can start with today is a simple focused meditation as a group, and we'll see what happens, shall we?"

Callie was about done with meditation for the day and could not stop thinking about her mother. She took deep breaths, trying to avoid the constriction in her throat that threatened to become a sob. She had thought she was on top of her grief, but this room and something she couldn't quite understand was bringing it to the fore. *Get a grip!* she told herself, pressing her fingernails into the soft flesh of her arm.

"There now, I think we're all prepared for an interesting session," Dorcas went on. "Just don't push yourself to make anything happen. It will or it won't, and we'll have spent a nice relaxing time together. I know that many séances require a joining of hands, but since we're all new to one another we'll do that later, when we get better acquainted."

She moved to the dim corner to work with some device. A quiet, ambient melody circulated through the room by way of multiple speakers.

"This is known as binaural beats, so it may sound a bit odd," Dorcas said, "but it does seem to alter brain wavelengths to benefit connections. The type of meditation I would like all of you to try is one known as focused meditation. Please concentrate your thoughts on one intention: that we get a discarnate visitor. Any questions? No? Let's begin, then. Get nice and comfortable."

Callie sat back in the chair, which was not as comfortable as those in the telepathy class, and did her best to meditate on having a discarnate visitor. *Yeah, right.* Her mind wandered down a path that led to a beautiful day in October. She was at the big Charlotte Ren Faire inside Clair's little round tent. Callie was sitting on the ground while Clair braided her hair in an intricate fashion, adding in bits of shiny "fairy hair." The sounds of a hammered dulcimer, hawkers, and visitors came in through the tent's opening, and the scent of patchouli incense that always reminded Callie of her mom permeated the air. Dorcas must have changed the classroom music and lit an incense stick, Callie figured.

"Someone is trying to come through," Faye said. "I see a woman plaiting a girl's hair. The girl looks a lot like you, Callie. I think it's you and your momma."

Callie's eyes flew open. She stared daggers at Faye. *How could she take advantage of me like this!*

"I don't think you're getting a discarnate, Faye," Callie said. "I think you're picking up on my thoughts."

"No, I know the difference," she said. "She's here and she wants to communicate with you."

"No, she isn't. That's a bunch of crap. This is all a bunch of crap!" Callie yelled, standing up in front of her chair, hands flat on the table's surface leaning in toward a startled Faye, "I don't know what you're trying to prove, but séances are fake. My mom was not talking to dead people, and neither are you!"

She grabbed her bag and ran from the room, eventually reaching the meditation garden. She slowed down enough to avoid tripping on the uneven path, found a flat patch of grass, and collapsed onto her knees, sobbing. She covered her face with her hands and fell forward like it would never end. She knew people were walking along the path staring at and whispering about her, but she just didn't care. Back and forth between grief and anger, her uncharitable thoughts about Faye and the stupid mediumship class made her want to quit the Psy Syndicate. She could work with the clients she already had just fine, and to hell with Rhys-Doyle. If he was related to her in any way, it didn't matter, because he wasn't doing a damn thing about it. As Chillian had said, she wouldn't waste brain space on people who didn't care enough about her to be there. Once she calmed down a bit, she realized that she didn't want to quit the Psy Syndicate altogether, but this class was too much.

She wiped the snot and tears from her face with the hem of her shirt and took deep breaths. She was about to pull out her cell phone to get a ride from Peggy or Jonathan when she heard someone approach her from behind.

"That was quite the exit, Miss O'Callahan."

Callie turned her head to look up at Dorcas. "You won't have to worry about me, I'm quitting the class."

"I am so sorry you were caught off guard like that. I know it wasn't that long ago when you lost your mum," Dorcas said, sitting down on the grass by Callie. "But I want to assure you of one thing: Faye was not trying to play a game with you. She truly believes she was in touch with your mum."

"Then she's delusional," Callie said.

"Now, that is uncharitable, Miss O'Callahan. We don't make judgments like that around here." Dorcas's voice reminded Callie of a prim schoolteacher who had just dropped a paper with a big, fat red F on a kid's desk.

"Sorry," Callie whispered. She heard another set of footfalls nearby and glanced up to see Rhys-Doyle himself, his arms crossed in front of him as he stared at the pair. He said nothing and Callie looked back down at the ground.

"That's all right, my girl." Dorcas slid an arm around Callie's shoulders. "I'm sure it's just the shock of it all. How about you go home for the rest of the day."

"I really think I should drop this course," Callie said. "I don't think it's for me, at least not right now." Not to mention that she couldn't face the group again without being consumed by embarrassment.

Dorcas looked up at Rhys-Doyle. Callie noticed and looked up in time to see him respond with a small nod before turning and walking back up the path to the big house.

Dorcas sighed. "If that's what you want to do, Miss O'Callahan," she said. She got to her feet with a groan and then stuck her hand out to Callie. "Let's get inside, it's colder than a nun's gaze out here."

Callie took Dorcas's proffered hand and stood up. "Is there another afternoon class I can take?"

"I don't know about course schedules—you'll need to ask Kristin about a transfer," Dorcas said as they walked toward the big house. Rhys-Doyle was nowhere in sight. "It happens quite a lot, to be honest."

"Oh, good," Callie said. "I didn't want to be a pain." At least, not any more than she'd already been. "I'll go check on that. Please go back to your class—I'll be all right now."

"I figured you were made of sterner stuff," Dorcas said. "When you're ready, you give the mediumship class another try."

Callie took a few minutes in the restroom to wash her face. Her eyes were still puffy and her lips and cheeks were still bright red, but at least she didn't have snot all over the place. Once she felt comfortable with the girl in the mirror, she took a deep breath and stepped out into the hallway. Once at Kristin's office door, she shook herself until she felt less tense, plastered a smile on her face, and walked in.

"Hi, Kristin," she said as she approached the woman's desk. "I would like to transfer out of Mediumship into another class."

"My, that has got to be a record," Kristin said. "People usually make it through one class at least. Not a bother, I have the afternoon class list right here." She put a spreadsheet in front of Callie. "It looks like most are full, except for the lucid dreamwork class and the meditation courses."

"What's lucid dreamwork?"

"Let me pull out the course syllabus for you," Kristin said, turning to riffle through a file cabinet. "Here you are." She handed Callie the course sheet.

Callie read it over, seeing that it was just a course in training people how to control their dreams and get information from them. It sounded interesting but also safe. No crazy stuff, just dream examinations. This she could do.

"Is it too late for me to join that class today?" she asked.

"Nope, I'll just move you over in the schedule."

Kristin typed up another form and sent it to the printer. She handed it to Callie and said, "This is for the instructor."

Callie took the form with a thank-you smile for Kristin, who smiled back before she was heads down again working on whatever project Callie had interrupted. She gently closed the office door and wavered a minute, wondering if she should wait until next week to join the new class or just barge in now. She decided to barge away so she wouldn't be behind in the coursework.

Once at the classroom door, Callie took a deep breath and twisted the knob, hoping it didn't have squeaky hinges. Fortunately, it moved silently, revealing a dimly lit room full of people lying on cots spaced evenly with only one person—Callie assumed it was the instructor—walking around slowly, speaking in a quiet voice. He was young, maybe Sahil's age, and was dressed in a hoodie and torn jeans. He spoke gently but rapidly in a British accent, and had long, wavy hair with highlights that graduated from light blond to medium brown. His eyes were bright green. Callie stood in the doorway staring at him until he looked up and said, "Yes, may I help you?"

She shook her head to clear it, holding out the form Kristin had given her. "I'm here to take the class."

He took the form and perused it momentarily. "Transferring from another class? That must be a record."

"Apparently," Callie said. "Where should I, um, sit?"

"Anywhere you can find an empty cot." He was not what she was expecting, but she figured her time in the lucid dreamwork class was going to be as dreamy as the instructor. Looking around, she found a cot by the window and tiptoed quietly through the maze of cots to settle on it. She put her gear under it and lay back like the other students, waiting to hear some kind of instruction. On the wall next to her cot was a poster with a stylized font that said, "When I fall asleep, I will have control over my dreams." There was also a large digital clock with glowing red numbers, and a print of the famous Picasso painting called *The Old Guitarist*. There were several more posters and prints that had striking colors and subjects. She looked at the other students to see if she recognized anyone, but in their supine positions it was difficult to tell. The instructor was walking in her direction, checking in with each student as he went.

"Now that the others are well on their way to dreamland, I can spend a bit of time with you," he whispered. "My name is Marcus Pantazis." He put a hand out. She shook it, finding his grip gentle, his hand soft.

"I'm Callie O'Callahan," she said.

"Oh, the famous Miss O'Callahan. I believe the director is familiar with your mother."

"Yes," Callie said, "but I'm not that familiar with the director."

"Ah. Well, I need to give you a bit of instruction so you can catch up with what we're doing so far. As you can see, you won't get in trouble for falling asleep in class." He chuckled at his own joke. "Have you ever had a lucid dream?"

"I don't know if I have," Callie told him.

"It would be a very realistic dream, one that would be hard to distinguish from being awake."

"I guess, but nothing that I remember that much," Callie said. Then she remembered the dream about the figure in the white fedora and coat, and the smell of cologne in the air.

"In this class, we are trying to induce such realistic dreams using techniques developed by sleep researchers," Marcus said in his rapid-fire speech. "Do you see that poster there?" He pointed to the one with the stylized font. "I want you to get into a relaxed state, almost like meditation, but say that statement to yourself like a mantra. You may fall asleep without noticing it, so try to find something that wouldn't exist in reality to verify that you're in a dream. It may be that your hands are weird, or the clock doesn't change time, or any one of those posters seems different. Don't get freaked out in there, just go with the weirdness or you'll wake up. I'll go over this in detail with you after class is over. Any questions?"

Callie had a few dozen questions but said, "Nope, I'm good."

Marcus stood up from his crouch and walked around to check on the other students. The afternoon would at least be relaxing if not informative. Callie said the mantra *I will have control over my dreams* over and over, trying to keep all other thoughts from invading her mind. She felt remarkably relaxed, considering her emotional outburst earlier in the afternoon. The next thing she knew, Marcus was tapping the back of her hand.

"Keep your eyes closed. I want you to think about the dream you were just having. Try to remember as much as you can," he said, then walked to the next student and did the same thing.

Callie did as Marcus had instructed, though this was not something she would normally do, unless it was a nightmare or a dream about her mom. There wasn't much to this dream, just that she was on a rollercoaster ride that had a lot of water around it. She was with Melinda and Jonathan but couldn't remember anyone else being there. Sometimes when the water sprayed them, it was cold. The cars entered a cavern but it wasn't dark, just flat, with very little of interest there. She wondered why she needed to remember such a boring dream.

Marcus went to the dimmer switch and used the dial to increase the light in the room. The students began sitting up and writing on pieces of paper. Callie didn't know what they were doing, so she raised her hand. Marcus came over to her with a clipboard.

"Write down what you remember of your dream. This is called dream journaling. We'll go over the symbolism after our break."

She wrote down everything she could remember, in bullet format. As the other students completed journaling, they got up and walked out of the room. Eventually, she finished writing, laid the clipboard on the cot, and got up to get a soda. She passed the dining area on her way to the kitchen and noticed a bunch of elementary-school-aged kids eating snacks and drinking from paper cups. Callie wondered why they were there and made a mental note to ask Sahil when she saw him next. Several of the older students were milling around in the kitchen area drinking their beverages and talking among themselves. Callie didn't recognize anyone, so she took her soda back to the classroom in hopes of speaking to Marcus about what she had missed from the beginning of the class.

He was sitting with a laptop in a comfortable-looking chair, sipping from an oversized mug. He looked up as Callie entered the room. She said, "I was hoping we could discuss what I missed, if you have a minute."

"Sure." He closed the laptop and set it aside. "I will be sending everyone a course syllabus and book list via email, but the gist of our first class was a practice session for many aspects of dream recognition. We generally forget our dreams, but they are more important than we give them credit for. Since we have only a few hours for instruction, I've combined a few things to get everyone started. First is attempting lucid dreaming, second is dream memory, and third will be dream interpretation. It should be easy enough to catch up, especially if you read from the book list."

"I was worried about missing important details," Callie said as people filed back into the room.

"This is not a complicated class," Marcus said. "As you Americans like to put it, it's an easy A."

"Second-place girl," came a voice from behind. "I thought you were in that mediumship course across the way. Are you lost? This one is for lucid dreaming."

Callie visibly cringed, and Marcus raised an eyebrow. The icing on this cake of a day was standing behind her in the form of Winston. *Ah, wondrous.*

"I decided to take Mediumship another time," she said without turning around. "Are *you* lost?" She glanced inquiringly over her shoulder at Winston's smirking face.

"I'm bringing some documents for Mr. Pantazis," Winston said, intentionally brushing up against Callie as he bent down to proffer said documents to the instructor. "I am such a huge fan of yours, sir. I have all your books—I've read them so many times I nearly have them memorized."

"Thank you, er..."

"It's Winston Spivey. I'll be taking your advanced class when you offer one. This one is really too elementary for someone of my skill. I won the Psy Games this year and I'm on the fast track to join the Psy Syndicate."

Marcus took a sip from his mug as he considered Winston. "That is quite impressive, Mr. Spivey. I'm sure you will be an asset to the organization."

"I look forward to working with you," Winston said. Done with his fawning, he turned to Callie and said, "And I look forward to seeing you later. It will be so much fun!" He actually giggled as he left the room. Callie was both creeped out and mystified by his last statement. It would be a hot day on Pluto before she planned to be anywhere with that guy, so where had he gotten the impression that they would meet again soon?

"Interesting chap," Marcus said. "Why does he call you that?"

"Apparently, second place is like losing to him," Callie said. "I guess he thinks I'm embarrassed by my showing, but I'm not. Getting better than that jerk is one of my goals, though."

"I understand that competition breeds success at times, but do this for your own personal development, not because some people push your buttons," Marcus said before taking another sip from his mug and standing up. "If everyone could please take to their cots, we'll continue with the dream interpretation section of today's lesson."

Chapter Twenty-Seven

Callie

The autumn leaves were twirling down to the ground in the gentle breeze redolent with the smells of food, horse sweat, and hay. The breeze picked up dust from the tournament field that had been kicked up by Callie's steed, but she *would not* sneeze. Her opponent was dressed in a combination of chain and plate mail, and his standard of black and white with a rampant red dragon whipped back and forth. His horse snorted and stamped its front hoof, shaking its head as if impatient for battle. The rider held a long, sharp lance straight as a pine tree in the strap designed for it. The crowd was yelling cheers and jeers as the pair sat their horses several lengths apart, preparing to unseat each other. Her helm's small, rectangular slit focused Callie's view on that intimidating sight but she was ready for him. This time, he would be the one lying in the dirt and horse manure, shamed by a girl. The master of ceremonies, finished with getting the crowd ready for blood, called the opponents to the ready position on opposite sides of the long wooden railing. Callie placed her lance at the horizontal, bracing for impact so that when it met the small section of his armor where it protected his heart, she would remain firmly astride her horse as she rode past, watching him fall to the ground.

"Master and Lady, are you prepared?" the emcee said.

Callie saluted with her free hand, as did her opponent.

The emcee held a red silk scarf up in the air, keeping it there for long enough that the crowd's combined voices rose in anticipation.

Then the scarf fell. Callie spurred her dutiful stallion forward, bracing with her knees as it charged like a race car. She focused on nothing else but the sweet spot on that shining armor.

Suddenly, a flash of white crossed between her and her opponent, causing just the briefest distraction, enough for Callie not only to miss her target but to be slammed by the opposing lance right in the chest. She somersaulted over the back of her mount, falling face up into the dust. Groaning, she looked up and saw an immaculately white duster fluttering in the breeze. The sun was behind the figure, putting its face in shadow, but the white fedora gleamed.

"Awww, did you fall off your horse? What a shame," the figure said in a mocking tone. It dissipated a moment before Callie saw her opponent raise his sword, the hilt in both hands, the business end poised just above her heart.

"What the..." Callie said as she awoke. Her heart and lungs were pumping as if she'd just finished running a sprint. Sitting up in bed, she took deeper breaths and relaxed her shoulders to calm down. After three weeks of the course, Callie had become pretty proficient at lucid dream control. It was actually a fun way to live out her fantasy life. She'd always wanted to joust with the knights at the Ren Faires but it required too much work and dedicated training. Marcus had mentioned that dreamwork could also help her with any personal issues she was having. Right now, the issue bothering her the most was this elusive figure in white that kept infiltrating her dream world.

Pulling out the spiral notebook where she kept her dream journal entries and telepathy notes, she wrote down the experience, including the figure in white. Perhaps Marcus could help her decipher what this figure meant to her. It seemed like a completely different personality than her own and toyed with her at every opportunity, turning her dream fantasies into nightmares.

Callie was walking down the hallway at the Psy Syndicate when she was stopped in her tracks. "What did you say?"

"I was describing your dream from the other night," Winston said.

"My dream?"

"You know, you were on that stallion and almost managed to unseat that knight. Too bad you didn't have the focus to follow through."

"I...need to get some lunch," Callie said, and walked briskly toward the dining room, trying to outpace Winston. She had just finished her telepathy class and had been planning to discuss her dream with Marcus in Lucid Dreaming that afternoon. She couldn't believe what Winston was saying, but he'd gotten the details just right. Was he using telepathy on her, or was he the figure in white?

"Same here. I'm famished," he said from behind her, too close in her opinion.

They both entered the dining room. Callie made herself focus on the buffet, not Winston, putting food on her plate without even considering what she was getting and then finding a table with space to sit. Winston sat down next to her, chatting away as if Callie were a receptive companion.

"They say I'm about done with preliminary testing and that I'll be having a meeting with Director Rhys-Doyle soon to determine the next phase here," Winston said. "How is your testing going?"

"Huh? Oh, I'm plugging along," Callie said. "Can you tell me something?"

"Sure, what?" Winston asked.

"How the hell do you know about my dream?" Callie asked.

"I don't just know about your dream, I was in it," Winston said.

"How is that possible and why would you want to be in my dreams at all?" Callie asked.

"I'm what's called a dreamwalker—and as to why, well, you're fascinating, of course," Winston said. "I wanted to get to know you better."

A dreamwalker? "That's very kind of you to say," she told him, "but I don't feel comfortable with you doing that."

"You should get used to it," he said, "because I'm not going to stop."

At that point, Chillian walked into the dining room. "Hey, girl," she said to Callie. "Winston," she shot him a pointed look, "everything okay here?"

"Hi, Chillian—you promised me you were going to show me around today, remember?" Callie said. She just barely tilted her head toward Winston.

"That's right, how about now?" Chillian asked, catching the hint.

"No better time than the present." Callie stood up with her plate of food. "I'll take this into the kitchen."

Chillian and Callie bolted from the dining room before Winston could respond or follow. Callie wasn't done with her lunch, so she took the plate upstairs with her. "I hope you don't mind me eating in your room."

"Why would I care? I don't clean it," Chillian responded, bounding up the giant staircase, Callie following close behind.

"Good, because I'm starving and that jerk was affecting my appetite," Callie said.

Chillian led Callie to her bedroom, which had a keypad lock on it. Chillian quickly inputted the code and pulled down the handle to open the door. The room was three times the size of the one Callie had at Peggy's house. There was an en suite bathroom and a sitting room with an excellent view of the back garden, and the bed had an actual canopy with carved wooden posters.

Callie put her plate down on the desk next to Chillian's schoolbooks and looked around the room. "Nice place you got here."

"What did Winston do?" Chillian asked.

"I don't know if you'll believe me," Callie said, sitting down in the desk chair and starting in on her fruit salad.

"What I believe has expanded since I got here," Chillian said, "so try me."

"I've been taking that lucid dreaming course, right? And having these really clear and vivid dreams lately," Callie said after she swallowed. "There's been someone in my dreams wearing a long white coat and white fedora."

"Mm-hmm," Chillian said.

"One night, he was across the street from my house and playing hide-and-seek with me. Last night, he distracted me when I was about to unhorse a knight."

"That doesn't sound so bad," Chillian said. "What's got you so freaked out?"

"Winston just described last night's dream to me."

"How the hell did he know about your dream?" Chillian asked.

"He said he was the guy in white," Callie said.

"Whaaaat?"

"Yes, Chillian. I'm being dream-stalked by Winston the slime," Callie said. "Just before you walked up to us he said I should get used to it."

"I know what we can do," Chillian said conspiratorially, "we can lure him out of the house and beat the crap outta him."

"That's a no," Callie said. "He'd call the cops on us for assault and get us kicked out of Psy Syndicate. If you're lucky, Rhys-Doyle would just ship you back home."

"That's not lucky," Chillian said, "but you make a few good points. You could go snitch on him to Rhys-Doyle. There might be something he can do to help."

"The director hasn't been particularly helpful so far. In fact, he seems to actively avoid me," Callie said. "Maybe my lucid dreaming instructor might have some ideas."

"Yeah, maybe," Chillian said. She plunked down in a chair. "I wanted to ask you something."

"Of course! You rescued me from Winston, after all," Callie said.

"I would love to go out somewhere without the Psy Syndicate handlers hovering around me. I don't know anyone here, so I was wondering if you'd be interested in going out with me sometime, like to the mall or something," she said, looking everywhere but at Callie.

"I'm such a selfish idiot!" Callie said. "My mom would slap me for being so rude. I should have been the one to offer to take you out. I'm so sorry."

"Look, don't do me any favors," Chillian said defensively. "I don't need your charity."

"No! That's not what I meant," Callie said, putting her hand on Chillian's. "Look, I feel like we have a connection ever since our first day in telepathy class. I should have been the one to offer to show you around since I've lived here as long as I can remember."

Chillian still avoided Callie's eyes but she didn't move her hand away.

"You will love the Misfits," Callie said. "How about we do dinner and a movie with them? Jonathan is this aspiring filmmaker and Mels is a costume diva. Grey is hilarious."

"Yeah, we can do that," Chillian said, "but another time. I'd rather just hang out with you first. I need to get something for my mom and grandma for Mother's Day."

"That *is* coming up soon, isn't it," Callie said. She had been through her first motherless Christmas and New Year's; now this holiday was coming up and she had no mom to give a gift to. She did have Peggy, though, and that woman deserved as big a gift as Callie could afford. If she just focused on who she had in her life, she could get through the day.

"I didn't leave on the best terms," Chillian said. "I need to send them a peace offering or I won't be welcome there anymore."

"I understand," Callie said. "I wish I still had my mom. I would do anything." Tears fell down her cheeks. Chillian stood up and put her arms around her as they wept into each other's shoulders.

Chapter Twenty-Eight

Callie

"That is quite fascinating, in a creepy way," Marcus said. The rest of the lucid dream class had finally left the room after hanging around to speak to the young instructor for the last time, and Callie had just described her situation to him. "It doesn't feel very fascinating to me. I want him to stop but he won't, so I have to make him somehow. Any ideas?"

"I have read literature about dreamwalkers for my book, but I didn't give them much credence. No one has studied them, as far as I'm aware," Marcus said. "Nor have I read about how to remove them from dreams. I will have to study it further and get back to you."

"I'd really appreciate it," Callie said.

"Meanwhile, I would go visit the director if I were you and make a formal complaint against Mr. Spivey," Marcus said. "He could encourage the boy to find another hobby or be removed from the Psy Syndicate."

Callie sighed, then thanked Marcus for his help and for the lucid dream instruction she'd received. It had to happen eventually, she'd just been putting it off: It was time to confront Rhys-Doyle.

Rhys-Doyle's office was situated right down the hall from reception, but he wasn't always in since he traveled extensively. The room was furnished sparsely with bookcases, a large desk, and a trio of chairs. Though there were several items other than books on the shelves, books dominated the room significantly.

"How can I help you, Miss O'Callahan?" Rhys-Doyle asked. He was leaning against the front of his ornate desk with his arms crossed. He was immaculately dressed in a dark gray pinstripe suit, a dove gray shirt, a pale pink tie, and a matching pocket square. Callie was in the overstuffed dark leather chair in front of him, fidgeting despite herself. The man could fill a room and make you feel like an annoying little bug.

Callie had been practicing what she would say to the director so that she wouldn't come off as being desperate, either about his relationship with her mother or about Winston. Taking a deep breath, she said, "I'm having some odd trouble with one of the other students."

"Really? Who?" Rhys-Doyle asked.

"It's Winston Spivey," Callie said.

"What trouble is he giving you?"

"This is the odd part," Callie said. "He claims to be inserting himself into my dreams. To be honest, I'm having a hard time believing he can do this in the first place."

Rhys-Doyle uncrossed his arms and walked around to his desk chair. He sat down elegantly while intertwining his fingers and resting them upon the desk.

"You are new to this," Rhys-Doyle said, "so I'm not surprised you don't know about dreamwalkers. You are not the first person who has had dream visitors at this facility."

"I don't want a dream visitor, and especially not Winston," Callie said. "I want him to stop."

"He isn't violating any rule, Miss O'Callahan," Rhys-Doyle said. "There is nothing I can do to make him stop."

"Can't you threaten to kick him out of the Syndicate?"

"As I said," Rhys-Doyle said, "he hasn't violated any rules, so I have no grounds to 'kick him out,' as you say."

"But he's stalking me," Callie said. "Isn't there some sort of law against that?"

"I suppose you could try to tell the police that you're being stalked in your dreams," he said, "but I imagine they will simply refer you to a mental health facility."

"I see," Callie said. "If that's your stand on this, then I don't think I'll be able to continue here any longer."

"Do you think quitting the Psy Syndicate will stop Winston's entering your dreams?"

"You don't?"

"No, I don't," Rhys-Doyle said. "Stalkers rarely give up."

"Then I'm trapped, without any recourse at all," Callie said.

"You don't want to end his foray into your dreams yourself?"

"How could I possibly do that without being arrested?" Callie asked. "I've already told him I don't want him to do it anymore, and he told me I needed to get used to it."

"You have just as much control in your dreams as you want," Rhys-Doyle said.

"I've been controlling my dreams but I haven't been able to control him," Callie said. "How do I do it?"

"This process takes time," Rhys-Doyle said. "I will give you instructions to take home with you. Follow them and you'll have the ability to eject Winston from your dreams if you want."

"Fine," Callie said. "I'll try it your way."

Rhys-Doyle unlocked and opened a drawer. He riffled through folders until he found what he was looking for and pulled out a sheet of paper.

"Here you are, Miss O'Callahan," he said. "Take this home with you and follow the instructions."

"Thanks." She took the paper and walked out of the office.

She was fuming inside. Rhys-Doyle had shown no sympathy for what she felt was a major violation of her privacy. She had hoped for more, especially an opportunity to segue into a discussion about her mom, but he was just as cold as the day he had stared at her in the garden. As usual, Callie was left to fend for herself.

"Hi, Callie," Sahil said, flashing his gleaming smile. "How are you today?"

"I've been better, Sahil," she said, "but maybe testing will get my mind off my current issue." They were walking up the stairs toward the testing area.

"Anything I can do to help?" Sahil asked.

"Maybe."

Callie was thoughtful as she considered whether to tell him about Winston. Sahil was a psychology grad student and might have another insight into dreamwalking.

"I've been having a problem with another student here. Do you remember the boy who won the Psy Games?"

"You mean Winston?" Sahil said. "Who could forget that guy?"

"He does make an impression," Callie said. "I've asked for help but I would like another opinion."

They reached the testing room and Callie sat down at the table across from Sahil. He gave her his full attention, which distracted her a bit. *He is really cute.* She cleared her throat and found the table very interesting all of a sudden.

"I can try," Sahil said. "What's he been up to?"

"Have you ever heard of dreamwalkers?" Callie asked.

"No," Sahil said.

"Apparently, these people use telepathy to get into other people's dreams," Callie said, "and Winston has decided to target me."

"That's bizarre," Sahil said. "What's he doing?"

"You know I've been taking that dreamwork class," Callie said. "I've been practicing lucid dreaming, where I control what's going to happen. He has been jumping into my dreams and altering them so I almost die. I'm so scared when I wake up."

Sahil put his hand on Callie's and gave it a gentle squeeze. "I'm so sorry."

Callie's heart rate jumped up. She cleared her throat again before saying, "I went to Rhys-Doyle but he's not very compassionate. He just gave me some instructions and basically told me there's nothing he can do."

"Really?" Sahil said. "He isn't going to kick this kid out?"

"According to Rhys-Doyle, Winston hasn't broken any rules, and even if he were to kick him out, it wouldn't stop him. He said it might even make it worse for me."

Sahil sat back in his chair, removing his hand from Callie's and running both his hands through his hair. He sat staring at the wall for a minute, considering Callie's predicament.

"I'm afraid the director is right," Sahil said. "Winston might blame you for getting him removed from the Syndicate and escalate what he's doing. Right now, it sounds like he's toying with you. If I were you, I would try those instructions the director gave you and see if they work."

"Yeah, I guess so," Callie said.

"Do you still feel up to doing some tests? We could reschedule," Sahil said, sitting forward again.

Callie took a deep breath. "I'm fine. Let's do them and see if these classes have made me better."

They worked with Zener cards first, then another series of tests that Sahil performed while Callie was in something called the ganzfeld room. It was quiet and dark with a comfortable reclinable chair in the center. She wore a pair of opaque goggles over her eyes and earphones playing white noise to prevent sensory input. While Sahil watched a short film in another room, she tried to pick up impressions from him and say what she saw or felt into a microphone. Callie was thankful she had not done this particular test when she was exhausted, because the threat of falling asleep was quite strong under these conditions. She performed three of these tests in a row, then three more times without Sahil actually watching the films; she tried to get her input directly from the computer playing them instead.

It was dinnertime when Callie emerged from the ganzfeld room. She felt relaxed by the experience, having been in a semiconscious state almost the entire time. She and Sahil walked down the stairs together discussing what the testing had shown.

"We know your talent for reading people is strong, but we wanted to gauge your telepathic ability, first with a human target and then with an electronic one," Sahil said. "Many people do better with electronics because there is no mental filter to sift through."

"That's interesting," Callie said. "I hadn't considered that before."

"So, what are your plans?" Sahil said as they reached the front door.

Callie looked at him in surprise. *Is he asking me out?* "Plans? Wh-what plans?" she stammered.

"What other classes were you considering? You have the summer off, I assume, so you could take quite a few."

Callie's heartbeat went from a flustered flutter to a disappointed thump. "I don't know what my plans are yet—I have to get through finals before I can think about that."

"I understand," Sahil said. "I've got to get through mine, too! Just let me know what you've decided on when you do."

"I will," Callie said, wishing he would see her as more than just a test subject. "By the way, I'm having a party—my adoption is final and we're celebrating. You can come if you want."

"That's wonderful!" Sahil said. "I'll have to check my calendar, but I am really happy for you even if I can't make it."

"Yeah, I'll text you the invitation," Callie said.

"That'd be great, thanks!"

As if on cue, Winston showed up when Callie was dreaming that night. She was a passenger in the car he was driving, way too fast. They were careening around corners and catching air over bumps in the road.

"Isn't this exhilarating?" he said, turning the wheel left and then right again.

"Why are you hijacking my dreams, Winston?" Callie said over the sound of the loud car engine and squealing tires.

"Because I want to, Callie. You should relax and enjoy the ride."

"Doesn't it matter to you that I don't want to do this?"

"You'll enjoy it if you just let yourself," Winston said. "You don't have a choice, so you might as well."

"Right," Callie said, and tried to make herself wake up just before the car sped off the cliff.

She was sweating and breathing hard and her bedsheets were twisted around her legs. Well, it was a dream, so she wrote down what she experienced, fuming and cursing the whole time. After that, she went to the bathroom and got a glass of water before she went back to bed. She lay there staring at the darkened ceiling, terrified to close her eyes, but then she got angry again at Winston's audacity. She was nobody's victim. Sitting up, she turned on her light and went looking for the psychic self-defense paper Rhys-Doyle had given her. It was a scary simple procedure that she could adapt to her dream realm. Having some semblance of a cure for her dream stalker, she set up her cell phone to play relaxing rainfall sounds to help her get a couple more hours of sleep.

"You'll be fine," Chillian said, sipping on her soda. "You just have performance anxiety."

"What?" Callie asked. She was chewing on her burger so it came out as a muffled "Wha?"

"You know, stage fright," Chillian replied. "You don't know how you'll do, so you're anxious. What do they tell you to do if you have to talk in front of a crowd? See people in their underwear, right?"

"I really don't think I want to visualize Winston in underwear," Callie said. "I'd like to keep my dinner down."

"Well, what would make him seem less threatening?"

"I don't know." Callie tore another bite out of the burger while she considered it.

"Just make him look like a little kid or something, or a cockroach," Chillian said.

"I'll try it," Callie said. "Thanks for trying to help."

"I would do more, but I don't want to be arrested," Chillian said. "It's no fun."

"No, this is my battle to win," Callie said. "At least he's leaving you alone."

"He doesn't have the guts to screw with me," Chillian said.

"Yeah, I'm an easy target, I guess." Callie sighed in resignation and realized she had consumed an entire burger without even noticing it. They dumped their trash and gathered their shopping bags.

"This little trip has been just what I needed," Chillian said as they walked through the massive mall toward the entrance. "A little girl time, a little shopping, some mall food. You guys have some cool stores here that we don't have in Philly."

"I don't really go shopping much, especially the last couple of years," Callie said.

"I can tell." Chillian looked Callie up and down. "You're not going to win any fashion contests. What *are* you wearing?"

"It's one of Melinda's old T-shirts that she didn't want anymore. She has a tendency to get tired of things quickly and I benefit."

"If you want to call it that," Chillian said. "Don't you have someone in your life you're trying to impress? That Marcus dude who taught your lucid dreamwork class looks pretty edible."

"I agree, but he sees me as just another student."

"I think we owe it to your future social life to get you something other than these cartoon shirts you keep wearing. Maybe these college boys will see someone more mature and interesting if you switch up that wardrobe a bit," Chillian said.

Callie bowed theatrically. "I bow to your prowess, m'lady. Find this sad Cinderella some proper attire for the ball."

"You are so crazy," Chillian said, giving Callie a playful shove.

Chapter Twenty-Nine

Callie

Callie spent her Uber ride home from the mall trying to come up with a way to morph Winston into something defeatable, but couldn't decide on what would work. Then epiphany struck and she put together a plan of action for his next unwanted visit. She cackled in mock glee, rubbing her hands together like a mad scientist with a planet-altering scheme.

The driver looked at her from the rearview mirror. "Something wrong, miss?"

"Oh no, just a plan coming together," Callie said.

When she arrived at Peggy's house, Callie saw that the kitchen light was on, so she stopped in there to find Peggy sitting at the table.

"Hi, Peg," Callie said, "anything wrong?"

"No, I'm just reading over tax documents. How was your mall trip?" Peggy asked, removing her reading glasses.

"Chillian has become my fashion advisor," Callie said. She pulled out a few of the cute tops they had found on the clearance rack. Callie had refused to spend more than twenty dollars on a piece of clothing, which made Chillian roll her eyes in exasperation. Still, the new items were quite a bit better than her usual attire.

"These are very nice," Peggy said, "and they look much more mature than those cartoon shirts you like to wear."

Callie squinted. "Did you guys plan this?"

"I don't know what you mean." Peggy smiled and batted her eyelashes.

"Fine," Callie said, gathering the clothes back into the shopping bag. "I didn't realize that my wardrobe decisions were so bad."

"That's not it at all, Callie," Peggy said, grabbing her hand. "You're getting older and people expect you to grow out of these phases."

Callie added a frown to her squint and was preparing a rejoinder but Peggy cut her off before she could get anything out.

"I don't like it any more than you do, sweetheart. People just treat people differently depending on how they dress and what they do with their hair. You had to dress like Clair for her clients so they'd take you seriously, right? This is the same thing, only for the broader world."

Callie couldn't argue that point, given how she had dressed the part for the Ren Faires and for her clients. She sat down across from Peggy. "I'm sorry, you guys are right. I've been ignoring my own needs for so long now, it's just been a habit."

"There you go," Peggy said. "Now get to bed, it's a school night."

"Yes, Mom." Even though Callie's tone was light, they looked at each other seriously, recognizing the importance of the moment. Callie swallowed the lump that had taken up residence in her throat. "Right, I will see you in the morning, then. Sleep well!" And she bounded up the stairs as fast as her shopping bags would allow.

After putting the new clothes into her dirty clothes hamper, she got ready for bed and pulled out her dream diary. This time, she wrote down in great detail what she wanted to have happen in her dream. Marcus had recommended this tactic to have lucid dream control. Every once in a while as she scribbled, Callie giggled at her creation. Dreaming was going to be very different tonight.

She walked into town, a lone samurai just looking for a place to get some food and a bed to sleep in for the night. It was dark except for the gentle luminescence of the paper lanterns that lined the street. Suddenly, the shadows began to move and coalesce into darkly clad human forms. With uncanny speed, she ducked into an alcove as a shuriken lodged itself into the wood by her head, just missing her. She pulled out her sword with her back to the wall, and realized immediately that it was a bad idea to put herself in a corner. *It's a dream, make your own rules*, Callie thought. Suddenly, she was on the roof, bow in her hands and an arrow nocked to shoot. She shot true and caught a ninja in the arm before he could throw a shuriken at her. She heard a sound behind her and whirled to face another ninja, who was twirling nunchucks meant to disarm her. She pulled back the bowstring and shot him in the leg; he went down with a cry, clutching his thigh. She nocked another arrow while looking for her next target. She saw the man in the white duster and fedora flying into town. He began to fight the ninjas in hand-to-hand combat, moving impossibly fast and with incredible strength. Winston had come to her rescue when she really didn't want or need it. Now was the time to turn the tables on her unwanted visitor.

"I don't want you here, Winston," Callie said. "This is my dream and my fight."

"Oh, but Callie, you make such a fun place to play, how can I resist visiting you?" Winston replied, punching a ninja in the face.

"It's my playground now, not yours, you freakin' jerk."

"That's not nice, Callie," Winston said. "You should share with me."

"Have it your way," Callie said.

She jumped down to the street, landing superhero-style on one knee, and lifted her face to stare at Winston, who was piledriving a ninja into the ground. He stood and looked at her—looked *up* at her: She was growing like Alice in Wonderland after eating a mushroom. Realizing that everything else was growing larger around him, he looked down at himself. He was no longer wearing the white coat and hat; as a matter of fact, his arms were no longer human. He wasn't sure, but his arms and torso were looking more like that of an insect. When he looked up at Callie again, he saw multiples of her and realized he was seeing through compound eyes. He fell to the ground as his legs changed and two more protruded from his thorax. Antennae were dancing before his eyes and he was still shrinking. When he looked up a final time, he saw the heel of a boot coming straight down on him.

Chapter Thirty

Amber

Amber would have almost preferred to have the beatings resume rather than what was happening since Gary had placed the shock collar around her neck. There were some benefits; she was no longer black and blue, nor did she have the perpetual aches and pains from bruising or broken ribs. He was even starting to feed her better. Her body was filling out and her hair had started to grow back to its lustrous blond. But the creepy stuff he had started to do made her want to go back to the bad old days. After dinner, he would let her sit down next to him while he watched TV but would start to stroke her neck and back. Then he would take her hand and make her stroke his groin while he made these noises. If she didn't do it, or if she failed to do it the way he wanted, he would generate a shock. It didn't just make her jerk, it made her feel like she was going to pass out from the pain, but it left no mark on her skin.

One night after Gary was done with her and she was back in her prison, she cried out, "Mommy, please help me! Please don't give up, please find me!"

She sobbed so hard her head ached, but it was nothing compared to the humiliation and guilt she was feeling. She cried until sleep crept up on her, exhaustion winning out over despair. But just before she slipped into that welcome state, that line between reality and dreams, she felt herself rise up in the darkness, lighter than a wisp, and in an instant she was in someone else's bedroom.

Every color she perceived was more vivid and sparkly, like the sunlight playing off water, but other colors were more muted than usual. Light wasn't necessary for her to see things around the room and she seemed able to take in everything all at once. She was oriented above the floor and facing a twin bed with a human-sized lump in it, apparently asleep and breathing deeply. The hair splayed across the pillow was long, so Amber assumed it was a girl. She looked around the room, noticing the dulcimer in the corner, knowing what it was without ever having seen one before, and there were pictures stuck along the tall mirror that sat in front of a desk. Shoes and other flotsam were strewn around the floor and clothing was draped over the desk chair. School books were on the floor by the bed as if they had been shoved off. Amber looked at the books and determined that the girl was a high school or college student. She also noticed books about telepathy and remote viewing, which were subjects she knew nothing about. What really mattered was that she was free, sort of, and somewhere with another person who might be able to help her.

Amber approached the bed somehow; without legs, walking was not how she seemed to propel herself. Since she had no hands, she simply thought about touching the girl's shoulder in order to awaken her. Suddenly, the girl sat up and whirled around, which shocked Amber right back into her own body lying on the cot in the pitch-dark room. She breathed hard and fast. Had she left her prison, or was it just a dream? Who was that girl and why had Amber visited her? She considered the questions and the experience until the blissful state of sleep overtook her.

Chapter Thirty-One

Callie

It was the last day of her sophomore year and Callie was past ready for summer break. The adoption party was in three days and she had a lot to do for it, not the least of which was making party food, cleaning, and decorating.

"Hey, sleepy head," Peggy called up to her, "you're running late—get down here or you won't have time for breakfast."

"Sorry, I'll be down in a minute," Callie called back. She had lost track of the time while she wrote in her dream diary. She decided to forgo a shower and put on deodorant and a spray cologne to cover any offending odor. She brushed her hair so fast and hard it hurt. She grabbed a T-shirt and capris to wear and shoved her feet into flip-flops. She flopped down to the kitchen with her bookbag, which she dropped onto the table, getting her bowl of cereal in record time and shoveling it into her mouth like a starving person.

"Whoa," Peggy said, "no need to choke yourself."

Callie smiled a cereal-filled smile and chewed more slowly. Peggy put juice in front of her.

"Last day as a high school sophomore," Peggy said. "Time sure does fly. I remember when you started middle school like it was yesterday." She sighed. "I've got to get ready for work. Oh, there's an envelope on the table there for you. Looks important."

Callie glanced at her phone, noticing how late she was, and grabbed her bookbag and the envelope before quick-walking to the bus stop. The bus was just arriving, so she had only moments to notice a strange man out of the corner of her eye. He seemed to be watching her intently. When she sat down on the bus seat, she looked out the window to see who it was. *Probably Winston*, she thought. The man had disappeared, so she shrugged it off as her imagination as the bus pulled away from the curb. The envelope was still in her hand. Curious, she looked at the sender; it was from the Psy Syndicate. *What's up with the snail mail*, she wondered. Normally she got emails from them. Inside the envelope was a fancy, formal letter addressed to her as if it were an acceptance letter from a university.

Dear Miss O'Callahan,

Every year, the Psy Syndicate teaches and tests new psychic candidates for entry-level positions within our organization. Your abilities first came to our attention with your better-than-average placement at the Psy Games. Your subsequent training over the past few months appears to have increased your abilities to a point where your test scores are significantly higher than your baseline scores. Coupled with your ability to solve a difficult problem involving another student with only a set of instructions, we find that you would be an excellent addition to the Psy Syndicate.

The position we are offering you is a paid internship for the summer months, which will also provide college credit if you are so inclined. Along with the internship, we would like to rent a meeting space to you for a modest fee, to provide a safe place to counsel your current and future clients.

If you are willing to accept this position and the rental space, please schedule a meeting with our representative as soon as possible.

We look forward to working with you,

Cyril Rhys-Doyle, Director, Psy Syndicate

Callie was gobsmacked. She had no idea that she had been under evaluation from the moment she had won second place at the Psy Games. It gave her a creepy feeling that threatened to morph into indignation. Then she thought about the paperwork she and Peggy had signed, accepting the winnings from the Psy Games and the terms of agreement. There must have been some fine print in there saying that they would be evaluating her, watching her every move. The next thing to add to her freak-out was the phrase "your ability to solve a difficult problem involving another student with only a set of instructions." Was Winston's foray into her dream realm some sort of test? Was that why Rhys-Doyle was unwilling to stop him? What in the actual hell?

They were at the school before Callie knew it, and she was still fuming and going over everything she had done while at the Syndicate. Was Chillian involved? Oh, that would be the end if they had made her befriend Callie just to keep an eye on her. As if by muscle memory, Callie got to her homeroom desk while contemplating Winston, Rhys-Doyle, the internship, and a possible betrayal by her newest friend, Chillian.

"Ladies and gentlemen, please take your seats," Callie's homeroom teacher said. "I will be handing out your final grades for the year."

This distracted Callie from her doom spiral. Since she had been able to concentrate on her finals with no clients or Psy Syndicate classes to worry about, she did well enough to keep her position on the honor roll, with mostly As and a couple of Bs. Her eyes filled with tears when she thought about how proud her mom would be. *I'll keep doing this for you, Mom, because you believed in me.* She felt a light touch on her cheek, almost imperceptible, as if someone were gently stroking it. She must have imagined the touch, as it was something her mom often did during a tender and proud moment.

Later that day, she met the current Misfits at lunch for the last time. Jonathan was graduating and off to UCLA to start his career in filmmaking. It would be only Callie, Grey, and Melinda left to hold down the fort. They still had until July before Jonathan left on his grand adventure, and his parents had sprung for a giant beach party for him and his friends. Callie didn't want to think about losing yet another important person in her life, but she knew this day was coming and he had promised to stay in touch.

"Hey, guys," Callie said as she approached the table.

"Callie-o," Jonathan said happily. "I'm so glad it's over and so sad it's over. Isn't that weird?"

"I can imagine," Callie said.

"I can't wait," Melinda said. "I don't want to do this for another year."

"I know," Callie said. "I am so ready to get to college and I have *two* more years."

"You guys will be long gone before I get outta here," Grey said glumly.

They discussed their final grades and Jonathan's summer party.

"At least you have something cool to do over the summer," Melinda said to Callie. "You get to do stuff at the Syndicate. I have to work at the Piggly Wiggly for cash."

"Interesting you should mention that," Callie said. "I got a letter from them in the mail. They want me to work for them as a paid intern and offered to rent me a space to see my clients." She pulled the letter out of her bag to show her friends.

All the Misfits erupted in simultaneous congratulations and questions. Callie had to use her hands to gesture them into silence.

"I don't know if I'm going to accept—they've done a couple of things I find questionable," Callie said.

"What, did they show you where the bodies are buried?" Melinda asked.

"No, Mels," Callie said in an exasperated tone. "The letter implies that they've been watching me carefully. It also implies that they sent another student to stalk me."

"*What?*" Melinda said, nearly sliding out of her chair. "That can't possibly be legal. No way. Don't work for creeps like that, Callie."

"He didn't actually *stalk me* stalk me," Callie said, "he kind of joined me in my dreams at night. Technically it wasn't illegal, just morally ambiguous." She didn't bring up Chillian's possible involvement, since the Misfits hadn't met her yet. She also didn't have any proof of her collusion.

"A paid internship and a safe place to work," Grey said. "It sounds like a dream job to me, no pun intended. Aren't they your kind of people?"

Callie should have been offended by his statement, except he was right. She had felt so comfortable there for the most part. Winston was the outlier and she had dealt with him handily, once she knew how. Her telepathy was stronger now, to the point that her clients had noticed and were referring more people her way. A safe place to meet with the local clients in exchange for a rental fee would increase her credibility even further.

"True," Callie said. "I'm just not sure I want to work for people who are so manipulative."

"All they did was watch you do your thing," Grey said. "It's not like they put cameras in your bedroom. My dad talks about how his managers love to use all these metrics to evaluate his work. It's a lot like that."

Grey's wise words gave Callie something to think about. As long as Chillian wasn't part of their "evaluations," she would take the job.

Changing the subject, she asked, "Everybody is coming on Saturday, right?"

"Remind me, what is happening on Saturday?" Jonathan asked in a mockingly thoughtful tone.

"Seriously? My adoption party, and if you don't come I'll haunt your dreams for the rest of your life!"

"Of course I'm coming, silly girl," Jonathan said. "Wouldn't miss it."

"Well, I was thinking of skipping it," Melinda said, "but if you're going to haunt people's dreams, I guess I can make it." She gave Callie a long-suffering look before she smiled widely and hugged her around the neck. "Even if Myrtle showed up on the same night to sew my cosplay for me, I would tell her 'no I have somewhere else to be.'"

"Grey?" Callie asked.

"Of course," he said.

Callie was grateful to her oldest friends. They would have one last job to do as a group: help her suss out a possible Psy Syndicate spy.

Callie had not had a gathering at Peggy's house since her mother's wake several months before. She spent time rearranging the furniture and putting up bright, joyful decorations to make the living room and dining room look like a cabana in Hawaii. Callie was wearing a gaudy full-length floral dress she had found online, while Peggy sported a red and white muumuu and straw hat. Clair's old friends, like extended family to Callie, arrived with covered dishes and gifts, giving her kisses on the cheek as they passed by. She hadn't seen these folks since the wake, either, and hoped they would consider that particular subject off-limits. The Misfits arrived in Jonathan's car, carrying on like they were arriving at a frat party. Fortunately, the neighbors were aware of the celebration and wouldn't complain. Melinda had a giant balloon arrangement in one hand and a gift in the other. Jonathan carried sodas and Grey had a covered dish. Callie held the door open as they piled in.

A few of the Ren Faire musicians set up their instruments and played tunes by request; another expertly juggled multiple balls in the air, trying to show some of the other guests how it was done.

Peggy was talking animatedly with a couple of other local shop owners, giving Callie time to pull her friends together.

"I need your help with something," Callie said. "Another girl is coming tonight who works at the Syndicate."

"Oh cool, another psychic?" Melinda said. "Maybe she'll read my fortune."

"No, I mean, yeah, she's a psychic, but that's not what I need your help with. I think we've become friends but I'm afraid she's just been hanging out with me to spy on me."

"So you want us to get some answers for you." Jonathan spoke like an actor from a gangster movie.

"Something more subtle, I guess," Callie said. "If she's for real, I don't want to scare her away, but if she isn't, then I don't want to work for the Syndicate. That's just too much for me."

"How do we figure out if she's a spy?" Grey asked. "It's not like she'll confess if we ask her."

"No, I will talk with her, but what I need you guys to do is get ahold of her phone and look through her texts and emails to see if she's been talking about me to Rhys-Doyle," Callie said.

"Oh wow," Jonathan said. "For-real spycraft. What about her password?"

"Easy," Callie said. "I'll ask her to take and share photos with us. Her phone will be open and we'll just pass it around. I can distract her while you take the phone and pretend to be looking at the pics. Then you give it back to her when you're done."

"Remind me not to get on your bad side," Melinda said. "I'll help—how about you guys?"

Jonathan and Grey nodded their agreement. A while later, Chillian arrived wearing a form-fitting neon green dress with Sahil holding her by the forearm. Grey's eyes popped open wide. "Is that her?" he asked, jabbing Callie in the ribs with his elbow.

Callie turned from her conversation to look toward the door. Her smile locked into place as soon as she saw the pair. Seeing Sahil with Chillian sent many confusing thoughts through her mind. *Was he in on the spying? Were they dating?*

Chillian looked around at the crowd until she saw Callie coming toward her through the throng. Chillian's smile seemed sincere enough, and Sahil let go of Chillian to give Callie a warm hug. Chillian hugged her too and handed her a tray. "A gift from Chef Lucia," she said.

"So glad you both could make it. You look amazing, girl! Let me take that for you. Come and meet the Misfits, they've been dying to meet you!"

Callie dragged Chillian by the hand toward the Misfits, leaving Sahil to follow behind them.

Callie introduced Sahil to the group, saying, "He tests my skills at the Syndicate," and then introduced Chillian, who put her hand out to each of them as Callie said, "This is Chillian from the Psy Syndicate, originally from Philadelphia."

Melinda said, "We've heard so much about you. Gorgeous dress!" Sotto voce, she said to Callie, "I would stay at the Syndicate just for Sahil."

Callie asked Chillian, "Are you hungry? We have sooo much food! I'm starving, been prepping all day."

She and Chillian headed over to the table covered end to end with casserole dishes and salads. Sahil stayed behind to talk with the Misfits.

"What do you think?" Callie said, posing in her Hawaiian attire for Chillian to review. "I mean, it's not as amazing as yours, but it's a theme party."

"It's smashing, darling," Chillian said in a haute couture tone. "No, really. I don't think I've seen you in a dress before."

"I'm not a fan of girl clothes unless they're Ren Faire," Callie said. "I grew up wearing that style."

"Weird," Chillian said.

"Which is why you don't see me in them," Callie said. "A bit too odd for high school. Hey, we ought to get some pics to commemorate the occasion. Do you mind being the photographer? I've seen your stuff and you're good at it."

"Flattery will get you a photographer then," Chillian said.

Callie dragged everyone at the party into at least one picture with her and Peggy to make sure there would be a huge number of photos before she ended with the Misfits.

"Chillian, can we take a look at your pics? I'd like to download them so I can make Callie a photo album," Melinda said.

Callie shot Melinda a look that said how impressed she was with her performance. Chillian gave Melinda her phone and showed her how to send photos to email. Once Melinda, Jonathan, and Grey went off into a corner with the phone, Callie took Chillian aside to distract and interrogate her.

"What do you think of the Misfits?" Callie asked.

"They seem nice enough," Chillian said in a cautious tone.

"I think they like you," Callie said.

"Mm-hmm," Chillian said.

Realizing that this topic wasn't going to yield much discussion, Callie changed tack. "I didn't get a chance to tell you—the Psy Syndicate offered me a paid summer internship."

Chillian's demeanor changed. "That is great! If you take it, we'll be able to spend the whole summer together! I was afraid that I would only be around a bunch of old psychics using crystals or tarot or something. You're going to say yes, right?"

Callie was heartened by Chillian's reply, which seemed authentic enough. Still, the whole episode with Winston needed to be dealt with.

"I have to ask you something," Callie said, fidgeting with her skirt. "Did Rhys-Doyle ask you to spend time with me when I started taking classes at the Syndicate?"

"Not really," Chillian said. "He was concerned that I was spending too much time on my own and he mentioned you and Siobhan were around my age. It seemed like an innocent recommendation to me at the time."

"Did he ask you about me? Specifically about Winston harassing me?"

"He did, now that you mention it," Chillian said. "I gave him a piece of my mind that he didn't do something about that scrap of preppy refuse."

Just then Sahil joined them. "Callie, you have the most eclectic group of friends I've ever met. I had no idea how much fun a Ren Faire could be. Everything okay here?"

Callie realized that she and Chillian must've looked quite serious for a pair at a party. "We're fine," Callie said, beaming at him. "We were just talking about a letter I got from the Syndicate offering a paid internship. I'm not sure I want to take it."

"I thought you would jump at the chance," Sahil said. "It would give you an opportunity to work with other professional psychics if nothing else. Why are you waffling?"

"I think it's about Winston," Chillian said. "He really weirded Callie out, and the director didn't do a thing about it."

"In his defense, there wasn't much he could do," Sahil said. "Not only is Winston a talented psychic, I hear his family is donating quite a bit of money to the Syndicate to ensure that he gets a position there. Rhys-Doyle is nothing if not dedicated to the Syndicate and has to deal with prickly and demanding investors."

"So I was expendable," Callie said.

"I don't think it was that simple," Sahil said. "As far as I can tell, he doesn't want to lose a single psychic. Maybe that's why he's offering you this internship, as a kind of peace offering."

"Really great pics, Chillian," Melinda said as the Misfits joined the Syndicate group. "I found quite a few that I can put in the album."

Sounds of furniture being moved came from the living room. Curious, the group went in to see what was going on. A large space had been cleared in front of the makeshift band. "It's time for the happy family to share their first dance with us," said a bearded Rennie. "Peggy and Callie, time to show us your skills."

Callie's face flushed with embarrassment, but Peggy was game as usual. She grabbed Callie's hand and pulled her onto the floor as the Ren players struck up a reel. Callie hadn't danced a reel in ages, but it came back to her as Peggy led them through the joyful dance. After just a minute on the floor by themselves, others joined them as much as space allowed while the less courageous guests clapped in time with the beat.

After a couple of upbeat dances, the band changed to a more sedate tune.

"Mind if I ask you to dance?" Sahil said, suddenly at Callie's side.

Turning to look him in the eye, she said, "I would be honored."

He took her hand to lead her to the floor and put one hand on her hip as he guided her through the slow waltz.

"You are a man of many talents, sir," Callie said.

"As you are a girl of many talents," Sahil replied. "It seemed the only opportunity to get you alone tonight."

Callie's face flushed again and she looked away from his dark eyes.

"I think it would be a huge mistake to turn down that internship," Sahil said. "I've worked with others who spent time with the talented psychics they have there, and they developed incredibly. I don't think you are even half the psychic you will be."

So his only interest was professional. Why had she gotten her hopes up?

"Yeah, I get it," Callie said. "I'm tired, Sahil. Thanks for the dance."

She left the living room in search of her friends, the people she had been able to trust as long as she could remember. She found them at the breakfast table sharing a plate of food.

"I am beat," Callie said. "How do these old people have so much energy!"

"They suck it out of the young," Grey said.

"We've been waiting to talk to you," Melinda said.

"I found her email account and looked back as far as February," Jonathan said. "There were a bunch of emails between her and the director so I had to look for your name as a keyword. There were only three and of those, only one was about that Winston guy."

"She was really letting the director have it," Melinda said.

"I think you can consider her an unwitting accomplice at most, and an ardent defender of yours," Jonathan said.

Callie breathed out a sigh, not realizing until then just how much she had feared that Chillian was only pretending to befriend her.

"You guys have always had my back," Callie said. "I know this was weird, but you didn't even question it. Thank you so much." She gave them each a hug. "Did you really mean it, Mels? You're going to make a scrapbook for me?"

"Not by myself I'm not," Mels said. "We're going to work on that particular project together."

"Hey, Callie." Chillian had come into the kitchen. "I'm about dead on my feet—we're going to head back to the Syndicate." Sahil was right behind her.

"I really appreciate you coming tonight," Callie said, giving Chillian a hug. "Let me walk you out."

When they got to the front door, she said, "I wanted to let you two be the first to know. I've decided to take the internship."

Chapter Thirty-Two

Callie

"Goodbye, Mrs. Farrington," Callie said, "I'll see you next month."

She guided her client through the back entrance of the Psy Syndicate. Callie was renting office space in the conference building, but the room looked like it belonged to a psychologist rather than a psychic. Callie hadn't had time to decorate in the usual gentle colors and Ren Faire kitsch that she was comfortable with. Mrs. Farrington's reading had gone longer than the allotted hour, which made Callie late for her first meeting with the psychic group she had been assigned to. She began running through the building and abruptly halted in front of the conference room, smoothed down her professional-looking outfit, and caught her breath. Quietly and slowly, she opened the door.

"You will be shadowing the psychic who most closely...Ah, Miss O'Callahan," Rhys-Doyle said as Callie walked in.

"Sorry I'm late," she said, "my reading went long." She took the closest available chair and sat down.

"As I was saying," Rhys-Doyle continued, "you will be shadowing the psychic whose gift most resembles yours."

There were three other people in the room with Rhys-Doyle: Faye Matthews from Callie's telepathy class; Siobhan Reilly, the young, elf-like girl; and Winston.

Winston. Great...Just great, Callie thought. He saluted, winked, and smiled at her when she looked his way. She rolled her eyes and then switched her attention to the director.

"You will be honing your specific skills with your psychic mentor as they work on cases for which the Psy Syndicate has been contracted," he said. "When a detective brings a case to us, each team member will utilize the information or evidence provided, drawing on their particular ability to give additional clues to the detective. We use more than one psychic to help confirm the clues given. If only one of the psychics gives a particular clue that cannot be corroborated by another psychic or by the evidence, then the clue is considered weak. However, if multiple psychics concur on a clue, it is considered strong."

As if on cue, the door to the conference room opened. Three people filed in and took seats at the table. One was a striking, tall blond woman who looked to be in her late thirties or early forties. The next was the older man whom Callie remembered from Rhys-Doyle's magic show, and the third was a diminutive Black woman with large eyes and a bright smile.

"Thank you for coming in today," Rhys-Doyle said to the newcomers. "Could each of you please introduce yourselves and tell us what your psychic skill is."

Siobhan went first and said she was a dowser. Faye said she was a medium-in-training, Callie said she was a mentalist and telepath, and the tall blond woman, whose name was Laura Etheridge, said she was a medium. The older man, Teddy Smith, was a remote viewer, and the Black woman, Veronica Miles, said she had multiple talents, one of which was dowsing. Then Winston claimed he was also a remote viewer with the ability to dream-project.

"Excellent," Rhys-Doyle said. "I will now assign you interns to your mentors so that you can get acquainted with one another before we begin our next case. Winston will be working with Teddy, Faye with Laura, and Siobhan and Callie with Veronica. Since it is time for luncheon, you may retire to the dining room. The detective will meet with us in here in an hour."

He rose from his chair to open the conference room door for everyone, standing outside in the hallway until everyone passed through. They began talking among themselves as they walked through the garden and into the house.

"Callie, right?" Veronica said, looking up at her.

"That's me," Callie said. "It's nice to meet you."

"And you're Siobhan?" Veronica asked, turning toward the other girl.

"Correct."

"Siobhan, how long have you been dowsing?" Veronica asked.

"All my life," Siobhan said. "My family all dowse."

"And Callie, you said you were a mentalist. How long have you been doing that?"

"I traveled with my mother when she was doing shows and fairs as a medium. I picked it up as a kid," Callie said.

They turned into the dining room. Lucia had made an assortment of sandwiches and salads to choose from at the sideboard. Callie grabbed a turkey sandwich and ladled pasta salad onto her plate. She sat down next to Siobhan while Veronica took a seat across from them. The other interns sat at tables with their mentors.

"Let me tell you a bit about myself, then," Veronica said. "I have been at this all my life as well. My grandmother taught me how to hone my abilities, especially with dowsing. I grew up in a small town and people weren't so willing to accept what I could do, so I was lucky to have her help me figure it all out. So, besides dowsing, I am clairaudient and a precog."

"You have future sight?" Siobhan asked. "How does that work?"

"In my case, it happens in my dreams," Veronica replied. "I keep a dream diary, writing down what feels like a prescient dream event. I send the information to the Psy Syndicate's precognition database and they let me know if what I saw comes to pass."

"I just finished taking a dream course here, but I haven't had anything like a precog dream," Callie said. She didn't want to relate her issues with Winston, since he was on their team. "How does it feel different?"

"The normal dreams are hard for me to remember, but the precog or telepathic ones are more luminous, or real and memorable," Veronica said. "I still try to remember all my dreams and write them in my journal, but those others go into the database.

"Siobhan, what kind of dowsing do you do?"

"We, I mean I, do mostly pendulum dowsing for lost objects, but my family contracts for locating minerals or water using the L-rod," she replied.

"You are familiar with dowsing using a map or a grid?" Veronica asked.

"I use all kinds of tools for dowsing—maps, grids, diagrams, and alphabets."

"You might be able to show me a trick or two, then." Veronica smiled.

Siobhan blushed and looked down at the table. "That's very kind, but I'm sure you have much more experience than I have."

The three of them spoke a while longer, talking about their respective backgrounds, before walking back into the conference room. An older man was in there, looking quite fit in a business suit, setting up the projector and a laptop. Once everyone else had returned and was settled in their chairs along the table, Rhys-Doyle gave the man the signal to proceed.

"Hello, everyone," the man said. "I'm Zachary Simpson from the Helion Detective Agency out of Memphis. I'm here on behalf of a family whose wife and mother has been lost for eighteen months. I've handed out some background information on her along with the investigation into her disappearance. I also have a PowerPoint presentation to show you so that we can discuss each aspect of the case. Please turn to page one in your packets."

All the psychics opened their glossy folders with the agency logo on the front. The detective used the remote to turn on the screen behind him and dim the room lights before beginning his presentation. The first slide was a picture of a dark-haired woman bracketed by three children of different ages and a man standing behind her, in what appeared to be a family portrait.

"This is Andrea Gonzalez and her family," Zachary began. "She failed to return home from her work shift eighteen months ago. She works second shift at the local hospital as a nurse and was last seen getting into her car in the hospital parking garage."

The projector showed a still photo of her from a security camera's footage.

"There has been no known sighting of her after this. Mr. Gonzalez and the children were unaware that she was missing until the following morning, at which point they contacted the police. As you may know, law enforcement is unwilling to perform an official search for a missing person until forty-eight hours have passed. Mr. Gonzalez took a day off from work to call friends and family to see if Mrs. Gonzalez may have gone to visit them. I have given each of you a list of contacts Mr. Gonzalez provided. The police placed Mrs. Gonzalez on the missing persons list forty-eight hours after Mr. Gonzalez contacted them.

"The members of the Church of Saint John put posters out with Mrs. Gonzalez's photo and performed searches with the police, but no further evidence has been obtained. The church members have also provided a reward for information. Although there have been a few calls, there have been no leads, nor has there been any activity on her accounts. There was no evidence that she planned to leave her family insofar that all her personal effects are still at her home and she has a good relationship with her husband and children. She is considered to be a devoted wife and mother who attends church regularly and is involved with her community."

"Was there any change in her behavior before her disappearance?" Laura asked.

"Mr. and Mrs. Gonzalez's friends say that she did not seem to be different in any way. They were planning a vacation and Mrs. Gonzalez seemed quite happy about it."

"Was there history of addiction of some sort?" Veronica asked. "Or a lover?"

"We thought of that. If you look on page five, you'll see we performed our own assessment based on an evaluation of her finances and witness testimony. She didn't have any missing time or large sums of money added to or removed from her accounts. Her work associates didn't see any behavior that may have indicated drug use, though we were unable to obtain a drug test. That being said, the hospital she worked for had a zero-tolerance drug-use policy, so any positive drug test would have meant immediate dismissal," he said.

"Does your agency have any hypothesis as to her whereabouts?" Rhys-Doyle asked.

"We really don't," Zachary said. "It seems like she simply vanished. It's why the family has asked me to employ psychics. They've got no other options at this point and would appreciate any help you can give them."

"Thank you, Mr. Simpson," Rhys-Doyle said. "Do any of you have further questions for Mr. Simpson?"

Veronica piped up, "It will help our group to have something of importance that belongs to Mrs. Gonzalez."

"Oh, of course," Zachary said. He riffled through his large bag and pulled out a plastic pouch with something purple in it.

"According to her husband, this is her favorite shirt." He handed it to Veronica.

"Anything else?" Rhys-Doyle asked. When no one replied, he said, "Thank you again, Mr. Simpson. We will send you a report as soon as we have any data for you."

"Thank you all," Zachary said. "The family is very grateful for any help you can supply."

With that, he gathered his laptop and bag and departed from the room.

"Ladies and gentlemen, let's do what we do best," Rhys-Doyle said.

Callie, Siobhan, and Veronica went to Callie's office to work in private. Veronica sat down at the desk and pulled out the plastic bag with the purple shirt. She then produced an atlas of the United States, flipping through it to Tennessee and perusing the pages for Collierville, the town where the Gonzalez family lived and worked. When she found the page, she placed tracing paper, a ruler, and a pencil over it. She then pulled out a crystal hanging from a chain. To Callie's eye, it appeared to be quartz, with the natural formation ending in a point like the graphite of a sharpened pencil.

"What's that for?" Callie asked.

"This is a pendulum used for dowsing on a map," Veronica said. "Siobhan, do you have one?"

"Yes," Siobhan said. She lifted a pendant from her neck. It was also a crystal with a pointed end; Callie thought it looked like an amethyst.

"Callie, this part is really pretty simple," Veronica said. "Siobhan and I will take turns dowsing using this map. Why don't you have a seat over at the couch for a while, Siobhan."

Veronica removed the purple shirt from the bag. It had stylized white lettering that spelled out "Eagles." Veronica wrapped the shirt around her forearm and then held the chain to her pendulum in her hand so that it came over the top of her crooked forefinger, allowing the crystal to dangle over the map. Small movements of her wrist caused the pendulum to swing in a clockwise direction. While the pendulum swung, Veronica slowly moved the ruler. When the pendulum stopped, Veronica drew a line along the edge of the ruler. She did this three times until the intersecting lines created a triangle. She marked the city streets on the tracing paper so that she could find the triangulated area again on the map, and then put it aside. The whole process took about ten minutes.

"Okay, Siobhan," Veronica said, "let's see what you get."

Siobhan had been meditating on the couch, so it took her a minute to come to awareness and walk over to the desk to join Veronica and Callie. She used a different method to hold her pendulum, grasping it tightly between her thumb and forefinger and wrapping the excess chain around her wrist. She laid the shirt on the table next to the atlas and placed her other hand on it. She found the suburb of Memphis and located the hospital where Andrea Gonzalez had last been seen. She allowed her pendulum simply to point directly to that spot until it began to swing back and forth in a southeasterly direction. Her movements followed the streets. Callie assumed that she was trying to follow the same route that Mrs. Gonzalez had taken in her car. Eventually, her pendulum stopped moving and pointed to a single area on the atlas page. All three of them leaned forward to see where the spot was.

"Is that what you got?" Siobhan asked Veronica.

"Yours is more specific than mine, but it's in the same area. Let's take a photo of the map so we can add it to the report."

"Do I get to do anything?" Callie asked.

"You can try receiving something telepathically," Veronica said.

"Okay," Callie said slowly, "but I've never tried to read a stranger at a distance before."

"When it comes to Ψ, time and space mean nothing," Veronica said. "Those are simply limitations we have placed on ourselves."

Callie raised an eyebrow and said with a sigh, "I'll try."

"Maybe if you put the shirt on the couch, as if Mrs. Gonzalez were sitting there," Veronica suggested. "Here, let me put it there for you."

Veronica laid the shirt on the couch, spreading it out as if a very flat person were wearing it, and then turned to look at Callie, hands on her hips. "How's that?"

Callie dragged her chair over to the couch and sat facing it. *How am I supposed to get a reading from a shirt?*

"I think you'll feel more comfortable if Siobhan and I leave you to it," Veronica said. They left the room, closing the door with a soft click.

Callie sat back in the chair and regarded the shirt. "Okay, Mrs. Gonzalez, what question can I answer for you today?"

As Callie had expected, the shirt said nothing.

She sat, chin perched in her hand, concentrating so hard on the shirt that her eyes began to lose focus. In a huff, she stood up, snatched the purple shirt and the keys to the room, and stomped out, slamming the door behind her. She fumbled with the key as she tried to lock the door. "Will something please work already?" she cried out. She continued her heavy gait to the main house, slamming that door as well.

Callie had actually been excited to work on a missing persons case. At first, it had felt like being in the middle of a true-crime reality TV show, but the importance of it had really hit home when she saw the pictures of Andrea and her children. If Callie had anything to say about it, not another kid would lose their mom. However, after watching Veronica and Siobhan effortlessly dowse a location, Callie felt useless. What could she do after all? Her ability to read people depended on them being in the room with her, seeing their small reactions, whether their hands clenched or were relaxed, looking into their eyes for changes in pupil size. She decided to go get a snack from the break room to calm down a bit.

"Hi, Callie," came Sahil's voice from behind her.

She turned, startled.

"I'm sorry, I didn't mean to scare you," Sahil said, putting his hand on her shoulder. "This is your first day with the psychic team, isn't it?"

"Yeah," Callie said, turning back to her soda and apple. She viciously bit into it and hunched over the table where the purple shirt lay.

"Not going well, it looks like," Sahil said.

"I've got nothing," Callie said. "The two people I'm working with got something within minutes, but not me. I'm useless."

"You're not useless," he said. "It's your very first day. Cut yourself some slack." With that, he patted Callie's shoulder a couple more times, grabbed a soda, and left the break room.

She grasped the shirt with both hands, trying to get any kind of psychic ping from Andrea. Still nothing.

I have no idea what I'm doing here, Callie's inner voice said to her. *I should just cut my losses and blow this joint. My clients will still come whether I'm here or not. I don't need this job!*

She grabbed the shirt and bolted down the hall, not knowing what more she could do. She was thinking that she should just go home, never to darken the Psy Syndicate's door again, when she ran into Dorcas in the hallway, nearly knocking the older woman to the floor.

"I'm sorry!" Callie said, catching Dorcas before she fell.

"Callie, are you feeling all right?" Dorcas said, concern in her voice.

"Just...I can't do this," Callie said. "I thought I could, but I'm not any good at it."

"I think you can," Dorcas said. "Let's go sit down and talk somewhere in private."

"Fine, but I don't think it'll make a difference," Callie told her.

Dorcas led Callie down the hall to the classroom where she had taught Mediumship and gently closed the door. Callie plopped onto the couch by the window. She couldn't meet Dorcas's gaze as the woman sat down next to her.

"What made you so upset?" Dorcas asked.

"I've just been assigned to a missing person case and I was asked to get some sort of telepathic message from her. I've never done something like this before and I got nothing when I tried."

Dorcas smiled and placed her hand on Callie's. "Don't get discouraged, dove. You won't always get through." She looked somber for a moment. "Sometimes no answer is an answer, just not a happy resolution."

"I don't even want to go there," Callie said.

"Is that what's bothering you? That the missing person might be deceased?"

Callie nodded, knuckling a tear from her cheek none too gently.

"Oh, my dove," Dorcas said, giving Callie's hand a squeeze. "This is just like the mediumship class, isn't it? You are hit harder than most because you've recently lost your mum."

"I can't see another child lose their mother, Dorcas," Callie said. "It's just not right."

"I know, dove. But it's already happened one way or another. You know that your mother passed, but this poor mother's family and friends don't have any answers at all. You'll be giving them information they need to move forward."

Callie sighed, then said, "Even so, how do I get ahold of someone I don't know and from a distance?"

"You'll need to try different ways to wrap your head around that," Dorcas said. "It's all very personal and depends on the confidence you have in your gift. If you don't think you can do it, you won't succeed. If it helps, I think you're sensitive and clever enough to achieve whatever you set your mind to."

"One of the psychic mentors said that time and distance don't matter," Callie said.

"She's right, but I know that it's hard if you haven't even met the client to try to get that connection," Dorcas said. "So you need to use something to help make that connection happen—a picture, for instance. I'm going to be offering a course on psychic skills that transcend time and distance, if you're interested."

"Okay, I'll try that next time," Callie said. "Thanks so much for your advice—I'll take that class, I promise." She gave Dorcas a hug.

"Anytime you need it, I'll be happy to help," Dorcas said.

Although Callie didn't feel like bolting from the premises any longer, she was still disappointed that she didn't have anything to offer. The thought of admitting that to the team filled her with dread.

Since she had no particular reason to stick around and Chillian was not available to hang out with her, Callie had decided to go home and watch some TV to get her mind off her failure. She had found nothing compelling enough to watch, so she mindlessly flipped through the channels for a while. After that became too boring to endure, she made herself useful by cooking dinner.

"What's gotten into you?" Peggy said. "You usually eat like a horse."

"Not hungry," Callie said, picking at her broccoli.

"Are you sick? I can take you to urgent care—"

"I'm fine, okay?" Callie slammed her fork down on the table. "Just leave me be!"

"I don't know what's going on with you, Callie, but I'm just concerned. No need to bite my head off."

"Sorry," Callie said.

"How about you tell me what's got you in such a mood?"

"It's nothing you'd understand." She grabbed her plate, dumped the contents into the trash, and put the plate in the sink. "I'll do dishes later," she said, and went upstairs to her room.

She collapsed onto her bed, staring at the ceiling and hoping for some kind of epiphany or even just a little whisper from Mrs. Gonzalez. When nothing came to her, she fell asleep, and her dreams didn't send her any clues, either.

Chapter Thirty-Three

Callie

C allie arrived at the Psy Syndicate a few minutes before the meeting was set to begin, so she helped herself to some hot tea, knowing that the British swore by its ability to solve all ills. Taking a deep breath, she opened the conference room door. The others were seated around the table engaged in quiet conversation. Winston looked up and smiled in his sideways fashion. Callie opted to ignore him and found a seat that blocked his view of her. She held the mug of tea in her hands like a talisman against evil. Rhys-Doyle arrived with Kristin following just behind him, carrying her laptop.

"Thank you, ladies and gentlemen, for taking time to be here today," Rhys-Doyle said, taking his usual position at the head of the table. "Unless you have any questions, we will start with our dowsers, Veronica and Siobhan. Please let us know your impressions and your confidence levels."

"We performed our dowsing separately and were able to get very strong impressions that Mrs. Gonzalez had gone in a southeasterly direction from the hospital for quite some distance before her trail ended near the highway," Veronica began. "I've emailed a photo of the location."

"Got it," Kristin said. She hooked the cable from her laptop to the central console that controlled the projector. After a couple of moments, a map of Collierville showed up on the screen. Veronica got up to point out where Mrs. Gonzalez had stopped.

"It's right about here," she said, indicating a triangle bracketed by two highways and a state route. There didn't appear to be any businesses or buildings of any kind in the area.

"Do you concur, Siobhan?" Rhys-Doyle asked.

"Yes sir, with high confidence," Siobhan said in her quiet, lilting voice.

"Teddy and Winston, were you able to obtain anything relevant regarding her location?" Rhys-Doyle asked.

Teddy raised his head much like a turtle emerging from its shell. He cleared his throat before saying, "I got the impression of a bunch of trees and underbrush."

"I got the same information," Winston said.

"It seems we have a location for Mrs. Gonzalez, and the sense of her in the woods. Now let's determine her disposition. Laura and Faye? What were your impressions?"

Laura said, "I was able to get some visions, but they were not strong. I felt sharp pain in my chest and a feeling of being enclosed in a small, dark space. I feel that she may have been harmed by someone and is not suffering from a sudden illness. I cannot say with complete confidence, but I think she has passed."

"I wasn't able to communicate with Mrs. Gonzalez," Faye added.

"Miss O'Callahan? Anything?" Rhys-Doyle asked.

Callie simply shook her head, unable to trust her voice. At that moment, she saw a devastated husband facing his young children with the news that their mother would never, ever come home again. The mug in front of her blurred as her eyes filled with tears.

Veronica spoke first. "Callie, are you okay?"

"I wish people would stop asking me that," Callie snapped. "I don't know how you all can talk about her like some object that someone lost. She was a wife and a mother and those kids...they won't ever see her again!" She leaped up from her chair and fled through the conference room door.

That's it. I'm done whether I want to be or not, Callie thought. She had run into the Psy Syndicate house, but without a ride home, she didn't know where to go. *Chillian should be upstairs*, she thought, and ran up the steps two at a time. She pounded on the door.

"I'm coming, I'm coming! Jeez!" came the muffled sound of Chillian's voice.

Callie was shaking and breathing so hard, she began to see stars dance before her eyes. She felt faint and displaced and nearly fell through the door as it opened. Chillian moved aside as Callie pushed through.

"What happened to you?" Chillian asked.

"I am probably fired," Callie said as she sat carefully on Chillian's messy bed.

"Really? What did you do?"

"I threw a fit and ran out of a meeting."

"Yup, that's pretty unprofessional," Chillian said. She sat down next to Callie. "Why did you run? Did Winston have something to do with it?"

"No," Callie said, "it's the missing person case, Mrs. Gonzalez. I wasn't able to get anything from her, and then everyone was just so impersonal when they gave their reports, like she was nothing more than an object, not a mom or a wife or a friend. The mediums weren't sure but thought she was already dead."

"I can understand why they acted that way," Chillian said. "All the years I've been seeing how and when people die, I've had to remove my feelings from it or I would be a hot mess."

"You don't feel anything at all for those people?"

"Death comes for all of us," Chillian said, "and death isn't the end of our story—at least that's what Grandma always told me."

Chillian lay back onto her bed and stared up at the canopy. Callie did the same.

"I used to get very upset when I had my visions. I was just a little kid," Chillian said. "Grandma would hold me tight until I stopped crying and tell me stories about the other side. She said that no one dies alone—even when they've had the most violent end, they will be met by someone they know and love."

"Did that help?"

"I mean, in a way, sure," Chillian said, "but it's a person, you know? And they leave people behind who have to live without them."

"That's what bothers me the most. Those kids and their dad will be devastated."

"Right, they will be," Chillian agreed, "but you didn't cause that pain, someone else did. You're just reporting the news." She turned onto her side to look at Callie. "You're giving them the gift of knowledge. What they choose to do with it is up to them."

"I guess so."

"You know what I do here, right? I'm finding people who are going to die soon and I'm letting the Psy Syndicate know."

"That's what you told me," Callie said.

"They're using that information to take out low-cost life insurance policies on these people," Chillian said. "The Syndicate gets some, but the family gets the majority of the insurance money."

"That sounds pretty mercenary," Callie said.

Chillian said, "Just imagine if the family not only lost their loved one unexpectedly but also had to live without their income on top of that. Money doesn't replace a father or mother or child, but it does keep them from poverty."

"Do you tell them that you see them dying?"

"I'm not allowed to talk with them, in case they react badly," Chillian said. "I wish I could sometimes, especially if it's something they can avoid, like a car accident."

She lay there quietly inspecting the ceiling. Callie wondered what it would be like to have someone's fate in their hands the way Chillian did.

After a minute, Chillian sighed and said, "At least the Gonzalez family will be able to find Mrs. Gonzalez and give her a proper burial, find whoever did this to her and get some justice. That's what you guys are offering them: closure."

"I didn't think about it like that," Callie admitted.

"You haven't had to deal with this before," Chillian said. "It will take time to get over the emotional fallout." She sat back up, pulling Callie to a sitting position next to her, and put her arm around Callie's shoulders. "Now, you have to go back to that meeting, face those people, and apologize."

Callie groaned and covered her face with her hands.

"Come on. I'll go with you for moral support."

Callie hoped the meeting would have concluded before she had to face the psychic group, especially Winston, who would not let her live this one down, but they were all still there. Callie was standing in the open doorway when Chillian gave her a little shove to get her into the conference room. Callie looked back at her and Chillian mouthed, "Go ahead, it will be fine."

She stepped into the room, avoiding everyone's stare by looking at the surface of the conference table. She cleared her throat and said, "Um. I apologize for how I acted earlier. The recent loss of my mother has made me susceptible to strong emotions. I promise it will not happen again."

"Miss O'Callahan, please take your seat so we may continue," Rhys-Doyle said.

Callie didn't meet his gaze and was unable to discern from the tone of his voice if he was angry with her. She sat down in the chair that she had unceremoniously vacated in her haste to be gone from the room earlier. Chillian came from behind to give her a quick hug and then closed the door as she left.

Chapter Thirty-Four

Callie

"How was your day at work?" Peggy asked as Callie came through the back door.

"Fine," she lied.

Before Peggy could ask any more questions, Callie raced up to her room, closed the door just shy of a slam, and fell facedown onto her bed, letting the pillow absorb her tears. With a heavy sigh, she rolled over, trying not to think of what a fool she had made of herself. Her phone buzzed in her bag. She yanked it up onto the bed and rummaged through the mess, hoping it wouldn't be a text from anyone having to do with the Psy Syndicate. Fortunately, it was from Melinda.

"Whatcha up to?" Melinda had texted.

"Just had a crap meeting at work."

Mels replied immediately. "Want 2 meet for shakes?"

"Luv 2."

Another quick reply from Mels: "OMW."

They were sitting on the hood of Melinda's parents' car sipping on their shakes, shivering from the combination of the cool evening and the frozen treats, when Mels asked, "How are things going over at the Psy?"

"I think I'm done there, actually," Callie said. "I'm gonna put in my notice if they don't kick me out."

"Why's that?" Melinda asked.

"Not only did I strike out trying to find a client's wife, I threw a fit and ran out of the room. I came back and apologized, but I don't know if that will matter," Callie said. "And they're charging me a fee to use their facilities to meet my clients. Peggy doesn't charge me anything if I use her back room. I don't know why I've wasted my time with them."

"I don't understand," Melinda said.

"What do you mean? I'll do better on my own. I always have."

"No, I don't agree," Melinda said. "You have been involved with them for a while now and you've been pretty happy there. Are you going to bail because of one bad meeting?"

"I'm just a hack compared to the people in that room," Callie said, "the descendant of a carnival medium who is really good at reading people and telling them what they want to hear. The rest of them have worked for the government or written books or been doing this psychic stuff all their lives. What can I bring? Nothing, that's what." She shoved off the hood of the car and chucked the remains of her shake into the trash can. "Can we go now?"

"Okay," Melinda said, sliding off the hood and getting into the car. "You know that is totally wrong, don't you?"

"What's totally wrong?" Callie asked.

"That you're a hack. I've been there when you've done your readings. Your clients are amazed by what you can do. And, don't forget that Rhys-Doyle dude offered you a job. I bet you a dozen donuts he would have kicked you out by now if you weren't so full of potential."

"I guess," Callie said.

"Well, *I* know," Mels said, "and you know that I'm awesome and I love you like a sister, so get over it and go back there and demand a second chance if you have to."

Just then Callie's phone pinged; it was a text requesting that she see the director in his office the next morning before she had her client meeting at nine a.m. She was sure that he was done with all her outbursts and demands, behavior that was very much out of character for her. That would be her argument, that she was just having a few problems and would behave better if he gave her another chance.

"You'll be fine," Melinda said, giving Callie a hug.

"Thank you so much, Mels."

Right on time the following day, Callie waited at the entrance to the Psy Syndicate. The house seemed to be preternaturally quiet and loomed over her as she stood in its shadow.

Just pull the Band-Aid off quickly, Callie said to herself. It was her mom's favorite adage about getting things you didn't want to do done and over with. She muttered her arguments under her breath, practicing the speech for the hundredth time just so she wouldn't falter before the director.

"Good morning, Callie," Kristin said.

"Yes ma'am," Callie said, not wanting to elaborate one way or the other. "The director sent me a request to meet with him before my client comes in. Would you mind having the client wait for me in case I'm delayed?"

"Not at all. I'll take care of them for you," Kristin said. "Good luck with the director."

Callie thanked Kristin as she walked down to Rhys-Doyle's office. His door was closed so she knocked gently on the hard wood with her knuckle.

"You may enter," he said.

Callie twisted the knob and poked her head through the doorway. "You wanted to see me this morning?"

"Yes, I did," Rhys-Doyle said. "Please come in and sit."

Callie stepped fully into the office and planted herself demurely in the chair he had indicated.

"Please let me start off by saying that I'm truly sorry for my outburst at the meeting yesterday. I don't normally have such difficulty mastering my feelings, but I promise that I will keep them in check and behave more professionally if I'm given another chance." There, the speech was delivered just the way Melinda had coached her.

Rhys-Doyle said nothing. He stood up and buttoned his suit jacket as he walked around his immense desk to stand directly in front of Callie.

He leaned forward. "You were in a room with extremely talented people discussing the possible demise of a woman by nefarious means," he said. "I'm certain that you felt not only out of your depth, but also a commiseration with the young Gonzalezes for having lost their mother, am I right?"

"Yes, that's a good way of putting it," she said.

"And you think that, now that you have this out of the way, future cases won't be equally as emotional for you?"

"I don't know."

"Precisely," he said, leaning back on his desk. "So don't promise something you cannot deliver. You will be haunted by some of the cases brought to us, perhaps for the remainder of your days on earth. If you cannot cope, I will remove you from the team and we will use your talents elsewhere, am I understood?"

Callie's trepidation turned to anger and anger steeled her resolve. "Understood perfectly."

Chapter Thirty-Five

Callie

Dear Miss O'Callahan, the letter began in a child's scrawl, *thank you for helping to find our mother for us. We know she is with the angels in heaven. May God bless you.* The note was enclosed in an eight-by-eleven-inch manila envelope along with a letter from the Helion Detective Agency and a bonus check of two hundred dollars for her "efforts regarding the disposition of Mrs. Gonzalez."

Callie held the child's note in one hand and the check in the other, feeling unworthy of both. It wasn't as though she hadn't taken money from clients before, but it felt different this time. She laid the note on the table and was about to rip the check apart when an idea struck her. Why not put the money in an account that would go toward helping the Gonzalez children? She had used a funding campaign to help with her mother's treatments and had benefited from other people's generosity; now she could help another family in need. Callie's bruised ego healed a bit with the intention to do something good.

The psychic group had not convened in the week since the Gonzalez case, so Callie had spent most of her time working with her clients and tweaking the decor in her office with Chillian's help. It was neither clinical-psychologist-style nor Ren Faire kitsch. Instead, it was a tasteful reflection of how Callie wanted to portray herself: a competent, caring young person. The rest of her time was spent testing with Sahil.

"How much time are you spending on meditation?" he asked now.

"I really don't meditate," Callie said.

"You should take it up. I understand from the others that it gets the conscious brain to stop interfering with the signal," he said. "There's a meditation class starting next week—my good friend is teaching it. Maybe Chillian will join you if you ask her."

"Fine, I'll sign up for it," Callie told him.

"Great! I will want to test you again after you take the class."

Callie liked any opportunity she could get to spend more time with Sahil, even if he was only into her for her psychic skills. She had put on makeup and worn the outfit Chillian had recommended, but he was still just being his typical friendly self.

When the psychic group met next, another man from a different detective agency stood in front of the group of mentors and their mentees, with Rhys-Doyle at the helm of the conference table as usual. This detective was also a mentee; his corpulent mentor sat nearby in case he needed any prodding.

"Thank you for seeing us today. I'm Dennis Blackenthorp of the Regis Agency and this is Milton Masterson. We are here to discuss a case that you've probably heard about in the news a few months back. We've been hired by the Biggs family to find their daughter Amber."

Callie thought the name Amber Biggs sounded familiar. Others in the room whispered to one another, apparently in recognition of the name as well. Callie was sure that Rhys-Doyle relished the positive press the Psy Syndicate would get if any information psychically gained led to Amber's whereabouts.

"Amber Biggs, age twelve at the time of her abduction, was reported to have left school after detention."

He brought up the blond girl's school picture.

"She was walking home and texting a friend when she disappeared. The friend received no more texts after four eighteen p.m. Amber's phone was recovered on the lawn of a home three blocks from her residence. Witnesses in her neighborhood claim to have seen a white van leaving the area at the time of the alleged abduction."

He brought up a photo of a windowless white van, the kind used by contractors everywhere.

"The local police brought in the FBI very quickly on this abduction case due to pressure from the family and the press. Neither agency was able to conclusively locate the van. Appeals for information along with a sizable reward have provided only fruitless leads. There are currently no suspects and there has been no contact from either Amber or the alleged abductor. Although people have claimed to see Amber since the abduction, the locations are far flung and their veracity is suspect. The family is desperate for any information you can offer."

"Thank you, Mr. Blackenthorp," Rhys-Doyle said. "Any questions?"

He looked at each of the psychics in turn and was met with shaking heads.

"Shall we get to work?"

With that, the group was dismissed.

"Wow, the Amber Biggs case," Veronica said as they left the conference room. She was leading her charges to Callie's office so that they could, once again, ply their skills in peace. Veronica had obtained Amber's favorite tattered teddy bear from the young detective and held it by the paw as she walked.

"What's so special about this girl?" Callie asked.

"Some stories get plastered all over the news for whatever reason. It would appear the Biggs family is well connected, to get national news coverage and FBI assistance," Veronica said. "Not all of us get that kind of help."

"Even so, it hasn't helped with finding her yet," Siobhan said.

They arrived in the meeting room, where Veronica cleared the table to set up the map of Amber's town and an atlas in case she had been taken across state lines. Veronica let Siobhan start her dowsing first while she sat down with Callie on the couch.

"I know you had a really tough time with the Gonzalez case. Are you ready to try this again?" Veronica asked quietly.

"I've dealt with it," Callie said. "I'll be fine."

"Okay, but if you need any help at all, let me know. It's what I'm here for."

"Thanks," Callie said, giving Veronica a smile.

She pulled out a picture of Amber Biggs and spent time examining it. She looked familiar somehow, as if Callie had seen her before. It must have been when the news was on TV or one of her news feeds. Amber's blond hair framed her face in long waves and her bright green eyes showed an impish quality that probably caused her parents no end of worry. There was an innocence in those eyes, as if nothing would, or could, ever go wrong in this girl's life. Callie wondered how those eyes might look now, if the girl was still alive. Callie mentally shook herself of that particular thought, since it wouldn't help. She placed the picture on her knee as she sat comfortably on the sofa. She allowed her mind to clear and then focused on a mental picture of Amber walking home from school, her head inclined toward her phone as she texted at lightning speed, earbuds blasting her favorite tween band's top tune, completely unaware of any danger lurking behind her.

Okay, Amber, give me a sign. Callie sent out a telepathic ping, hoping for a response. Now in a light meditative state, she listened quietly. She let all other thoughts and distractions simply wash from her mind as she continued to send out a ping toward Amber. Callie felt a presence, as if she were being watched from the corner of the room. When she looked up, she saw nothing there, and the two dowsers were too engrossed in their work to notice Callie watching them.

She closed her eyes and let her breath in and out carefully, slowly, and asked, "Amber, are you here with me? Can you talk?"

Just the faintest of whispers came to Callie's awareness: *Alive...Help.*

Suddenly, she felt a hand on her shoulder. She opened her eyes and blinked rapidly.

"Any luck?" Veronica asked.

"Just a faint whisper," Callie replied. "I feel like she's still alive."

"I think we've got a location to give the detectives," Veronica said.

"That's good news."

The three of them walked back to the conference room and saw that it was empty, so they decided to take a break and discuss their findings.

"I'm feeling really good about it this time," Callie said as they walked along the path toward the main house. "I'm going to see if I can get through to her a bit better tonight using lucid dreaming."

"I'm so glad you got something," Siobhan said. "I was so upset after the Gonzalez case, my mom threatened to bring me back home."

Callie had not noticed that the quiet Siobhan had been so affected, and felt better now that she had company in her misery. She put her hand on Siobhan's shoulder. "I'm sorry, I had no idea."

"That's okay. I know how hard it was for you, too," she said. "Did you get a note from her children? That made me feel loads better."

"Yeah, they got what they needed, even if it didn't turn out that their mom was coming home to them," Veronica said. "I hear they have a suspect in custody already."

"If it's the guy, at least he won't hurt anyone else," Callie said.

They enjoyed their beverages while talking among themselves in the break area until Kristin came in. "Mr. Rhys-Doyle is ready for you in the conference room."

Callie had finished only half her soda but suddenly didn't feel like putting anything more into her stomach, since butterflies had decided to settle there. She followed Veronica and Siobhan down the hall to the conference room, where the rest of the psychic group and the two detectives sat waiting.

"Now that we're all present, we'll continue with our findings," Rhys-Doyle said.

Kristin took a seat with her laptop open, prepared to take notes on the proceedings. The younger detective had a notepad and pen in front of him to take notes of his own.

"Mr. Smith, Winston, we'll begin with your findings," Rhys-Doyle said.

Teddy Smith prodded Winston, who said, "We believe she is being kept in a single-story house in a neighborhood not far from where she was abducted. She may be in a basement room, since there appear to be no windows and it is pitch dark. I've drawn a picture of the layout as I saw it." He pushed a diagram toward the young detective, who took it and looked it over briefly before passing it to the older detective, who glanced at it as if it were a child's doodle.

"Mr. Smith, do you have anything to add?" Rhys-Doyle asked.

"It's one of them cookie-cutter neighborhoods with similar floor plans," he said. "I got the impression it's relatively new. Otherwise, I agree with Winston's findings."

"Thank you, gentlemen, that will be quite helpful, I'm sure," Rhys-Doyle said, turning to Laura Etheridge. "Ms. Etheridge, please provide us with your report."

Unlike Teddy, Laura didn't have Faye, her apprentice, speak for her. "I did not get a reading from the other side, so I believe she is still alive. I have no other details at this time."

"Thank you. Ms. Miles?" Rhys-Doyle said, turning toward Veronica and Siobhan.

Veronica cleared her throat. "We began at the alleged abduction site near her home and were able to follow a trail across town to a neighborhood called Bright Trails in Wendell. Kristin, could you bring up a map, please?"

Veronica waited until the map of the neighborhood, with its broad, winding streets and cul-de-sacs, appeared on the screen at the head of the conference table. She said, "This house here gives us the strongest impressions," and indicated a house on one of the cul-de-sacs.

Kristin hovered the cursor over the house to get its address. The young detective scribbled it down on his notepad.

"Very good. That will be helpful, I'm sure," Rhys-Doyle said, turning to Callie. "Miss O'Callahan, anything to add?"

"I wasn't able to connect with Amber directly, but I got the feeling she's still alive. I just don't think she's in great shape."

Chapter Thirty-Six

Amber

"I want you to sit there," Gary said, pointing to a chair, "and look at the camera like you want a candy bar."

Amber was wearing a sheer dress with a slit up the front that came to her upper thighs. Gary came over and pushed her knees apart so that her lace underwear would be visible to the camera. He fixed her hair so that it fell over one eye and moved her head a bit one way and then another. She let him pose her like she was a mannequin. He had meticulously painted her nails bright pink and applied makeup to her face. Her mother had never let her put on makeup or nail polish, saying she was too young for that. It felt odd, like a mask. Gary hadn't hit her face in ages, so there were no bruises to hide, and the clothing he had her wear hid the shock collar.

"Okay, now look down at the floor," he said.

He positioned Amber's hand so that her index finger was touching her lower lip.

"Now make a pout."

He had transformed the spare bedroom into a photography studio. He was using a high-end camera and one of those white umbrellas with a light in front. Amber remembered one like that from when her family had gone for professional portraits. This was a new activity for Gary, but at least it wasn't painful, disgusting, or arduous, like everything else she had to do for him.

"Go lie on the bed," Gary said. "Lie on your side."

He made her hold her head in her hand as she balanced on her elbow, and arranged her legs to look like one of the women in paintings at the art museum. He went back to the camera and took more pictures, adjusting her a few more times on the bed.

Gary had kept Amber in her cell for days at a time, letting her out only to get cleaned up, but he had provided her with a light to see by and some books to read. He had brought her food three times a day when, normally, he would have brought it only when he felt like it. He didn't make her clean the house either. This, she could live with.

"Change back into your other clothes. Leave those on the bed."

Amber was left alone in the spare room. She heard his fingers clicking away on his laptop in his bedroom as she discarded the lacy garments onto the bed and began to put on the clothes she'd had on before. She was pulling up her pants when she heard Gary talking.

"Did you get the pics I sent?" he was saying.

After a pause, he said, "Yeah, I can get her for you. What's your offer?"

Ice went down Amber's spine. She tiptoed to the bedroom door to hear better.

"Look, that's not nearly enough. She's got skills, I've been training her," he said.

Another pause.

"I'll tell you what, talk to your boss and get back in touch, okay?"

Amber heard the trill of a cell phone as it disengaged a call. She walked rapidly and quietly back to the spare room, where she sat on the edge of the bed and put on her shirt, pretending she hadn't heard anything.

"Let's get you back downstairs," he said.

She started toward the stairs with him following close behind. He locked her in the cell without a word and left her alone to ponder what she'd heard. It sounded like he had sent pictures to someone and was going to sell them. But what had Gary meant by "she's got skills"? Maybe he was planning to sell more than just pictures—maybe he was planning to sell *her*. Of course, Gary might have been talking about another girl, but the coincidence was too great.

Amber began to panic. If Gary sold her to someone else, she wouldn't know where she was. She had been lucky to find the address to this house, and she was sure that wouldn't happen again. The news had plenty of stories about girls being abducted to other countries and their parents fighting without success to get them back. What if he sold her to someone in a foreign country? She would never see her parents or her best friend, Ashley, ever again.

Chapter Thirty-Seven

Callie

Callie imagined that the information the psychic group gave to the two detectives would lead the authorities to Amber, and she would see the triumphant emergence of the abducted girl on her social media news feed. At least that was what she chose to think; she didn't have the time or inclination to think otherwise.

It was when Callie was falling asleep that night that a mental video appeared of Amber sitting on a raggedy cloth near a lake equipped with the usual ducks and sunning turtles on half-submerged limbs. She was there with two adults who Callie assumed were her parents. The woman laughed at something the smiling girl had said and hugged her around the shoulders. Then she rummaged through the basket next to her for a bag of bread. Amber snatched it and ran to the edge of the lake, taking bits of bread out and throwing them toward an oncoming family of mallards as her parents watched with smiles on their faces. Suddenly, Amber seemed to look directly at Callie and mouth the words "Help me."

Startled awake by the vision, Callie picked up her cell phone to see what time it was. Only 2:30 a.m. She put her phone down and smashed her extra pillow over her head to block out any other unwanted thoughts so that she could go back to sleep.

Callie was in a room where she had never been before with a nondescript man she had never met. A girl was sitting on a stool, her back to Callie, with white umbrellas arrayed around her. The man brought an expensive camera up to his eye and clicked the shutter. He moved toward the girl, adjusting the angle of her face and swiping a bit of her hair to the side, then he stepped back to take more photos. When the man was distracted by his camera, the girl, who turned out to be Amber, fully made up and coiffed, faced Callie and mouthed, "There isn't much time." Callie pulled herself out of the vision, breathing hard, her heart thundering as if she'd just had a large spider land on her.

So, Amber was communicating rather loudly now. After writing the details of the dream in her journal, Callie got up to see if she could distract herself with some television and maybe get some sleep before she needed to meet with her first client. She held a mug of warm milk in one hand and the TV remote in the other, getting comfortable under a light blanket. Since there was not much on early-morning TV to interest her, her mind returned to the dream. Amber believed she didn't have time left but didn't seem to be in imminent physical danger. What did she mean? Was she going to commit suicide or was she ill? Why was that guy photographing her? More important, what should Callie do next? The obvious answer was to speak with the Regis Agency about the dream, especially about time being a factor. Kristin would have their contact information. Callie yawned. The mug of milk was empty, there was nothing to watch, and she had decided on a course of action regarding Amber. It was time to try to fall asleep again. Lying down in her bed, she sent a mental ping to Amber: *I hear you and I will help.*

Peggy had time the next morning to drop Callie off at the Psy Syndicate. "You look like ten miles of bad road," she told her.

"I had some really interesting dreams that kept me from sleeping," Callie said.

"What were they about?"

"Psy Syndicate business," Callie said. "I'm not allowed to discuss it with anyone yet."

"Wow. Top secret squirrel," Peggy said. "I can keep a secret if you need to talk about it."

"I'm aware of how well you keep secrets," Callie said, remembering how she had kept her mother's impending death from her. She sighed. "I will talk with you about it if I need to."

They had arrived at the entrance to the Psy Syndicate.

"Do you need me to pick you up later?" Peggy asked.

"I don't know yet, so I'll text you when I do. Have a good day at work," Callie said.

"You too," Peggy said, and then drove away.

Callie punched in the security code and the door clicked open. She then tapped on the door to the office where Kristin was typing rapidly on her keyboard.

"Good morning, Kristin," Callie said.

"Hi, Callie, good morning. Something I can do for you?"

"I need to speak to that Blackenthorp guy from the Regis Agency about the Amber Biggs case," Callie said. "I couldn't find his direct phone number."

"I'm on it," Kristin said. She pulled up the detective agency on her screen and wrote the man's phone number down on a scratch piece of paper.

"Great, thanks," Callie said. "Have a good one!"

Callie typed Blackenthorp's phone number into her cell phone as she walked to her office to meet with her morning client.

"Blackenthorp here," he said.

"Hi, Mr. Blackenthorp. This is Callie O'Callahan from the Psy Syndicate calling about an update in the Amber Biggs case."

"Oh, hello, Miss O'Callahan," he said. "Give me a moment to scrounge a pen and paper."

Callie walked into her office and said, "Hi, Janice. I've got an important phone call to finish. I'll be with you as soon as I'm done."

"No problem, Callie," Janice said. "Take your time."

Callie closed the door and Blackenthorp returned to the phone. "Go ahead, Miss O'Callahan."

She described the dreams to the detective as she paced up and down the hall. "What do you think they mean?"

"Well, I'm no good at dream interpretation," Blackenthorp said, "but if I were to take them literally, it sounds like Amber might be a victim of child porn. Was she dressed or naked?"

"She was dressed very nicely from what I could see, and she was made up," Callie said. "It was like he was taking portrait photos of her."

"Hmmm," Blackenthorp said. "It might be something else."

"Like what?"

"I'm not sure. I'll get this information to the lead investigator at the FBI."

"Please be sure to tell them that her time is running out," Callie said.

"I will do my best," Blackenthorp said. "Thank you for the information."

Callie finished up her client meetings for the day and went to the meditation class with Chillian, who swore it would help alleviate stress. Instead of clearing her mind, though, she considered the conversation she'd had with Blackenthorp. Her confidence that the FBI would consider psychically derived clues was about as strong as wet toilet paper. Yet she had to admit to herself that there was a time, not that long ago, when she also would have taken any advice given by a psychic with a full shaker of salt. But what more could she do? She was just a telepathic teenager without a badge.

Chapter Thirty-Eight

Callie

"Checking up on Amber?" Chillian asked.

Callie was scanning her phone. "Yeah, nothing new on the news feed. What the hell is taking them so long!"

She threw the phone on Chillian's desk in exasperation.

"It sucks not to know," Chillian said, "but you have to learn to set things free. It isn't your responsibility anymore. Let the cops do their job."

"She won't let me sleep," Callie said. "She wants to know when I'm coming to save her."

Chillian got up from her yoga mat. "Have you told the agency that?"

"I call them daily," Callie said, "enough that they let voice mail answer my calls."

"Maybe Rhys-Doyle can give them a nudge. Have you asked him?" Chillian wiped sweat from her face with a towel.

"I haven't seen him lately. I think he's been out of the country," Callie said. "But I'll talk with him. I figure he would want the publicity from such a high-profile case."

"Yeah, can he talk to the press?" Chillian asked.

"I don't think he can," Callie said. "We all signed confidentiality agreements."

"Still, there might be something he can do. This may sound harsh, but you need to end the contact with Amber. It will drive you crazy to have her in your head like this, especially since you can't do anything more to help her."

"You really think there's nothing more I can do?" She stood up and glared at Chillian. "I'm supposed to give up on her just like that? Well, maybe you can do it, but that's not something I can live with."

She grabbed her phone and her gear and stormed out of the room, ignoring Chillian's apologies. As she went down the staircase, she tried to calm down by slowing her breathing. She really had to stop popping off whenever things got emotional; it was going to give her a bad reputation. If Rhys-Doyle was in his office, she could bring this to his attention to see what more the Psy Syndicate could do, himself specifically. She decided to knock on his door to see if he was in.

"Come," came the answer from the other side.

She turned the knob and pushed the door open to see him in his shirtsleeves looking at the top sheet of a pile of papers. "Ah, Miss O'Callahan. What can I do for you today?"

"I haven't had a chance to brief you on the Amber Biggs case and I could use your help," Callie said. "Do you have some time to go over it?"

He sighed as he leaned back into his office chair. "I would love an excuse to take a break from this infernal paperwork. Please take a seat and give me your report."

Callie discussed her dreams about Amber and how they seemed to be directed at her personally. "There is a feeling of urgency, like something is going to happen to her soon."

"This report was given to the Regis Agency?" Rhys-Doyle asked.

"I've given them a daily report. They are no longer taking my calls, though."

"Interesting," Rhys-Doyle said.

"Is there anything more we can do? Maybe speak to the press?" Callie asked.

"We were hired by the Regis Agency, not the family, so we aren't allowed to speak with them directly. There is also the confidentiality agreement on top of that. Quite honestly, we've done our part and it's now up to law enforcement."

"I've been following the news about her case and nothing is coming up. She's haunting my dreams, telling me to help and to hurry," Callie said.

She clasped her hands tightly in her lap to help remain calm, but she wanted to stand up to this attitude and yell at the director. There had to be something more.

He steepled his fingers under his chin as he regarded Callie. "Remember our discussion from the Gonzalez case?"

"Yes," Callie said.

"You will need to find a way to get through this part, Miss O'Callahan, as hard and as cruel as it may seem," he said. "Perhaps speaking with Dorcas will help."

Callie counted to ten in her head as she took in and then let out a breath. "I understand the position that the Psy Syndicate and you are in. Thank you for your perspective and your time."

"You are welcome," Rhys-Doyle said.

Callie got up from the chair with nothing more to say and left the office. She understood the position they were in legally, but they had a moral obligation, too. Leaving this to law enforcement alone was not going to get Amber home safely.

Callie would normally have been eating a giant breakfast at a leisurely pace on a summer Saturday morning, but today she had time for only a banana. She had told Peggy she was going by train to Charlotte to visit some of her Ren Faire "family," and would be home late and not to wait up.

"Can I come with you?" Melinda asked. She had been suffering from an extremely dull summer working as a cashier and desperately wanted some adventure. She was parking the car at the train station to wait with Callie until the train was ready for boarding.

"I'm not doing a show, I'm hanging out with a bunch of uncles and aunties I knew back when Mom did the Ren Faire. You would be just as bored," Callie lied. She couldn't remember a time when she'd deceived her friend and it felt terrible.

"No, I wouldn't. They're cool and tell great stories and let me have mead," Melinda whined. "Pleeeeease?"

"Maybe next time." She heard the announcement for her train over the loudspeakers. "I've got to go. Thanks so much for the ride."

She and Melinda shared a quick hug before Callie grabbed her bag and joined the queue for the train.

Her plan was simple. Callie had inputted the pedophile's address—the one Veronica had dowsed and Amber had confirmed in her dream—into her cell phone, allowing the maps app to guide her to Amber. She had found out that the town where he lived was not terribly far away, just a couple of hours by train. She had devised a plan in the middle of the night, unable to sleep since everyone else had given up, then worked on the details as if it were a séance and got the gear together to make it happen.

She stared out the train's window, not seeing the fields and small towns they rumbled through. Time and again she found the calm, logical part of her brain trying to talk her out of this crazy plan. Her lack of sleep and stress were causing her to make bad decisions; she could just get off the train at the next stop and get a ticket home; Rhys-Doyle and Chillian were right, it was up to law enforcement. But then Amber's pleas and the sense of urgency would remind her that she should still try something...anything.

Callie found the bus station not far from the train station and got as close as she could to the Bright Trails neighborhood by bus. She walked the mile or so to the entrance of the neighborhood, where she put down her duffle and put together her persona. She then walked along the street, knocking on doors and speaking to the residents as a salesperson selling magazine subscriptions. Then she was at *the* door. *Amber, if you can, come to the front door so I can see you.* Callie rang the bell, and the photographer from her dream answered a few seconds later.

"Hi. My name is Callie. Can I have a moment of your time?"

She started to push her way past Gary into the house and launched into her spiel. "I'm selling magazine subscriptions like *Photography* and *Outdoorsman* at a reduced rate."

He tried to put his arm across the doorjamb to stop her entry, but she just ducked it and looked around the room. "Nice place you have here. Lived here long?"

"Look, girl..." he began.

"Name's Callie," she said, loud enough for Amber to hear.

"Look, Callie, I don't want no magazines and I don't like people barging into my house uninvited." He went to grab Callie's arm but she managed to dodge him.

There Amber was, peeking around the wall that connected the living room to the breakfast nook.

"Who's that?" Callie asked. "Your daughter?"

"No, that's my niece." He managed to snag Callie's arm and bodily pulled her out the front door.

"Ouch!" Callie said. "No need to be physical."

"Leave. Now," he said.

"Fine, I'll go." She walked rapidly down the street, pulling out her cell phone. She dialed 911 as she walked.

"Emergency Services, where is your emergency located?" the call center responder asked.

Callie gave her the address.

"What is the emergency?"

"I was just out doing my job and when I knocked on this guy's door I saw this girl. She looks like the one who was abducted, Amber Biggs. Then the guy grabbed me and tossed me out."

"Are you still there?"

"Yes, I'm just down the street," Callie said.

"I will dispatch the police to your location. Are you able to wait there?"

"I can wait here," Callie said, giving a description of herself. After twenty interminable minutes, a police cruiser pulled up beside her.

"Are you the person who called in a complaint about Amber Biggs?"

"I am."

"Please wait here, I'm going to check on the house," the officer said. He drove past and parked in the driveway. He got out and walked up to the door. It took a while for the man to answer it, but he eventually did and after a short discussion, let the officer in, closing the door behind him. It was all Callie could do not to sneak up to the house and watch through the window. Several more minutes passed as Callie imagined seeing more police cruisers arriving, the pedophile removed from his house in handcuffs, and Amber carried out swathed in a blanket to an awaiting ambulance. She was surprised instead to see the officer leaving the house alone, speaking briefly to the man as he left and returning to his cruiser. He drove up to Callie and spoke through the window again.

"Miss, I saw no sign of this missing girl," the officer said. "Mr. Smith let me check all the rooms and out in back. Are you sure you saw her?"

"I'm positive. She has to be in there somewhere."

"Well, without a warrant I can't do any more, but we'll keep our eyes on him."

"I don't think you understand." Callie had to struggle not to sound unhinged. "She doesn't have that kind of time!"

"I'm sorry, miss. I can't legally do anything more."

"Thanks for trying," Callie said. She watched the officer drive away.

Chapter Thirty-Nine

Amber

There she was. The older girl in the jeans with the auburn hair. It wasn't a dream this time, because the girl was actually real. Not only that, but she had done what she had promised, to come help get her away from here. Gary was so mad, but the girl hadn't even flinched, she was so brave! He might have hit her or, worse, thrown her into the dungeon with Amber. Then they'd both be stuck here. She had said her name was Callie, loud enough to be heard in the kitchen, so Amber had risked coming into the living room. They would leave together, running down the street. But Gary had shoved the girl out of the house and slammed the door. He turned around so fast that he caught Amber staring at him. He came at her with all the anger built up from the encounter with the girl and smacked her down to the floor with the back of his hand. She just stayed there, terrified to move or speak, waiting for the next blow to land.

"Are you done cleaning in here yet?" he asked.

"No sir," she replied.

"Get to work, then," he said.

She continued to wash the dishes and wipe down the countertops until she heard Gary exclaim, "The cops, dammit!"

He barged into the kitchen and grabbed Amber by the arm, dragging her to the bookcase, which he swung open to reveal the secret door. He scrambled to unlock it and shoved Amber inside. She put her ear up to the door and heard the bookcase slide into place.

Even though she made her breathing shallow and had her ear hard up against the door, she could hear only muffled speech.

The voices wafted and waned as Gary and the police officer walked through the house and out into the backyard. Amber felt tears sliding down her cheeks and she realized that the officer would not find her here, not unless she had the guts to scream. She opened her mouth but couldn't generate any sound. Twice in the span of an hour, she had been given a chance to run, to save herself, to make a sound. Twice she hadn't had the courage to do anything.

When she heard the front door close and quiet pervade the house, Amber slid down to the landing, put her head on her knees, and cried.

Chapter Forty

Callie

"Have you absolutely lost your mind?" Sahil asked.

"I know this is risky, Sahil," Callie said, "but a girl's life is at stake and I've done everything else I can think of."

Callie had called Blackenthorp about her Amber sighting, and he had replied that an FBI agent would follow up on the police report in the morning. After thanking him for absolutely nothing, Callie decided to drag Sahil into her plan.

"Do you have any ideas?" Callie asked him.

After a pause, Sahil replied, "No. I can't think of anything more you can do. I'll be there in a couple of hours—text me the address where to meet you."

"Sahil, you are my knight."

"Just promise me you won't do anything until I get there," Sahil said.

"I promise. Besides, I need to get some things at the store."

Callie hopped a bus and went shopping at the local mall. First she got a sandwich because she hadn't had anything to eat since breakfast, then she went to a giant box store for the supplies she would need for her breaking-and-entering foray. Her life with the Rennies had been nothing if not educational. She recalled one story in particular that would serve her well, in which one of the Rennies had to break into his ex's house to get his dog, who was under custodial contention. Along with the tools, she purchased a dark hoodie, dark pants, and dark stage makeup. She waited at the mall until Sahil texted her that he was almost there.

"I'm at the food court," Callie texted back.

Sahil walked into the food court searching around for Callie, who waved her arms for him to see. He approached the table looking like a storm was brewing behind his eyes. "Let's get going" was all he said.

The ride to Gary's house was quietly tense. Callie was trying to communicate with Amber, who seemed oddly quiescent. She felt that the girl was still alive but potentially unconscious. Did Gary beat her senseless after the policeman left? She was sure he would be panicking now, trying to plan an exit strategy that would save his skin if not Amber's. Callie hoped he would keep the girl alive long enough for her and Sahil to execute a rescue.

"Park where you can see the house but he can't see you, if possible," Callie said, breaking the heavy silence in the car.

He did as she instructed, finding a spot at the bottom of the cul-de-sac where he could see the front of the house.

"What exactly is your plan?" Sahil asked. He was looking at her with undisguised intensity.

"I'm hoping he's not in the house, but if he's home, I'll go in when he's asleep," Callie said.

"Sounds very well thought out," Sahil said, sarcasm coating his words.

Callie pretended not to notice, staring at the house as darkness descended and the neighborhood lights went on.

"Here goes nothing," Callie said, beginning to open the passenger door.

Sahil grabbed her left wrist, pulling her back toward him. "Do not risk your life, Callie," he said quietly.

"I won't," Callie said. "Just call the cops if you see anything weird."

"I have them on speed dial," Sahil said. "Are you sure you don't want me to come in with you?"

"I think it would be best if one of us was a lookout," Callie said. "Besides, this isn't your mountain to climb."

He let go of her arm and she left the car carrying a backpack. She loped toward the house, her face and hands blackened by makeup, the jacket's hood over her hair. Sahil watched her progress.

First, Callie needed to see if Gary was still home. She snuck into the driveway and peeked into one of the garage windows. It was too dark to see anything so she pulled out her cell phone and used the flashlight app. No car. Callie sighed in relief. Things would go so much easier with Gary gone, but since she didn't know when he'd be home again, she had to move as quickly as she could. She sent a quick text to Sahil: "No car in the garage. Going through the back."

Also in Callie's favor, there was no fence surrounding the backyard. She slipped by the side of the house, searching for an exterior door she could use. The only entrances she could find were windows and a sliding glass door. She pulled out a large pry bar and placed the flat end of it under the door, heaving upward and levering it out of the track. Callie pushed it aside with effort and found herself in the kitchen. It was dark and quiet with only the appliance clocks to light it.

She used her phone's flashlight again to illuminate the living room. There was a door that led to a utility room and the garage. She passed a bookcase and a hallway that led up to the bedrooms, but, after a circuit of the living room and hallway, she couldn't find another door.

Amber, please wake up. I'm in the house and I can't find where you are!

She felt Amber's consciousness awaken, which gave her a moment of relief. In a flash, she saw the bookcase she had passed in the living room. Amber's vision showed a door behind it. Callie approached the bookcase, shining the flashlight all around it until she saw some marks on the wall. She put the cell phone on the floor and grasped both sides of the bookcase, jiggling it until she found how it moved. She undid a latch and swung it aside, revealing a door.

The door had a padlock through a tongue-and-groove panel. Callie pulled out a can of supercooled air for cleaning electronics. Then she picked up her cell phone so she could see to aim the nozzle just right. She sprayed the air until frost appeared on the padlock, then she picked up a hammer from her bag and, with all her might, broke open the lock, which fell uselessly onto the carpet. She opened the door and saw a set of stairs leading down.

Heart pounding, she found a light switch and flicked it on. The narrow stairway led down to another locked door. This time, she would have to tackle a deadbolt lock with a keyhole instead of a padlock. She pulled out two small picks, inserting them the way she had seen it done by the Rennie who had to retrieve his dog from his ex. Sweat trickled down the side of her face as she focused on her task, which seemed to be taking more time than she had expected. Finally, the lock turned, and Callie stood up and opened the door...and saw Amber. She was sitting on a cot, one hand held up to protect her eyes from the light. She blinked a few times before she could see, and then, when awareness dawned on her that it was Callie and not Gary standing at the door, she leaped up with a cry and almost knocked Callie over.

"OMG! I can't believe you actually came back!" Amber hugged Callie tightly.

"You're okay now," Callie said. "I've got you. Can you walk?"

"I can," Amber said. "Let's get out of here before he comes back."

Callie couldn't lock the door again, so she simply left it slightly ajar. She pulled out her cell phone before flicking off the overhead light, and together they left the dungeon that had been Amber's home for over a year. Then Callie heard the noise.

"So, you came back," Gary said.

Chapter Forty-One

Sahil

Sahil watched Callie run on cat's feet up to the house and peek through the garage window. She pulled out what appeared to be her cell phone to see what was in the garage better. Then his phone buzzed with a text: "No car in the garage. Going through the back." He sagged in the seat with relief—at least she wasn't going to be confronting a potentially dangerous man. He watched her move around toward the side of the house and disappear. He had the hardest job of all, waiting. He had almost gone up to the house several times to make sure Callie was still safe, but she was right, it was best for him to watch for the man to return home. He had already composed a text, so if that happened all he had to do was hit Send. Then he was to call Emergency Services to get the police there immediately. His eyes swiveled from the house to the rearview mirror. What was taking her so long? He looked at the time on his phone. It had been twenty minutes already. Then the worst-case scenario occurred: A car appeared in the cul-de-sac, turned into Gary Smith's driveway, and pulled into the garage. Sahil hit Send to get the emergency text to Callie, then he dialed 911.

A woman answered. "Emergency Services. What is the address, please?"

Sahil gave it to her. "Please hurry, I think he might be armed."

"Yes sir, I have a priority dispatch to your location. Are you able to stay on the line?"

"Yes, yes I will," Sahil said. "How long?"

"They will be there as soon as possible."

Sahil kept the phone to his ear and without much thought for his own safety, got out of the car and ran up to the house. Gary had left the garage door open, having retrieved something from the car trunk first. By the time Sahil got to the house, the overhead garage light had gone out, so he carefully made his way around the car.

The woman's voice on the cell phone startled him. "Sir, are you still there?"

Sahil jumped and whispered, "I'm still here."

"They are on the way," she said.

Sahil continued to step quietly toward the door leading to the house. He slowly turned the knob. He was now in a darkened utility room that had another door at the opposite end. He let his eyes get used to the darkness before he slowly opened it.

Chapter Forty-Two

Gary

"I didn't know how you managed to fool the cops," Callie said, "so I had to come in myself to see how you did it."

"You can never be too careful," Gary said. "People like to snoop around in other people's business. That's how I knew you were here."

He showed Callie his cell phone with a picture of her on the back porch as she was breaking in. Apparently, she missed the security camera.

Amber began to shake in Callie's arms. Gary lifted an object in his right hand and pointed it toward the girls. It was hard to tell what it was in the darkness, but Callie assumed it was a gun.

"Believe it or not," Gary said, "I'm actually glad you came back. I know some buyers who would love to break an assertive girl like you."

"Look, people know I'm here," Callie said. "Let me and Amber go and we'll tell the cops you never came home and we don't know where you went. You'll get a head start."

"With what money?" Gary asked. "I need the funds from this sale to get away." He started walking slowly toward them. "Now be good and go downstairs to the cell so I don't shoot you."

At that very moment, Sahil appeared in the living room. Callie saw him and yelled, "Sahil, get out!"

Gary turned around and fired the gun at Sahil. Callie screamed, let go of Amber, and ran toward Gary to stop him from firing again. She managed to grab his gun arm, spinning him back around, and attempted a maneuver to disarm him, but all she managed was to bring his gun arm down. He squeezed off another round into her left leg, which gave way, forcing her to the floor and taking Gary down with her. She continued to wrestle him for the gun, but he was now on top of her and much, much stronger. She managed to get it out of his hand by biting his wrist. It skidded away from them in their struggles. Callie unleashed an unholy, wrathful scream, and Gary began to beat her with his fists.

Suddenly, there was another gunshot. Gary stopped moving and fell across Callie. Amber stood above them, gun in both hands, acrid smoke rising from the barrel.

Chapter Forty-Three

Callie

Callie was floating. Literally, she was hovering above her body. Her body was in a surgery suite with lights shining down and a mask over her nose and mouth. It was covered with a white sheet except for her left leg, which had a blood-spattered drape surrounding a nasty wound, the white of her femur shining through the blood. A surgeon's bowed head blocked her view of the carnage. She didn't care and she felt no pain, simply a pull toward the corner where the wall met the ceiling. There was a tunnel of pure energy drawing her upward, at an angle to the room.

"Hello, my Callie," a voice said in her mind.

"Momma?" Callie replied. "Are you taking me with you?"

"No, my love, it isn't your time yet. You will be going back soon."

"But I don't want to go back," Callie cried out, "I want to stay with you."

"You will see me again in time, love. Now you need to return and be strong. You have a lot left to do, but you won't have to do it alone."

Callie's consciousness slammed back into the body on the surgical table and all went dark. The following few days she awoke only occasionally and briefly from the intense pain, which was lessened by the press of a morphine drip button on her IV. She knew that Peggy was there, and thought she saw Melinda and the other Misfits.

Sahil was there, too.

"Callie, you did it!" He gave her such a big hug, and a kiss.

"*We* did it, Sahil," Callie said. "I couldn't have done this without you."

"Just remember," Sahil said, "whatever happens, it was my choice and not your fault."

Finally, she was awake long enough to have a conversation with Peggy.

"If you didn't make it, I was going to kill you!" she exclaimed. "What on earth were you thinking?"

"I couldn't let her down," Callie said. "No one would or could help. I tried everything else."

"I know," Peggy said. "The police mentioned that you called them at least twice."

"How is Amber?"

"She's doing well. She did come by to see how you were doing."

"Good," Callie said, "I can't wait to talk with her. Has Sahil come by? I remember him visiting, I think."

"Oh, no, hon, he didn't visit you," Peggy said. "I was told that I can't talk with you about what happened. The police have questions to ask now that you're awake and lucid."

They were interrupted by nurses and the attending physician coming in to examine Callie and discuss with her and Peggy the treatment plan for Callie's recovery. She would be able to walk, but with a limp, which would be less pronounced if she followed her physical therapy regime as directed.

"Miss O'Callahan?" a man's voice asked from the doorway.

"Yup, that's me," Callie said. "Who's asking?"

"I'm Detective Romero from the police department. How are you feeling today?" He walked into the room and stood by her bed.

"Like I got shot in the leg and beaten by a pedophile. How are you?" Callie asked. She used the bed controls to help her sit up and winced when she moved her leg.

"Better than you, I think. Can you answer some questions for me?" He looked back and forth between Peggy and Callie. Peggy nodded, her mouth in a grim line.

"I suppose I ought to get it over with," Callie said.

"We have the recording from the Emergency Services call that Sahilesh Ramamurthy made during the incident, and we also spoke with Amber Biggs—she is your biggest fan, by the way—so we only need your statement," the detective said.

Callie went over her story with him, including the entry to Gary's home without his permission. Her voice wavered at the point where the gun was fired for the first time.

"Is Sahil alright?" Callie asked. "You didn't mention taking his statement, only about the phone call he made. Is he..."

Callie could tell by the look on Peggy's face and then the detective's that something really bad had happened.

"I'm very sorry to inform you that Sahilesh did not survive the gunshot," the detective said. Peggy held Callie's hand.

"No, I just saw him, he was fine," Callie said in a barely audible voice.

"He died at the scene, almost instantly."

"Not again, Peggy!" Callie said, tears spilling over her cheeks.

"I know," Peggy said. "You've had more than your share. I'm here, sweetheart."

"At least the bastard who did it is dead, right?" Callie practically yelled.

"No," the detective said. "He survived his wounds and will be arraigned next week."

"Are you kidding?" Callie said. "That piece of filth is still alive and Sahil..."

"I'm sorry, Miss O'Callahan. I wish I had better news for you."

Callie was well enough to go home after a few more days in the hospital and physical therapy, which she would continue as an outpatient. She was wheeled outside the hospital and immediately accosted by Amber, her parents, and members of the national press, who yelled questions at her.

"You are so my hero!" Amber said, wrapping her arms around Callie's neck.

"Callie, we cannot begin to thank you enough," Amber's mother said. "If there is anything at all we can do..."

"Over here, Callie!" one enterprising photographer yelled.

"Callie, how did you know where to find Amber?" a well-coiffed newscaster asked.

Peggy began to push Callie's wheelchair away from the throng and toward the hospital parking garage. Hospital security directed the crowd away from them so that they could get to the car.

"You're a celebrity now," Peggy said.

"Great," Callie said. "Just what I've always wanted." Sarcasm dripped from every word. "I would rather have Sahil back."

Callie stared out the car window on the two-hour drive back home. Peggy didn't press her, just asked the basic questions about whether she was hungry or needed to go to the bathroom or to stretch out. Otherwise, she listened to the radio and let Callie be. Callie's emotions ran the gamut from elated that she had been able to save Amber's life to devastated that she hadn't saved Sahil's. She was in physical pain and emotional turmoil. She knew she would have to go to the Psy Syndicate and speak with Rhys-Doyle, which increased her level of trepidation more than the possibility of facing the murderous pedophile in court, another fun thing to look forward to.

When they arrived at the house, Callie noticed press vans parked along the street and a bevy of reporters on the sidewalk. One of the neighbors must have called to complain, because two police officers were standing on the lawn keeping the peace. When Peggy pulled her car up to the driveway, one of the officers came up to the driver's-side window.

"Hello, Officer. This is my house," Peggy said.

"May I see your identification, ma'am?"

Peggy took out her ID and showed it to him.

"Thank you, ma'am," he said. "You'll need to hire private security to deal with these folks. We don't have the manpower."

"Thank you, Officer," Peggy said. "How the heck are we going to afford that?"

"I'll see if I can stay at the Psy Syndicate so the press will leave you alone," Callie said. "They can handle it, and Rhys-Doyle will probably love the notoriety."

"If that's what you want to do, I'll support your decision," Peggy said. Callie could tell she was both relieved and concerned about her staying there.

Peggy helped Callie out of the car. The press were yelling questions or just yelling her name so that she would look their way. The cacophony continued until they were inside and Peggy closed and locked the door.

"Let's get you on the couch and comfy," she said. "Can I get you anything?"

"I'd love some iced tea," Callie said. "I'll see what I can find regarding personal security."

Happy to find something to distract from the mental and physical pain, she pulled out her cell phone from her bag. While she was scanning through personal security companies, there was a knock on the door.

Peggy went to answer it. The same police officer stood there with a man in a military uniform. "Excuse me, ma'am," the officer said, "this marine said he was family. Can you vouch for him?"

Callie tried to peek over the top of the couch at this person. He was lean and tall, with close-cropped sandy blond hair, and his chest bore an impressive array of colorful ribbons.

"Neither of them knows me," the marine said, "but I'm Callie's father."

End of Book One

Author's Note

THIS NOVEL IS THE PRODUCT of six years of investigation into the world of parapsychology. My first intention was to write a novel about a woman who had recovered from a car accident to find that she could psychically see things when she touched objects (psychometry). To find out more about this, I walked into the oldest American parapsychology research center, called the Rhine, in Durham, North Carolina. They were having their weekly research meeting and I just wanted to sit in, listen, and ask the odd question or two. What I thought would be a simple journey of a few months stretched into these many years, and I've enjoyed every minute of learning about the subject. Sally Rhine Feather, daughter of the center's founders, JB and Louisa Rhine, asked if I would write a novel for younger readers when I was done with my psychometry novel. So many young people suffer from the stigma that psychic ability has in Western culture and are wrongly diagnosed with a mental illness. I decided to shelve the psychometry novel and start on *Calliope O'Callahan and the Psy Syndicate*.

I had to learn much more about parapsychology than I had originally intended. I must thank John Kruth, who became my psychic sensei. He spent countless hours discussing the phenomena of psi with me and allowed me to access the Alex Tanous library at the Rhine. He has utilized me as a research subject in at least three experiments, and we have been discussing the possibility of two more.

I must also give my gratitude to Jeffrey Mishlove, Ph.D., and the volunteers at the New Thinking Allowed Foundation, who have allowed me access to even more amazing information beyond parapsychology but potentially linked to it as well.

The psychic team in *Calliope O'Callahan and the Psy Syndicate* is based on real psychics whom I have met and interviewed, though

I will keep their identities to myself. It was important to me that this series be as accurate as possible in the portrayal of psychic experiences, so I have kept much of the information I have gleaned true to their real-life experiences.

As excited as I am about the potential that psi is a real phenomenon, I remain skeptical about many claims. There is an effect, albeit small, and the evidence is overwhelming but inconsistent. Many mainstream physicists, psychologists, and other scientists consider the study of parapsychology to be a waste of a good scientist. However, there are those willing to ride the waves of controversy because they have seen the evidence and cannot ignore it. They often have witnessed a psychic medium give very specific information they could not know or had a reading that was filled with detail. These intrepid seekers often change their scientific pursuits to that of parapsychology. There is currently no parapsychology program available through an accredited US university, so many have chosen a career in its sister science, psychology. There are also physicists and biologists who study Ψ from their perspectives.

No one has a "theory of Ψ" because the mechanism isn't known. Many materialist scientists think it is impossible because it would defy several laws of physics. Many quantum physicists might disagree, given that this subatomic realm constantly throws curveballs at their theories. Scientific history is laden with impossibilities that were eventually proven possible. The earth was once the center of the universe, and those who opposed that belief were at best censured and at worst put to the flaming stake. Parapsychology suffers from that earth-centered dogma today; though no parapsychologists have been physically harmed, their careers suffer and their research funding dwindles to nothing. There are non-scientist "skeptics" who will alter the Wikipedia pages of prominent researchers and write books and publish magazines decrying their "pseudoscientific" research as poorly designed. True skepticism requires an open but questioning mind, which many appear to have left in their cupboard somewhere.

If you have experienced something you cannot explain, follow the recommendation of William of Occam and find the simplest possible explanation. Is that a ghost making the bumping sound, or the guy driving by with the woofer turned up in his car? "Once you've eliminated the impossible, that which remains, however improbable, must be true." That is the realm of parapsychology.

Acknowledgments

ONE MUST ALWAYS GIVE gratitude to one's spouse, but in my case, my husband, Brian, has been more than just a cheerleader. He has many skills, one of which is a better-than-average understanding of physics and a willingness to read some sketchy research papers trying to espouse a theory of psi. He read this book and gave me some really good ideas, and he puts up with me, a tall order. We have almost daily intellectual discussions, which have kept me both on my toes and down to earth.

My son, Xander, is an aspiring filmmaker who had looked askance at my interest, but was willing to consider it and actually made a short film on the subject. My other kids, Risi, Flash, Tim, and Nick, and the grandkids (as of this publication), Victoria, Persephone, Ophelia, Lilly, Kai, and Mirabelle, are a constant reminder that love surpasses and mends all.

For the researchers at the Rhine, I cannot express how much I appreciate your patience and your willingness to allow me into your world. I hope that my small contribution will help in some fashion to bring more recognition to your life's work.

For Jeffrey Mishlove and John Kruth, there are few kinder people in the world who have the desire and wherewithal to educate the masses about this much-maligned science. You both had better things to do with your time than to blow it on me, but you invested and I am thankful.

For my mother and my stepmother, who saw this awkward, quiet, and philosophical kid, thank you both for educating me that there is more to this world, but that this world is also pretty darned amazing.

No one does anything alone. There are the teachers and adults who come into your life when you are young, the friends, coworkers, and acquaintances who drop little wisdoms or shape your perspectives as you grow. There are the experiences you have with others, all of which influence the person you become. Always give thanks to those innumerable people, as I do now.

www.ingramcontent.com/pod-product-compliance
Lightning Source LLC
Chambersburg PA
CBHW030655260626
47157CB00007B/2666